SHUTDOWN

ALSO BY HEATHER ANASTASIU

Glitch

Override

SHUTDOWN

HEATHER ANASTASIU

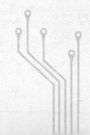

ST. MARTIN'S GRIFFIN

NEW YORK

SHUTDOWN. Copyright © 2013 by Heather Anastasiu. All rights reserved. Printed in the United States of America. For information, address St. Martin's Press, 175 Fifth Avenue, New York, N.Y. 10010.

www.stmartins.com

Library of Congress Cataloging-in-Publication Data

Anastasiu, Heather.
  Shutdown / Heather Anastasiu.—1st ed.
    p. cm.
  ISBN 978-1-250-00301-0 (pbk.)
  ISBN 978-1-250-02235-6 (e-book)
  [1. Individuality—Fiction. 2. Emotions—Fiction. 3. Thought and thinking—Fiction. 4. Psychic ability—Fiction. 5. Government, Resistance to—Fiction. 6. Science fiction.] I. Title.
  PZ7.A51852Shu 2013
  [Fic]—dc23

                                                          2013003055

St. Martin's Griffin books may be purchased for educational, business, or promotional use. For information on bulk purchases, please contact Macmillan Corporate and Premium Sales Department at 1-800-221-7945 extension 5442 or write specialmarkets@macmillan.com.

First Edition: July 2013

10 9 8 7 6 5 4 3 2 1

For Mom and Dad

Acknowledgments

First off, thanks as always to my agent extraordinaire, Charlie Olsen. You've been a solid in the very un-solid world of publishing.

Thanks so much to Terra Layton for your fabulous edit letter that kicked me in the pants and helped me get back on track both plot-wise and character-wise. Thanks also to Holly Blanck for your fine-tuning and to the rest of the awesome team at St. Martin's.

Huge love to all my beta-partners: Paula Stokes, thank you SO MUCH for helping me see that a big meandering section in the middle needed to be hacked down and for making me figure out how to make Adrien less C3PO and more Han Solo. Thank you to Lenore Appelhans—as always, you help make my books better. And Julie Cross, thank you for helping me key in on the emotional center of Adrien and Zoe's story.

Thanks to my writer's group, who put up with my sloppy first drafts and scenes (that usually have zero setting!): Natalie Boyd, Anne Greenwood Brown, David Nunez, and Lauren Peck. You guys make me a better writer every week.

And thanks to my sweet husband, Dragoş, for the continual support and encouragement. You always deserve my biggest thanks, no matter how many books I write.

SHUTDOWN

Chapter 1

THE SUNSET BLAZED FINGERS OF bright purples and oranges outward over the mountains. The breeze tugged at my
hair. I shivered even though it wasn't cold and wondered if I'd
ever get used to it: the open sky, the wind, the feel of sunshine
on my face.

I leaned against the rock wall where the transport bay opened
to the Surface and breathed in deeply. After months of practice controlling my mast cells with my telekinesis, my throat
didn't even begin to close up during an allergy attack. It was
still amazing to me to be able to stand here without fear of my
allergies killing me. Thanks to the Chancellor, I'd been allergic
to everything—plants, molds, even sunlight. But as I stood
here now, there was no shortness of breath, no swelling tongue,
no rash.

When Adrien had first told me of his vision of me standing
under the open sun a year and a half ago, I thought it would
mean I'd one day find a cure for my allergies. Instead, it was a
constant battle to use my telekinetic powers to internally sur-
round and suppress my mast cells from releasing deadly amounts
of histamine—at least any time I was outside of the Foundation with its complete air-filtration system. I couldn't say I did
it quite without thinking yet, but I was getting there. I let the
breath I'd held in my lungs out in a steady stream. Everything

was ready. I was the Resistance's strongest asset now, and tomorrow I'd leave for a mission that could change the world.

But then a lump formed in my throat that had nothing to do with an allergy attack, and everything to do with the empty space beside me. Adrien first showed me this spot near the top of the mountain where the transport bay opened to the Surface. Just six short months ago. Back when everything was . . . back when he was whole.

I shook my head, letting my hair fly in the breeze for one more short moment before turning back and walking through the transport bay to the elevator.

I stepped off the elevator and went through the allergen wash-down container. I tried not to let my thoughts wander. Empty mind, that was what Jilia always talked about in our Gifted Training class. The thoughts usually flitting through our head at any given moment were rarely about what we were doing now, but so often only worries about the past or the future. The trick of controlling our Gifts was to silence all thought and be completely present.

Emptying one's mind, however, was much more difficult than it sounded, especially when my mind was so full, like now. I used the breathing trick, counting my breaths in and out up to ten, then started over again. I'd catch a stray thought of worry about Adrien or the mission and consciously push it away until there were only the numbers. By the time I had tugged on my soft pants and pullover tunic, it was so quiet in my mind that I almost felt peaceful.

Until I opened the door and saw Max waiting for me.

Any peace I'd achieved was immediately replaced by anger. I brushed past Max, but he followed at my heels.

"You have to talk to me. We're going on a mission together tomorrow and you're not even going to say hello?"

I stopped midstride and spun on my heel toward him.

"You're going on a mission tomorrow because we need your Gift. That's the only reason. Believe me, you're the last person I want as my mission partner."

I continued forward, loathing the fact that we had no other choice but to take him on the upcoming mission. I had liked it better when he'd been locked away for months and I didn't have to look at or speak to him. Even once Henk had put a tracking anklet on him and released him for a few hours a day, I'd still managed to avoid him for the most part. Whenever he tried to approach me, I headed in the other direction. Which I intended to do now. We both knew our roles for the mission. There was no need to talk about it.

"You can't be mad at me forever," he said, putting a hand on my arm to stop me from walking away. His face softened. "We were friends once."

I stared at him open-mouthed. Did he really think we could just pretend the past year hadn't happened? That he hadn't let the Chancellor capture and torture the boy I loved? That he hadn't impersonated him for two months? But then again, Max's powers of self-deception had always been more impressive than his shape-shifting ability. He only cared about what *he* wanted, and he barely even noticed the people he destroyed to get it.

Max would pay too. He thought eventually I'd forgive him for what he'd let happen to Adrien. While Max was impersonating Adrien, Adrien was off being tortured by the Chancellor because his love for me had somehow enabled him to fight back against her compulsion. When even the torture couldn't make him tell her his visions, she'd cut out portions of his brain to make him compliant. The lobotomy had succeeded in making him obedient, but it also made him stop having visions altogether. And it had left him a shell of a person who, in spite of some groundbreaking tissue regrowth treatments, still didn't seem to be able to feel emotion.

I'd forgiven Max for every other horrible thing he'd done in the past. But he was wrong this time. He'd live his whole life and then die, and I'd still never forgive him.

I didn't know which was healthier—sadness or anger—but anger was certainly more productive. Sadness made me numb, like I wanted to sleep for a hundred years. Anger, on the other hand, made me active, gave me energy and purpose, and kept me busy planning my revenge against the Chancellor. Most of the time, if I kept busy enough, it even staved off the guilt. Or, at least, I had so many things to do, I could push it to the back of my mind and let it feed the anger instead of consuming me.

I pulled my arm away from his touch, biting back what I really wanted to say: that I looked forward to the day he went into a coffin box and was burned to ash in an incinerator. The thought surprised me as soon as it flitted through my head.

I never used to have thoughts like that. A year and a half ago, I hadn't even understood what the word *hate* meant. But Max was an excellent teacher.

"Zoe, I'm sorry for what I did. You know I am."

"You think that absolves you?" I shook my head. "Because you say you're sorry?"

"But Zoe, don't you see? It means that I'm trying, that I'm changing. That night, on our date when things got so," he leaned in, "so *heavy*, I stopped it from going too far. Doesn't that mean something? I realized in that moment that I didn't want to be the guy who just took what he wanted no matter the consequences. Even though I wanted it so, so badly. And I'll keep changing, every day. I could still be the kind of man you could love."

I scoffed harshly, and I didn't care about the look of hurt on his face. I tried to calm down the rage simmering inside me. It didn't matter what I felt. I needed Max for the mission. I knew the only reason he'd been so eager to help the Rez, in addition to hoping they'd lessen his imprisonment sentence, was to try to insinuate himself into my life again. He'd even let Henk implant a kill chip at the base of his skull since we'd have to take off the ankle tracker for the mission. Every vehicle that entered Central City was scanned, and the tracker would show up as anomalous. Once we left, both the team back here at the Foundation and I would each have a trigger switch. If he betrayed us again or tried to escape, he'd be dead within minutes.

He'd been trying to pretend he was a changed man for a few months now. Molla even talked Tyryn and the Professor into letting him have supervised visits with his baby son. After everything he'd done to her, Molla still loved him. I saw it in her eyes sometimes while he was holding their little boy— whom she'd named Max Jr.—how she believed that Max had suddenly become the man she'd always wanted him to be. Apparently incredible powers of self-delusion weren't limited to Max alone.

I brushed past him, and this time he let me.

I went to the Med Center. Jilia looked up at me. "Hey," she said.

"Is everything ready for the mission?"

She nodded. "Henk sent a message an hour ago. His team captured the two Uppers without a problem. You and Max should be able to replace and impersonate them without no one being the wiser."

I swallowed my nerves. There was no turning back now. "When do we leave?"

"An hour. You'll be in Central City by late tonight."

I fidgeted with the edge of my sleeve. "Do you know where Adrien is? I want to say good-bye before I go."

Jilia looked down as she arranged her instruments on a tray.

"He came by here half an hour ago for his daily injection. I think he said he was heading to the Caf."

"Thanks."

"Zoe." She put a hand on my arm. "Be safe on the mission."

I nodded, then turned and headed down the long hall that flanked the cafeteria. I peeked in almost hesitantly when I got to the door. The Caf was packed like always. More and more refugees had been flooding into the Foundation since it was one of the last few safe Rez sanctuaries left. Loud chatter filled the room. A few children laughed and chased each other around, but most of the adults wore subdued expressions. Some of them had been on the run for months. And they knew as well as I did that the situation here at the Foundation was tenuous at best.

With the Chancellor able to use her compulsion powers to make any Rez agents she captured tell her everything they knew, Rez numbers had dwindled to the lowest in recent memory. It also made sneaking in supplies harder than ever. Many of our supply contacts had either been captured, or were too afraid to help us anymore.

Which meant, even with stringent rationing, soon we wouldn't be able to feed the people who'd taken refuge here. Some of the refugees were already grumbling about the smaller portions. Last week we'd found several men breaking into the pantry, trying to steal food.

I shook my head and took a deep breath. It wouldn't be a problem, I told myself. After the mission next week, everything would change.

I finally located Adrien among all the other people. He sat at a small table in the corner, reading from his tablet. I paused for a moment, watching him. It was a picture I wanted to take with me.

The way he hunched over when he read was so familiar I

was stung by memories. For just a moment I could pretend that when I walked in and called his name, he'd look up and a smile would light his face. That special smile he used to save only for me.

I stepped in, wishing I could lengthen out the space of this moment, so full of potential, when hope was still alive that today might be the day I'd see that smile.

But then I came closer and he shifted his head, showing the angry red scars tracing across the left side of his skull. Evidence that nothing could ever go back to normal, not after what the Chancellor had done to him. At least his hair was finally growing back in, short and wavy against his head except where the scars were.

I swallowed hard and then sat beside him like I always did. Every afternoon, no matter how busy I was or how many demands were made of me as the ranking officer at the Foundation, I made sure to stop whatever I was doing and spend an hour with him. He used to let me take his hand, but for the past few weeks, he hadn't. I didn't know if this was a good thing—that he was developing a will of his own again, or a bad thing, because the Adrien I knew would never give up a chance to touch and connect with me.

"How are you feeling?" I asked.

"Nauseous and weak."

"Oh. I'm sorry. Is it the treatment?"

"It's the injections the doctor gives me. I don't like taking them."

I reached for his hand, but he put it under the table before I could make contact. I stared for a second. All month he'd deliberately moved away from me whenever I reached for him. I tried to still my quivering voice. "But the injections will help make you feel better," I said. "They're helping stimulate the new amygdala tissue that's been grown."

He didn't say anything, just stared at his tablet.

I tried another approach. "What about your emotions?" I asked. "How are you feeling emotionally today?"

Again, he didn't say anything. He never did when I asked him that question.

"What are you reading?" I tried instead, desperate to hear more than a cursory answer from him. Usually when I visited him I spent most of the hour talking since he rarely gave more than one-word responses. But I missed the sound of his voice. Sometimes I was afraid I was forgetting what it sounded like, just like I was afraid of forgetting what it used to feel like when his eyes brightened when I walked in the room, or the way he looked at me when he said the three most magical words in the English language: *I love you.*

He looked up briefly, then back at his text. "One time you called me a philosopher," he said. "So I'm reading philosophy."

I brightened. He remembered. I knew Jilia said he had all his memories—it was attaching emotion to the memories that was the problem. I kept hoping that the more he remembered, the more he'd be able to draw those emotional connections himself. I'd called him a philosopher during one of our first conversations when he was trying to convince me that people had souls, that we weren't only base physical parts strung together with electrical impulses.

"So what's it about?" I asked.

He finally met my gaze for more than a passing glance. "It's about the myth of Sisyphus. Do you know it?"

I shook my head. I hadn't read much beyond what the Professor assigned in Humanities. "Tell me about it." Anything was better than the math theorems he usually liked to study. He'd tried to explain them a couple times during past visits. Not only could I never follow, but he'd become so meticulous and absorbed in the problems on the page, I felt like he barely noticed I was even there.

He paused, and for a second it seemed like his eyes softened. "It's the story of this man who's in the Greek mythological version of hell. You know what hell is?"

An uneasy shiver went down my spine. I didn't like where this was going, but I tried to tell myself it was encouraging that he was engaging with me and actually asking questions. "Um, isn't that the bad place people in the Old World thought people went after . . . after they died?"

He nodded. "So this man is in hell, and they were very creative with their punishments there. They knew that it wasn't just unending pain that could torture a man."

"So what did they do to him?" My voice was barely more than a whisper. I'd wanted to get Adrien talking, but now I wasn't sure that I wanted to hear what he had to say.

"All day long and every night without rest, he had to push a rock up a hill. Then when he got it to the top of the hill, the rock would roll back down, and he'd have to push it up again. Over and over and over again. For all eternity."

"You know that's only a story, right?" I said uneasily. "That never really happened."

Adrien lifted his tablet briefly. "Well, I'm reading this philosopher named Camus who says that this is really what all our lives are like. Useless, monotonous. That we're lying to ourselves if we think anything different."

"No," I said, edging closer to him. My heart hurt in my chest at the things he was saying. "That's not all there is. There's love and beauty and courage."

He averted his gaze from mine. "Camus says love is a fiction. Make-believe. A story weak men tell themselves so they can believe there is something more to their pointless lives.

He says it's courageous to look at life in the face and call it what it is. All of us uselessly pushing our boulders up the hill."

"Adrien," I said, putting my hand on his forearm, but he pulled away again.

"Maybe I'm not as broken as you all think. Maybe I'm just one of the few people who can see clearly now." His voice was calm. It sounded like he thought it was a good thing not to be able to feel anything.

I didn't know what to say to that. I wanted to yell at him that he was wrong, to grab his shoulders and shake him until he remembered how to love me. Instead I got up and started walking away, not wanting him to see my tears. Because unlike him, I *could* still feel emotion, and he was breaking my heart.

I turned back at the doorway. "Okay, well, I'm going on a mission tomorrow. See you next week, when I get back."

He didn't nod or acknowledge me. He looked absorbed again in what he was reading. It was like that sometimes. He'd seem aware and engaged one moment and then gone the next.

It wasn't his fault he was like this.

Jilia said the neural pathways had to reconfigure themselves, that hopefully his body would teach itself to make those connections again. But it had been six months already with absolutely no change. I tried to stay positive and hopeful, at least in front of him. He had loved me once, but now he looked at me with no more interest than he would a stranger.

After so long with no evidence of emotion, even Jilia's assurances carried a tinge of doubt. She tried to hide it, but everyone could tell. No one had ever tried to repair the kind of damage Adrien had. There were no guarantees it would work. He might be like this forever. The Adrien we'd known and loved might be lost to the caged spaces of our memories.

Adrien's mother, Sophia, looked haunted and drawn whenever I saw her, which wasn't often. She made sure to visit Adrien in the mornings so we never crossed paths.

So yes. I understood hatred now. I hated the people who had done this to him—I hated the Chancellor, I hated Max, and I hated the system that gave the Chancellor so much power. But most of all, in the darkness of night alone in bed with nothing else to distract my thoughts, I hated myself.

Because how could I have let it ever happen? How had I been so self-involved I hadn't noticed when Max switched places with Adrien? Max might have the power to disguise himself and impersonate other people, but I should have known. I thought back to that night of our "date." At the time, I'd been so happy to have Adrien communicating and being open with me again, I hadn't noticed anything off about the way he held me and kissed me. I shuddered at the thought that it had been Max, not Adrien, touching me so intimately. I should have recognized it right away, and we could have rescued Adrien before it was too late.

But as had happened so many times before, I'd failed when it counted most. First with getting my older brother killed, then not finding a way to sneak my younger brother Markan out of the Community before the Chancellor set a twenty-four-hour watch on him, and now with Adrien. I knew that even if I succeeded in this mission, I couldn't atone for it all. My jaw clenched with determination. Still, maybe I could save others, even if they weren't the ones I loved most. As General Taylor had once told me, there's nothing more dangerous than someone who knows they have nothing left to lose.

Chapter 2

"DARL, DO HAVE SOME MORE of the bubbles." Max offered a full sparkling glass to me.

I tried to smile as if I thought everything at this overly lavish Uppers party was perfectly delightful and fun. *Fun.* I choked down the impulse to punch the especially fat man beside me who kept leaning over and talking at me with his mouth full of food. Sometimes little bits of spit shot out as he spoke, and I felt like I'd need to take an hour-long shower with blasting hot water when this was all over.

Last night we'd successfully infiltrated Central City by posing as the Uppers couple Henk's team had captured. The expansion of Max's powers allowed him to project the vapid socialite's face onto mine. As long as I stayed within a thousand feet of him, people would look at me and see her.

"Really, Darl, *darl*ing, bubbly makes you laugh, and everybody loves to hear your laugh," said Max, sounding greatly amused with the bad pun on the name of the woman I was impersonating.

I reached to accept the glass, and smiled tightly at him. Of course Max had suggested we take on the shapes of *this* particular couple back when the Rez started researching the perfect way to infiltrate the Uppers circle in Central City. Darl and Nihem Westermin were the optimal choice because of their connections, their wealth, and the fact that their partying ways would make them the last people on earth the Uppers would suspect as planning to sabotage the Link.

The fact that they were traveling to Central City at the same time Chancellor Bright would be absent had cinched it. Central City was the only place that had the mainframes capable of uploading the Rez's hack. We would disable the Link that connected billions of people together through the hardware chips in their heads that turned them into mindless slaves.

I'd been hoping for a nice sibling pair to impersonate— being a married couple meant I had to share a room with Max. Or better yet, I'd wanted to just slip into the city invisible, since Max's power had expanded so that he could do that too. But we'd discovered part of the security protocol for entering the city was a complete vehicle scan to make sure there were no hidden bodies on board trying to sneak into the city. Invisibility was out.

So instead we impersonated Darl and Nihem. Max gave us their faces, and we passed the retinal scan with the tiny film Henk had us put in our eyes before we left. We'd prepped for the DNA prick by pooling some of Darl and Nihem's blood under false pads on our fingertips. When we arrived inside the gates, we were met by the party organizer, who was asked to personally identify us before we were allowed past the last barricade into the city. Darl and Nihem were well known to him, so he allowed us in with only a passing glance. They took no chances when it came to security in Central City. Once you made it inside, though, there were far fewer precautions.

I put the glass of champagne to my lips and pretended to drink. I needed to be clearheaded tonight if I was going to manage my part of the mission. I would get my target alone, then flash the device Henk had given us in his eyes, and during the moment he was stunned, slip the key drive off the chain over his neck and replace it with the duplicate. The way the stunner worked, he would only feel a little disoriented, but wouldn't remember anything from the last few minutes and would most likely just shrug it off as a momentary lapse in concentration.

I hoped no one would notice if my glass stayed full all night. Apparently Darl was a notorious drinker, preferring the extra mind-altering vintages where the vines had been crossbred with opium. I looked down at my glittering dress and momentarily hated the person I had to be.

Max-as-Nihem leaned over and whispered in my ear, "You need to drink at least a sip. People are starting to notice you're not drunk. Now, there's your target." He nodded slightly to the right. I peeked up for a moment and saw the rotund, red-faced man he was looking at, Harole Warnost.

"And here's the red wine." He slid the goblet into my hand, smoothly exchanging it with my untouched champagne. "Make sure to douse him good with it. Then follow him to the bathroom and make the switch."

I smiled widely, pretending my husband was whispering something sweet in my ear. I barely kept myself from rolling my eyes. I was the one who'd come up with the plan, I didn't need a reminder of the specifics. All I had to do was follow my target to the bathroom. Max would make me invisible right after I stepped out of the party.

"And do take a sip," Max whispered. "Darl would never walk around with a completely full glass. Everyone expects her to be drunk by this point in the night."

Max pulled back, and I reluctantly took a small sip of the wine. I half choked with how strong the stuff was, but tried to turn it into a laugh instead.

"That's my Darl," Max said with a loud laugh before moving away, no doubt seeking out his own target. Tonight we'd get the two key drives, and tomorrow we'd infiltrate the programming station while everyone else was at the fight. "Drink up like a good little girl."

A couple people standing nearby laughed. I hated them a little more for encouraging Nihem's patronizing support of his wife's drinking.

Everyone's sparkling clothing seemed to gleam brighter after I'd taken a couple sips. The added brightness only made the whole scene more menacing in its frivolity. Earlier we'd all sat at a long table where course after course of food had been placed in front of us. I'd eaten protein patties and hypoallergenic supplements for my entire life, so I didn't even know what some of the foods *were*. Meats of many different kinds, rich creamy soups, pastas in buttery sauces, and vegetables of every color a person could imagine.

I learned after our brief dinner when we'd arrived last night not to eat as much as everyone else. My stomach wasn't used to the rich food, not to mention the drinks. All night long, I was in and out of the collapsible med container we'd brought for me to sleep in. Tonight I had only nibbled politely at every dish, leaving the majority of it on the plate. The woman who'd sat beside me had clucked approvingly at my smaller portions, saying that I was right to try to keep my figure with a husband like Nihem.

As much as it galled me to waste food—I knew the amount of food I'd left uneaten on the plates would have fed a family for a week at the Foundation—I couldn't afford to lose more sleep. It was exhausting enough to use my telek constantly to keep my mast cells in check so I wouldn't go into an allergy attack. Central City buildings were all above ground of course. The Uppers had never believed the lies they fed to their drone labor force about the surface of the earth being destroyed by nuclear weapons. It was just another way for them to control us, keeping us underground while they all lived happily soaking up the sunshine on the Surface.

But this was what I had trained for. The past four months had been spent perfecting my control so that I could come on this mission. There had been a few brief discussions about whether someone else should come on the mission instead of me because of my allergies, but in the end I'd convinced them it had to be me. If something went wrong, my particular Gifts would be needed if there was any hope of getting out of the city alive. But nothing would go wrong, I reassured myself. I would accomplish the mission and finally bring the Link system crashing to the ground. We would free my younger brother and all the rest of the drones, at least the ones under eighteen that hadn't yet had the last deadening adult V-chip implanted. It would change the world. It's what I'd dreamed of since I began to feel emotion for the first time—I wanted everyone else to be able to feel these amazing new things too.

I clutched my glass tighter and headed toward my target, pasting a wide smile on my face. But before I could get to him, the woman who'd sat beside me at dinner, Checil, came up to me. She was only a few years older than me, but her skin was sallow and the heavy bags under her eyes were only partially concealed by her too-heavy makeup.

"Are you amped for Fight Night tomorrow?"

I shrugged, trying to look bored. I glanced quickly over her shoulder. My target was talking with a group of other white-haired men. "It's really more of Nihem's thing," I said. "It's what he dragged us out here for in the first place. I'd rather be cozy back at home. As it is," I smiled tightly, looking around, "I'll need a stiff drink to get through it. Or four. Speaking of, I think I need something stronger than this wine," I nodded toward the open bar and tried to brush past her.

But she took my arm in hers and pulled me forward, almost

sloshing the wine out of my goblet. I had to stop myself from pulling back from such an intimate touch. Again I was amazed at Max's ability. No one ever saw through the disguise he'd given me, no matter how close they were.

"I know exactly what you mean. Have you seen *my* husband?" She waved at a man with thinning hair and a portly belly. He must have been more than twice her age. He was one of the men in the circle talking to my target, Warnost. He nodded back at Checil, but didn't move from his spot. He swiped another small cake from a passing drone server's tray.

Checil wrinkled her mouth in distaste.

"I loathe him, but not all our parents are legacy owners in Comm Corp like yours! The rest of us have to do what we can to keep our proper position in society. Even if it means marrying a saggy old man with perpetually greasy fingers." She steered me around the perimeter of the party.

I glanced back and swore internally. I needed to extricate myself from this clingy woman, and quick. The party was almost at its end. We'd waited intentionally for the later half of the night to strike so our targets' disappearances wouldn't seem out of the ordinary, but if I didn't act soon, I'd miss the opportunity completely.

Checil went on, oblivious that I wasn't responding to her. I learned quickly that she was the kind of person who could keep up a stream of chatter no matter her audience. I suspected she enjoyed the fact that I didn't speak much, and that she enjoyed even more walking and letting herself be seen with someone of Darl's position. As she'd said, Darl's parents were important people.

"Look, I really have to go—" I tried to interject, but Checil just kept talking.

"He's determined to put a baby in me." Checil went on as if I hadn't said anything. "Continue the pure line of Uppers and all the bash that gen goes on and on about. Even though he already has three children. At least one of his sons is debauched and delicious. I've had him of course," she laughed again. "If I ever do decide to let a parasite destroy my figure like my darling husband wants, I just might let the son take care of it. Then at least the little monster would look like family."

I tried not to let my abhorrence show on my face. This woman would betray her husband without thought, disgrace him, and laugh about it in the same moment. I'd heard other women talking about Checil last night when she wasn't there—about how her family had no money anymore and were only still Uppers because of the family name. Checil's marriage to the husband she so casually dismissed was the only reason she was able to still appear in society, wear fancy dresses, eat this fancy food, and have these friends. As we circled the party, some of those so-called friends looked right at her and then turned away and chattered some more, laughing behind their hands.

"Well, I think I better see where Nihem's gotten off to—" I glanced back at the circle of men. Several had left the group, but Warnost was still talking to Checil's husband.

Checil's smile faltered and her grip on my arm tightened. "To tell the truth, I'm just out of sorts because it's been too long since my last infusion," she said, her voice low. "There's a dealer here of course, but all on the quiet since Bud and some of the other old gens look down on it. I have to steal all the credits I can to even get my hands on a tiny bit." Her eyes flashed with anger before she turned to look sweetly up at me. "But I've heard you're quite the infusion enthusiast as well. I'd be happy to introduce you to Central City's most prominent dealer. Maybe we could steal away and go have a real party." She raised her makeup-darkened eyebrows and smiled. It was a desperate smile, almost feral.

I had no idea what infusions were, but I suspected it had something to do with her bloodshot eyes and dilated pupils. I almost felt sorry for her. Almost. I smiled sweetly and disengaged my arm from hers. "Thank you so much for the kind offer, but I'm fine for tonight. Now, I must go find Nihem."

I turned to go but she grabbed my arm again, her eyes wild. Her fingers felt like claws in my skin. "But you have to help me! I mean, I don't quite have enough credits for another infusion, but if you come, I'm sure the dealer will overlook that." Her voice wavered between persuasion and panic. "He really has the best clientele. He heard of your . . . your *interest*, and asked me to introduce you."

"Really, I can't right now." I couldn't keep the impatience from my voice. My target had shaken hands with Checil's husband and was walking toward the exit.

"But later? After the party?" Her fingers were still digging into my arm.

"Sure, whatever," I said, forcing a smile. Anything to get rid of her.

She nodded vigorously, finally letting me go. "Meet me at the fountain at midnight. We'll go then." It was a command, not a suggestion. I was sure Darl would have put her in her place for her attitude, but standing her up tonight would accomplish the same thing.

I hurried toward Warnost's retreating back. But before I could get to him, he exited through the double doors. I stopped, wondering if I should follow him down the hall. He'd be alone, just like we wanted. Maybe this whole thing could work to our advantage. But when I looked behind me, I saw Checil's bloodshot eyes on me, a small frown on her face. It would look odd if I didn't go find Max like I'd said I would. And worse if it looked like I was following my target out. The way these people gossiped, every one of them would know by morning.

I balled my hands into fists in frustration but then made my way over to Max until I saw who he was talking to. It was the second target, a woman who was far too old to be wearing the outfit she had on, a short red dress with so many cutouts that it looked like a hastily wrapped bandage.

The way she was leaning into Max's chest, I could tell his plan was working. I'd been skeptical when he'd been so sure he could get her alone without a trick like spilling wine, but now I saw why he'd been so confident. He was a natural at this, far more smooth than he'd been a year and a half ago when we'd still lived in the Community and he'd clumsily tried to seduce me. I was sure he'd had plenty of practice since then. I swallowed my disgust.

Then again, as I got closer I could see the tiny key drive hanging like a pendant from a glittering gold chain around her neck. As long as Max got results, that was all that mattered right now.

This might still work after all. We'd planned on getting in a public fight tomorrow afternoon to explain our absence from the main attraction of Fight Night, but doing it now would work just as well. And then maybe I could still leave to go track down Warnost without suspicion.

I stopped several feet away and put my hands on my hips with an exaggerated look of disgust on my face. I stood a full ten seconds, making sure the people around me could see me watching them. Nihem was an infamous philanderer, this was all well within character.

I went forward and knocked the cake out of his hand. "You bastard. The least you can do is *try* to hide your affairs."

Max smiled at the woman he was talking to before leisurely

looking my way. "Usually you're too bubbled to notice, *darl*ing."

"You know I hate it when you call me that," I said through gritted teeth.

"Oh, are we talking about the things we hate now?" The smile was still on his face. "My list is oh so long. Starting with the fact that you're in love with another man."

People all around had stopped to stare at us. They did love a good piece of gossip. I hoped we were performing to their standards.

I tipped my head to the side and laughed in Max's face. "He's more of a man than you'll ever be. You're just a bad imitation," I couldn't help adding, "A copy who could never live up."

His smile was gone now. "You never gave me a chance. Besides, there was a while there when I lived up just fine." He leered at me. "I didn't hear any complaints."

My face heated up. "Only because I was looking at you but imagining him."

He pulled back. "I should have known from the start you'd break my heart. You always were a cold-hearted bitch."

My hand flew to slap his face, but he caught my arm mid-swing. I glared at him, letting the hatred pour off me. I didn't have to fake it.

"If I divorce you, you'll lose everything," I said, getting back on script. "My father will make sure you end up with *nothing*." I spit the last word.

He only looked momentarily daunted, but then smiled. "Your father was glad to get rid of you. He's happy I have to deal with you now so he doesn't have to bother."

I glanced around at all the people watching now and tried to look embarrassed, even hurt. I glared back at my pretend husband. Then I let out an angry huff and stalked out of the room toward the door my target had left through. It was the perfect excuse to make a believable exit.

Once I was out, I hurried down the hallway toward Warnost's room, trying to let go of my anger at Max so I could focus. I hoped our little charade hadn't lasted too long and I'd catch Warnost before he disappeared behind the locked door of his bedroom suite. But as I approached, the door sealed shut behind him. I put my ear against the chrome door. If I buzzed, I could still slip inside after he opened the door and stun him. But then I heard two voices inside and swore silently. There was someone else there. I couldn't use the stunner on both of them at the same time.

"*Shunt*," I swore under my breath. I stood one second longer, frustrated at how close I was to getting the key drive. But it was too risky if I tried it now. I finally pulled away from the door. I was so frustrated I wanted to kick something. Or punch a certain doped-up socialite for getting in my way.

I headed down the hallway to my own suite. We hadn't intended on going to the preparty before the fight tomorrow, but now we'd have to so we'd have another chance to snatch his key. I didn't like cutting it that close, but there was no other choice. I flopped on the bed in our suite and let out a long breath. Imitating Darl was exhausting, and my feet were screaming from the too-tight shoes I'd been wearing all night. I took a long bath, as if I could wipe all traces of her off me.

I dressed and came back into the main suite. Cream-colored silks and other manufactured gauzy fabrics were draped all over the room. They cascaded from a bar along the top of the bed and were bunched along the sides of the windows. I backed away from the window on instinct. We kept the heavy drapes always drawn so no one could peek in, but I was still glad it was nighttime. Even though I could control my allergies now, the outdoors still unnerved me.

I curled up on the plush couch to study the detailed schematics of Central City's layout some more. Tomorrow we'd need to be perfect, especially now that we'd have to work in time to get the second key drive too.

Max came in a couple hours later. He tossed his shoes away and sat heavily on the bed. I looked at him and saw Max's own face again, but I turned away anyway. Max was no more welcome a sight than Nihem.

"I couldn't make the switch," I said. "That ridiculous woman kept clawing my arm, and by the time I got away from her, he was gone. We'll have to get it tomorrow."

Max nodded. "Okay."

"Any problems with yours?"

"Nope. She was more than willing to go somewhere to be alone with me. But nothing happened," he added quickly.

I frowned. "You didn't get the drive?"

"No, I got the drive." He reached in his pocket and produced the tiny device. My breath caught. As disgusting as Max was, what he held in his hand made it all start to feel real. We were one step closer.

"Good performance tonight, by the way," he said.

"Wish I could have thrown something at your head, but I didn't want to blow our cover if I accidentally knocked you out."

He laughed. "Oh, Zoe, I've missed you."

I turned back to him, barely holding my temper. "And I can hardly stand the sight of you. I'm going to sleep." I pulled out the collapsible med container from underneath the bed where we stored it. The seven-foot box was made of cloudy plastic panels that sealed together seamlessly. I couldn't control my allergy in my sleep, and this was the safest option. Max moved to help me pull it out, but after a hard glare from me, he backed away with his hands up.

His face was solemn. "Someday, Zoe, you'll see. I'm different now."

I didn't respond. Instead, I touched the button and watched the pleated collapsed side panels of the box slide up with a small whirring sound.

I went to the bathroom and opened the small cylinder bottle I'd brought from my bag, shaking out two little blue pills. I filled the cup of water and downed them. I still Linked myself voluntarily every night when I went to sleep to keep from accidentally unleashing my powers from a troubling dream. The Link kept me from going into REM sleep cycles. But still, in spite of the fact that it calmed all thought and emotion, I'd been having trouble falling asleep lately. I didn't know if it was because my thoughts were too tumultuous from all the stress I was under as the ranking officer at the Foundation, or if my power was again expanding in unexpected ways. I shuddered at the possibility of the latter. When I talked to the doc about the insomnia, she said not to worry and gave me the sedative to take on nights I couldn't sleep.

Just in case it had something to do with my power expanding again, I'd started spending more and more hours each day outside, using my telek to keep myself from going into an allergy attack. It was the best way I'd found to use up my excess power, and I had needed to learn control for long periods of time so I could come on this mission.

I lay down in the box, pulled the lid on over me, and latched it tight. The air-filtration system came to life with another click, followed by the familiar suctioning noise as the container flushed all the tainted air and contaminants out, replacing them with fresh air from the self-replicating oxygen system. I breathed out in relief. For the first time all day, I didn't have to control my mast cells. I slumped with the relief of it.

One more day. I could hold it all together for one more day.

Chapter 3

I WOKE THE NEXT MORNING and stepped out of my sleep chamber. I rubbed my eyes blearily and sat up. I looked around for Max.

But he wasn't there.

I cursed loudly, then jumped out of the med box. I checked the bathroom, but he wasn't there either. I pulled the kill switch out of my pocket. After everything he'd done, we'd been fools to ever trust him.

But right as I was about to push the button that would trigger the chip to release a deathly electric charge throughout his brain, a small projection screen popped up on the bed, probably activated by a motion sensor.

Max's face and upper torso filled the screen. He raised his hands. "Zoe, wait a second before you push the kill switch, just hear me out." It was a prerecorded video, but he'd known this would be my first response when I discovered his absence.

"I'm going out this morning to try to track down the second target to get the other pendant key. I overheard some of the other men talking to him about a casual meeting for morning coffee, and knew I could sneak in better if I went by myself.

"I'll follow him and try to catch him alone. I'll be back by ten o'clock, so I'm begging you not to push the kill switch till then." The projected image zoomed in on his face, probably because he'd leaned into the capture camera. "Please

Zoe, I'm putting my life in your hands." The projection cube went off.

I stared for a second, fury boiling up inside of me. Did he think I was stupid enough to believe him for a second? Volunteering for this mission must have only been a ploy to gain his freedom from imprisonment at the Foundation. What better place to disappear than in Central City with a ready-made identity all in place?

But he had to have known we weren't idle in our threats to trigger the kill switch if he ran. And there was his son. Would he abandon him so easily? Then again, I wasn't sure he'd ever really loved Molla. Spending time with her and their son could just be part of his cover to get us to trust him again.

I looked at the clock. It was nine thirty. I didn't usually sleep this late. Had he switched the pills I'd taken last night to give me an extra-heavy dose of sedative? I wouldn't put it past him. Early morning sun had been filtering in behind him in the video, so he couldn't have been gone for more than three hours already.

But Max was crafty, and there was no telling what he could have already accomplished in three hours. He could have arranged with a doctor in the city to try to get the kill switch chip out of his head. Any tampering was supposed to trigger it, but if he'd found a surgeon who was careful enough . . .

My hand tightened around the kill switch trigger. I took a deep breath and lifted my thumb over the red button. But then, just as I was about to push the trigger, I realized something: if I killed Max now, my own cover would be blown. I might be able to make it out of the city—I could call on my power easily these days, and I'd been constantly increasing my stamina and control. Heavy locked doors posed no problem for me. I was confident I could take down a squadron of Regulators too without much trouble. But still, even if I could get myself out of the city, I would have failed to accomplish what I'd come here for. It would be difficult to ever get another chance like this, especially if they realized we'd already infiltrated once.

My eyes shot back to the clock. It was only twenty-five more minutes to wait. If Max wasn't back by then, I'd have no choice but to try to escape. I couldn't pull off the plan without the second pendant key; there was no way I'd be able to get into the central Link coding station without it. Not to mention that walking around with the face of the most notorious fugitive in the country would get me caught within minutes of anyone recognizing me. If there was even the slightest chance that Max was telling the truth—and that's all it was, *slight*—then I had to wait for him. I hated him even more for putting me in this position.

I gritted my teeth and got dressed, then sat down on the bed with the kill switch in my hand. I pulled at the fringe on the edge of the pillowcase and watched the clock. The minutes inched by at an infuriatingly slow pace. I'd have sworn minutes never took this long before. Finally it was nine fifty. Then, what felt like an hour later, nine fifty-five.

At nine fifty-nine, a moment before the clock clicked to ten, the door to our suite opened. No one appeared to be there, but reaching out with my telek, I could feel the shape of Max's body. I leapt off the bed as he closed the door behind him and reappeared.

"Zoe, wait, I can explain—"

His words were cut off because I'd lifted him off the ground by the throat with my telek. I slammed him against the marble wall so hard his eyes bugged out in their sockets. Then I dropped him to the ground and flipped him onto his chest. I sat on his back, binding his arms to his sides with my telek, and searched the hair at the back of his neck. I couldn't see any incision points. I reached forward with the kill switch device, put it flush against his neck, and clicked the diagnostic option. After a few seconds it let out a small beep and flashed a message: ALL SYSTEMS CHECK.

I got off of Max and released him from my telek hold.

"Shunt, Zoe!" he said, massaging his throat. "I said you could trust me. Can't you believe that a guy can change?"

"Never," I said, my voice full of venom. "And if you disappear like that again without talking it through with me, I won't hesitate. I'll trigger the kill switch first and ask questions later. Got it?"

He stared at me, a heavy frown on his face, but he nodded. "Got it," he said.

"Good. So did you retrieve the secondary key?"

He sat down heavily on the bed. "No, I couldn't get it. He was surrounded by a crowd of people the entire time. I waited outside his bedroom in the morning, thinking I'd catch him alone that way, but his son met him right as he came out and they walked together. Then once they got to the coffee room, Warnost stayed clustered with the others."

He shook his head. "You'd think old men drinking coffee would have to use the facilities once in a while, but while almost all of the other men went to the bathroom at one point or other, Warnost never did. He stayed so long I had to leave before I could follow him when he left since I knew you would . . . ," he glared pointedly at the kill switch still in my hand, "overreact."

"Overreact?" My voice shot up an octave with disbelief. He had the nerve to call me overreactive after all that he'd done!

"Look," he held up his hand, "I don't want to argue. We just have to figure out some other way to get that key."

I paced the room, glad to get my mind back onto the task at hand. "Maybe we could catch him alone after lunch?"

Max shook his head. "The pregame shows are starting in an hour, and I heard him say he was going to meet his wife and head over to the arena as soon as he left.

I swore under my breath.

"But I think I may have a plan," Max said.

"Shall we?" Max held out an arm several hours later, like he was escorting me back to another vapid party. I just glared at him and he dropped it with a laugh. His plan was risky, but it was the best we had if we still wanted to have a chance at getting the key drive in time.

"Don't worry so much." Then he disappeared, there one moment and gone the next.

Even though I'd seen him do it before, it was still startling every time. I projected out with my telek and could sense the outline of his body taking up space in the room. I let out a sigh of relief.

Still, if this morning had taught me anything, it was how easy it would be for Max to disappear and leave me here. Maybe he'd tried to find a surgeon this morning but couldn't, and *that* was the real reason he'd come back. Of course, if Max had just wanted to escape, he could have done so any of the countless nights I'd been sleeping in the med container and not watching him. He could have slipped out, and without his power disguising me, I'd have been found out almost instantly. A cold shiver went down my back at how much I'd already been depending on Max without thinking about it. I knew from previous experience never to underestimate him.

I looked down at my own body and frowned.

"You're invisible too," came his voice from the air, "it just never looks like it to yourself."

I nodded. Of course. I never looked like Darl to myself when I looked in the mirror either.

Max pressed the door button and it slid open. He stole down the hallway in front of me. I kept my telek on alert, both so I'd know where he was, and to be aware of anything else we might pass. As we came to the central foyer that all the suites branched out from, I felt Max pull back up against the wall. I heard the voices coming toward us and imitated him, pressing my back against the wall. We might *appear* invisible, but we were still solid, and if someone ran into us, they'd know something was anomalous.

After the group of people passed, we hurried quietly down the ornate marble hallways. In my head, I matched the hallway to the schematics I'd carefully memorized. Just a little farther and we'd be at the stadium.

The main event would be starting any minute now. I heard a hive of voices buzzing ahead. We soon came to clusters of well-dressed people, faces that had become familiar in the past couple days, all talking and, of course, drinking. Checil stood talking with a woman in the corner whose eyes were also bloodshot. No doubt she was still looking for her next infusion hookup.

Several whooping boys ran through, bumping me into an older gentleman. I immediately backed up against the wall.

I held my breath, cursing inwardly. But the man just called after them, "Calm down. There will be enough excitement in the arena!" He must have thought it was them who'd bumped him, not me.

I stuck tighter to Max after that. He glided with an expert lightness to his feet. I tried to mimic the way he walked, rolling heel to toe, heel to toe.

A loud horn sounded right as Max and I had edged our way through the front of the crowd toward the narrow stadium entrance. Suddenly everyone on all sides began surging with us. I lost Max's shape amid all the others. People pressed against my shoulders. This lobby entrance was the only one that led to the premium center stadium seats reserved for the highest tiers of society. There was no time to keep trying to find Max. Soon enough, someone would wonder why it felt like they were bumping up against a person when it looked like empty air.

Finally the bottleneck of the entryway opened up and people fanned out into the wide aisles that surrounded the huge domed stadium on all sides. I was pushed forward and made it through the doorway just as a second horn blasted.

The crowd around me roared. I pulled away from the crush of bodies, trying to feel around frantically to find Max. But people were moving so quickly, pouring in and then filling their seats. It was impossible to try to determine which moving body among the hundred didn't have a visual match. I looked around frantically. Hundreds of rows of seats surrounded the oval pit sunk fifty feet below. Layers of balconies hung over each other for even more seating. Lights from the domed top of the arena blazed so brightly it looked like daylight, and huge screens were mounted along the walls.

I pulled back out of the crowd and stepped onto a raised ledge running along the bottom of the wall outside the entryway. At least this way I could get out of the flow of foot traffic. No one had noticed me, but only because I'd been lucky. I watched for a moment to squeeze back through the entry. But people kept streaming in, and I worried that if I tried to push back against them moving in the other direction, someone *would* notice something anomalous this time.

A third horn sounded, and the crowd responded with deafening noise, jumping to their feet, screaming and yelling and whistling. I'd never heard anything so loud in my life and covered my ears. The screens filled with images of Regulators and detailed stats about their hardware additions and kill records. I shuddered. I hadn't known it would be Regs fighting. It made a twisted sort of sense, I supposed. They wanted to pit the strongest fighters against each other. Who better than their police force of Regulators with their metal exoskeletons and hardware enhancements? They were still human underneath, but years of training and programming had converted them into killing machines.

Then I thought about Cole, one of the Regulators-in-training I'd rescued when I first escaped the Community. I'd been able to crush his V-chip and sever him from the Link, and he'd fought hard to regain his humanity. It was his personal mission to help other young Regs-in-training we captured do the same. Like the rest of the population, once Regs got the final V-chip installed at eighteen, they were lost to us. The Rez still hadn't found a way to remove the invasive adult V-chip without killing the person, in spite of countless attempts. Still, if Cole knew the details of this spectacle in front of me, he'd be horrified. These Regs had been programmed to fight for no other reason than for the sick entertainment of a pampered crowd.

A countdown clock started, and the crowd chanted along. "Ten! Nine! Eight!"

From the ledge, I could see over everyone's head down to the oval not far below. When the count got to zero, a large set of doors opened at one end, and a hulking figure walked out to the center.

I couldn't help but stop and stare. It was a Reg, that was clear from the metal that glinted in the arena lights. But it wasn't an ordinary Reg. Metal spikes covered his back. At first I thought he was wearing some kind of armor, but as the large wall screen zoomed in, I could see he wasn't wearing a shirt at all—the spikes were embedded along his spine. Bits of flesh peeked out from the metal woven into his musculature, but unlike normal Regs, he looked more machine than man.

I forced myself to look away from him. I had to find Max. I looked at the people streaming through the door, wondering if I should chance pushing through them all anyway.

Then at the other end of the stadium, a door opened and five more Regs came out, each of them with more strange and terrifying additions. One had a giant steel battering ram for an arm, another had heavy swords instead of hands. The ear-splitting horn sounded again, and the five raced toward the spiked Reg. The ground of the arena was covered in metal plating, and the huge *thunk, thunk, thunk* of their heavy sprinting footsteps echoed through the arena even above the sound of all the cheering and screaming.

The Reg with the battering-ram arm reached the spiked Reg first and launched himself forward with his hydraulic-reinforced legs. The spiked one had jumped too, twisting in midair so that his back was turned to his oncoming enemy.

The Regs met in the air with a giant crash. The spikes sliced through the exposed belly of the other Reg. Blood spurted out over the ground just as the rest of the Regs got close. The crowd jumped to their feet around me, roaring their approval of the kill.

The other four quickly attacked the spiked Reg. The metal from their various body parts sparked with the force of each impact. More blood spurted through the air, huge swaths of red filling the vid screen in the background.

I turned away, nauseated. But I couldn't block out the sounds of metal crunching against metal. I could tell from the way the crowd reacted that another Reg had died. I glanced back and saw three bodies on the ground. The two remaining Regs had turned on each other, one swinging a heavy spiked ball on a chain. The other hit the ball away with his sword, but the Reg was quick and swung again right away. The spiked ball embedded itself in the opponent's forehead.

And the crowd jumped to its feet, cheering louder.

I stepped down off the ledge. I didn't want to see any more. I already felt sick to my stomach. My power buzzed in my ears uncontrollably, straining to get out because I'd become so emotional. It hadn't happened in months, at least not when I was awake. I stumbled, the bile rising in my throat, and backed into someone who let out a grunt of surprise.

Chapter 4

BEFORE I COULD TURN AROUND to look at who it was, a hand slid over my mouth and a whisper sounded in my ear, "Shh."

It was Max. I let out a relieved breath and whipped around. I wondered how he'd found me. Could he sense me somehow, since he was using his power to shield me? Then again, the *how* wasn't important. All that mattered was that he *had* found me, and we could continue our mission. He grabbed my hand and tugged me forward. I didn't like touching him, but at the same time, didn't want to get separated again.

Most of the crowd was seated now, and the aisles were clear. Down in the arena pit, bodies were being dragged away and the stage reset for the next match. I forced my eyes away from all the blood.

With my telek, I felt Max moving ahead of me with confident steps, crouched low to the ground. I followed his lead as he walked toward the front row. There was a wider aisle in front of these seats to give ample legroom for the important few who got the front-row seats. And there was our target, Warnost, just a few seats away from us now.

The horn sounded again, signaling the start of the next match. Warnost sat forward in his seat. People were packed in all around him, and suddenly our plan seemed ludicrous. It had sounded so simple when we were discussing it in theory back in the safety of our suite. At least I didn't sense an ounce of hesitation from Max. There was no trembling in his hands, no stutter to his step. He squatted low right in front of Warnost and pulled out the stun device.

And then we waited, heart-thumping minutes while the crowd watched whatever was going on behind us. The crash of metal against metal was still deafening, but I forced myself to focus only on the mission. Warnost's face was getting sweaty with excitement as he watched. His eyes were glued to the action, and then, right after I heard a loud metallic slicing noise, he jumped to his feet along with the rest of the roaring crowd.

That was our cue. Max jumped up too and held the stunner to Warnost's face. Warnost froze in place, staring outward with dull eyes. Everyone else was so busy cheering, they didn't notice his blank expression or the quick flash of light the stunner emitted. I leapt up and tugged the buttons of the top of Warnost's shirt open, then reached in and slid the pendant off over his neck. Max pulled the fake replacement pendant out of his pocket, keeping the stunner to the man's eyes the whole time.

I grabbed the pendant from Max and put it around Warnost's neck, tucking it into his shirt. I glanced around quickly—some of the crowd was starting to sit down again. It was going to look strange if our target was the only one left standing, especially with such a weirdly blank expression. We had to finish quickly.

But once I had the new pendant in place, I couldn't get the buttons done up again. My fingers shook as more and more people sat down. Warnost's wife took her seat and looked up at her husband. I managed to get one button clasped and then left the top two undone. Hopefully it just looked like he'd left them open to relax for the fight.

I dropped down again, and Max must have felt me, because he joined me and then we began inching away carefully. I looked back at Warnost's face. He was blinking in confusion and looking around him. I swore silently. Did he realize something had happened to him? But then he sat down with everyone else, looking only slightly bewildered. The horn sounded, announcing the next match, and he leaned back in to watch as if nothing had happened. A wave of relief rushed through me.

We'd done it! We had both keys. I tried to tamp down my excitement. We were still far from done. We headed back toward the entry gate where once more there was a crowd of people entering and exiting. Max reached back and grabbed my hand again.

The gilt ornamentation on the lobby walls seemed so absurd compared to the blood being spilled inside. The lobby was mostly empty except for the cluster of people surrounding the food and drink station. We easily maneuvered around them by staying close to the far wall. Finally, we came to a bank of elevators.

When we'd arrived in the city, we'd been given two all-access cards, the kind given only to the richest and most important Uppers. Max flashed his in front of the elevator and the doors opened immediately.

Good. We were back on plan now. I bit my lip nervously. No more hiccups or distractions.

The elevator tube door pinged and opened. We hurried in and Max swiped his card again, then pushed the button for the highest balcony. When the doors opened again, I walked quietly, sharp to everything around me. These seats were just as full as those below, but the people here looked different. They weren't dressed in fine dresses and suits. Instead, they wore the dark blue tunics that signaled they were techers.

Techers weren't quite Uppers, but they were no longer

drones. They wrote and supported the code that kept the Community Link alive. Uppers rarely did any actual work, so certain drone children who tested as brilliant were pulled out of drone circulation. They never got the adult V-chip because it had been shown to negatively affect creativity. Techers were paid, but for security reasons they were never allowed to leave the city where they worked. While they had few luxuries, they were allowed certain entertainments, such as getting to come to Fight Night, even if they were so far away from the central oval that they needed special glasses to see the action.

But they cheered just as loudly as the crowd below when a huge booming crash echoed from the pit—the unmistakable sound of two Regulators colliding. Max pulled me back against the wall as two techers walked by. I felt him nod, and I closed my eyes. There were over two hundred techers in this section, but we were only looking for one. Rowun Cilde. An assistant programmer who had access to the central mainframe.

Before the mission, I'd studied the feel of his 3-D profile, memorizing the curves and lines of his brow, his too-large nose, his chubby rounded cheeks. Everyone was seated and I hoped I could work through the rows quickly and find our man. I immediately skimmed past all the women and spent a brief moment scanning anyone of the right height and build.

It was slow going, and I could sense Max's growing impatience every time he moved or twitched beside me. I tried to shut him out. I knew we were already behind schedule because we'd had to stop and get the other pendant, but there was still plenty of time. The games were just getting started.

Finally, after a solid five minutes of searching, I found Rowun. He leaned forward with his eyepiece, intent on the action below. I felt his brief reaction of surprise when my telek overran his body and forced him to stand. The muscles in his throat strained as he attempted to call out, but I kept them frozen and immobile.

A bead of sweat broke out on my forehead. I'd practiced this for weeks with Xona and Ginni and anyone else who didn't mind me taking over control of their bodies for a few hours while I worked to achieve perfect and complete control. All leading up to this moment.

I felt Rowun's resistance, his frantic internal attempts to push back against my control, but I kept the muscles of his face completely still. I forced him to walk past all the other techers who were too busy watching the game to notice anything strange about their companion. Part of me felt sick at taking control so completely away from another human being. I knew just how horrible it felt. An official had once plugged a subroutine program into my neck port, immobilizing me. But as much as I might not like it, it was the only way. Too much was at stake.

The techer started to fight harder the farther I pulled him away from the group. When he passed by Max and me, heading toward the elevator, I could feel his own energy screaming to get out. I closed my eyes as we went, walking by my telek sense rather than sight so I wouldn't lose my grip on the techer for even a moment.

No one stopped to question him as he moved toward the elevator. Why would they? Anyone who noticed him would think he was probably just going back to work. Even though techers were allowed to watch the games, they were still always on call.

Max and I followed behind Rowun into the elevator.

"Hold the door," said another blue-suited techer, catching the closing elevator door with his hand and stepping in with us. Max and I flattened ourselves against the walls.

Rowun kept trying to twitch or call out, anything to signal to the techer standing only inches away from him that something was wrong. Finally after what felt like an interminably long ride, the elevator pinged and the doors opened. We stepped off too since it was the techer level. I kept my grip around Rowun firm as I forced him out of the elevator and into the hallway.

After heading down several long corridors that were fairly empty, Max pulled out his mini console with the city schematics.

His head swung in both directions, as if looking to make sure we were alone, then came near and whispered in my ear. "Straight ahead. Make sure to follow me closely."

"I know, I memorized it last night."

Rowun's eyes twitched at the sudden voices coming from thin air. I ignored him and started forward again. We were only one quick shuttle tube ride away from the central access facility where all new programming was uploaded.

The arena and Uppers housing was located in a small node at the apex of the city, with the tube shuttle lines running outward like veins. My heartbeat raced as we walked across the shuttle platform. The sun shone brightly through windows lining the ceiling of the shuttle station. I took several deep breaths, unnerved as always by sunlight, and tightened my grip on my mast cells.

There were only a few other people waiting with us. Two Regs stood on guard at the back of the station. I had to hand it to Henk. He was the one who suggested we make our attempt during Fight Night. The city was almost deserted since everyone was packed in back at the arena. Our two targets wouldn't realize their pendants had been switched until they went into work the next day, and by then we'd have already crashed the Link.

But still, if I lost control for even a *second*, Rowun could call out to the Regs and we'd be done. I could take out a couple Regs easily enough, but our mission would be ruined. The city would go on lockdown. Sweat beaded on my forehead.

I felt an absurd relief when the shuttle finally arrived and we all stepped on. It wasn't any safer in reality—maybe less so because now we were stuck in a confined space, not to mention we were still in the heart of Central City—but at least it felt better than waiting out in the open.

The shuttle was filled with drones in the crisp white tunics of the service class. They all stood at attention, holding on to the looped handholds that hung from metal bars running along the ceiling. There were a few other unchipped workers like Rowun here and there, distinguishable by the color of their tunics, a few with the surgeon reds and repair-worker browns. Rowun was the only techer on board though, and that fact made me nervous. Would it look out of place for him to enter the programming facility during the festivities of Fight Night?

The shuttle made several stops, and I gripped Rowun even tighter during every exchange of passengers. The shuttle dipped underground and a half a mile later finally came to a stop at the entrance to the programming access facility.

We stepped out and were faced with an intimidating blockade door at the edge of the station platform. I forced Rowun to hold his wrist out. The ID chip implanted in his wrist registered with a *beep* and the door opened. Max led us deeper and deeper into the complex, Rowun's chip opening every door. Just as we'd thought, the facility was almost empty. The few techers who were working were too busy to even look up as Rowun passed.

We finally arrived at a small white room. The light-cells overhead all buzzed at their brightest setting.

Now we came to it. Excitement tickled up my spine. We were so close now. This was the only place we couldn't follow right behind Rowun. There were three doorways that ran full-body scans before letting anyone pass. Max's power could trick people, but not a scanning computer.

I stepped closer to Rowun and pressed a small drive into his left hand, forcing his fingers to close around it. Then I made him lift his right finger to a small pad and press. He didn't flinch when he was poked and the small drop of blood was extracted. He did this every day.

The thick door in front of him opened, and I could see beyond him to a small square room. Rowun went in and the door closed again. A flash of light came from the small window in the door: the full-body scan in action. My telek was able to pass easily through the barriers, and I kept Rowun still through it all.

When he was inside, I did a quick sweep of the room. All of the machinery was foreign to me. I touched my arm panel to pull up the file where I'd written the Foundation techer boy's instructions. I couldn't remember his name at the moment. That was the problem of having the best techer on your team also be a glitcher whose power made people forget him. I'd been careful to write down everything he said, knowing I wouldn't remember if he only told it to me.

The top of the file read: NOTES FROM SIMIN.

I nodded. Oh right, his name was Simin. I could always remember his name for a few minutes whenever I heard it. I read on hurriedly.

FIND THE BOX ALONG THE WALL RIGHT BESIDE THE DOOR, OPEN IT, AND INSERT THE SMALLEST DRIVE INTO THE PORT TO OVERRIDE THE BODY–SCAN SECURITY.

Okay, so there should be a box close to the entryway. I felt along the wall for it with my telek and frowned. There was a box in the middle of one wall, but it wasn't close to the doorway at all.

A frantic bubble of fear passed through me, then I gritted my teeth and searched the other walls. Two were covered top to bottom with server consoles. The third wall had some kind of interface area, but it was flat and didn't seem like the kind of box Simin described. It had to be the one on the first wall.

I made Rowun walk over to the box, flip it open, and lift the tiny drive. I prayed this was the right one and I wasn't about to set off a ton of alarms or something.

He slipped the drive in.

Max and I waited anxiously. I started tapping my foot until I realized it was making an audible sound and made myself stand still again.

Then, just a moment later, the heavy doors of the full-body scan room opened, and I finally let out the breath I'd been holding. We were in. We hurried through the small passageway to where Rowun stood.

Three hovering console screens were projected over the desk in the center of the room.

I felt Max take out one pendant from his pocket. I pulled out mine and we both moved to the key stations, one on each side of the programming console. We inserted the keys and twisted them simultaneously. The blank console screens suddenly came to life, spooling out start-up data before settling on the main interface screen.

I sat down in the swiveling chair. Halfway there.

I studied the screen for a moment. It looked exactly like the model Simin had provided for me to study. I'd taken basic programming and computer interfacing, but all of this was way beyond my sphere of knowledge. So I'd studied the model for hours and made sure I knew exactly what to do so I wouldn't make a mistake.

I raised my hand to the projected screen and clicked through several data directories until I got to the central programming vector.

I pulled out the fingernail drive Simin had given me with the rebooted Link programming. He'd worked on it for months. The Link feed in everyone's head should automatically stop, along with the submission impulse. We'd uploaded simple instructions to broadcast what had been done to them and where they could go to acquire weapons if they wanted to join the revolution. The adults would most likely mindlessly follow the new instructions and fight with us. We'd had qualms about forcing them to fight like that, but it was better than the alternative plan of releasing an EMP. Setting off an electromagnetic pulse in the upper atmosphere had been General Taylor's plan to destroy the Link hardware in all the drones' heads Sectorwide. While it would have freed everyone under eighteen from the Link's control, it also would have killed the millions upon millions of adult drones who had fully integrated V-chips. Making them mindlessly fight was definitely the lesser of two evils—it at least gave them the possibility of a future. Once we'd won, we could begin researching in earnest about ways to free them from their more extensive V-chips.

All around the country, Rez fighting cells were poised at strategic posts, ready for the takeover. With the drones on our side, even if only a third of them fought with us, we'd outnumber the Uppers thirty to one. We'd take Sector Six, freeing all the drones in the second-largest country in the world. And now, finally, we were here.

I slipped the drive into one of the console slots. Blue code started spinning in the columns in front of me. I checked my arm panel again to check Simin's instructions: WAIT ONE

MINUTE FOR THE ERASE OF CURRENT CODE. I tried to wait patiently, but my foot started tapping again. We'd been here too long already. I glanced behind me at the still-open security doors. If anyone came in, they'd immediately know something was wrong.

Finally the code stopped blinking, and a translucent command box popped up.

REWRITE? YES OR NO.

A rush of exhilaration flooded me. This was the day Adrien had always dreamed of. I wished it could have been him standing beside me instead of Max.

With shaking fingers, I clicked Yes, and then waited for the world to change.

I watched the screen, excitement already bubbling through me. A confirmation screen should pop up any second now, letting us know that the signal had been broadcast.

Instead, an alarm so loud it seemed to shake the room went off. Huge metal doors slammed down at every exit, locking us in.

Chapter 5

"NO!" I SAID OUT LOUD. This couldn't be happening! We'd planned everything so perfectly.

Rowun started laughing. I'd let go of my hold over him in my shock. "You thought you could upload code from one port and affect the entire Link? We have a hundred redundancy systems in a hundred different places." He laughed even harder. "It's part of the protocol, so if one station is breached with foreign code, all it does is trigger the alarm!"

"We've got to go, now!" Max shouted.

I grabbed the fingernail drive out of the computer, knowing even as I did that the information had probably instantly replicated. I replaced it with the kill-disk drive I'd also brought with me. I could only hope that it erased any of the code that had been logged and copied. Either way, I had to get word to the Rez quick, in case the Uppers could still see the code mentioning the Rez rendezvous sites.

I had an encrypted com, but all outgoing signals were too carefully monitored in Central City, and if the kill disk *did* work, calling my Rez contacts would give away their location to the Uppers just as quickly.

First we had to get the hell out of this facility.

Max grabbed my hand and pulled me away before I could see if the kill disk worked.

"Open the doors," he said and I nodded. I lifted my hand,

letting the telek build up inside me for a moment and then I unleashed it. The door slid back up in its track, grating with a loud screech as it broke free of the hydraulics system holding it in place.

"What the hell?" Rowun said from behind us. I didn't have time for him. I threw him backward into the wall of consoles with my telek, then focused again on the blockades in front of us.

We ran through the open space and down the hallway. Heavy metal lockdown doors awaited us at every step along the way, but I felt ahead and opened the blockades before we even got to them. I could only hope it would be quick enough.

When we got past the last one I started heading left toward the shuttle platform. "Zoe, what are you doing? We've got to steal the nearest transport we can find!"

"No," I pulled him near. "We'll never get out if we steal a transport. There's no reason we can't continue with the original plan."

He nodded, then gripped my hand. The tube shuttle was still working. They hadn't shut it down yet. We hadn't encountered any actual Regs yet either. We'd only hit automatic redundancy systems so far. If the alarm in the lab went off, the doors went down. No one expected someone like me, someone who could breech even the widest, heaviest of lockdown doors to escape. Anyone alerted to the situation would still think we were inside. Until they saw the twisted metal of each door we'd broken through.

The hum of the transport shuttling along its tracks would have been comforting if I weren't so terrified of what we'd find on the other end. My fingernails dug into Max's palms. The door opened and I breathed out a sigh of relief. We were quickly back in the arena lobby and took the elevator down to the Uppers quarters. We ducked into an alcove, and Max transformed us into Darl and Nihem again.

My hand felt strangely bereft after Max let go of it. Holding his hand had helped keep my terror at bay. But then again, now more than ever, we had to play our parts perfectly, and Nihem and Darl would never hold hands. We walked stiffly together, side by side but not touching.

We walked straight to the departure bay, and as we saw the attendant valet we started arguing.

"You can't even let us stop to enjoy the game?" Nihem said loudly.

"I said I want to leave NOW." I put an angry whine into my voice. "And if you have any hope of keeping our marriage alive and saving yourself from complete and desolate financial ruin, you'll come with me. My daddy will cut you off as sure as the morning sun."

"But Darl—"

I turned to the attendant and handed him our passkey. "It's the pretty one with the shiny silver stripe," I said.

The attendant stared at me a little blankly.

"Women." Max shook his head, stepping in front of me. "She means the purple BT6."

"Nihem!" I said, sounding exasperated. "It's things like this. You treat me like I'm a child. You are so patronizing I could just strangle you—"

"I'll be right back with your vehicle," the attendant cut in, then hurried off.

Max and I continued arguing in case anyone else was watching. Our purple BT6 soon came around the bend.

Max suddenly pushed me against the wall. My eyes instantly widened. Was something wrong? Had someone found us? A quick look over his shoulder only showed the attendant getting out of the car. And then suddenly Max was mashing his lips against mine. I was so stunned by the audacity of it that I didn't move at all for a second.

And then I felt fury. We had failed in our mission, we didn't know how many people were in danger, and he was taking this opportunity to steal a kiss when he knew I couldn't hurtle him across the room like I wanted to? Max hadn't changed at all.

I pushed him hard on the chest instead, conscious that I couldn't say everything I wanted because of the attendant. "You act like you've been forgiven already."

"You have to forgive me someday," he whispered, his eyes searching mine.

I bit my tongue to keep myself from saying more, pushed off the wall, and headed for our transport. I slid into the driver's side. Max made some joke with the attendant that I couldn't hear and then jumped in the other door. My telek buzzed loudly in my head now. So much had gone wrong, and so much still could.

But then the doors of the transport garage opened up and we lifted into the sky.

We'd made it out.

I stood under the allergen wash shower back at the Foundation with my hand against the wall as the heavy spray beat down on my head and shoulders.

I'd failed.

This had been our big plan, and it had failed so utterly and completely that I had no idea what to do next. I'd sent the abort signal out once we were far enough away from Central City, but some cells still may have gotten cracked.

"Zoe, oh my gosh, are you okay?" Ginni asked as soon as I

stepped out of the shower with a towel wrapped around me. "Simin said it didn't work."

"I'm fine," I said, gritting my teeth when I saw the rest of my team and several high-ranking Rez soldiers waiting for me. "I'll debrief everyone later about what happened. But yes, the mission was a failure."

"What happened?" Ginni asked.

"I'll debrief you all later," I repeated, my voice more snappish than I intended. Xona put a hand on Ginni's shoulder and led her away. I rubbed my eyes tiredly, then went to change in the dressing room.

All I wanted was to sink into my bed and forget the failure that weighed so heavy on my chest it felt like I could barely breathe. But I knew the other Colonels were waiting for me in the Sat Com office, and I was anxious to find out if everyone was safe.

Henk had set up the teleconference room in what used to be Taylor's office, at my request. I knew the Professor hadn't wanted me to—he'd wanted to leave all her things just as they'd been. But it was a luxury we couldn't afford in this underground bunker; space was too precious, especially now that we were flooded with refugees. Every closet doubled as an office, every dorm was at triple occupancy.

And now what would we do with them all? How long would we be able to feed them? I wondered if Henk had been able to get more supplies while I was gone. Another thing I'd have to check on before I slept.

I sat down at the desk with a bay of four projection screens around me, each screen displaying the face of a different Colonel in the Rez. They were camped out at the few other Rez hideouts that were still left scattered in and around Sector Six. None of us knew exactly where the others were stationed. It was safer that way.

I rubbed my face in my hands for a few long moments, trying to gather myself. But they were waiting for me, so I shook my hands out and took a deep breath before clicking on the camera so they could see me too.

"Did everyone get the message to abort in time?" I asked immediately.

"Two cells didn't, and Reg armadas discovered them before they could flee," said the redheaded woman, Sanyez. "A high-security alert must have gone out after the central mission failed. Reg armadas have been scouring the skies for hours."

"Just two cells?" asked Garabex. He was an older man with a thick gray beard. "That's less catastrophic than I expected, considering what a mess was made of the mission."

"At least if the cell leaders are interrogated," Sanyez said, "they were told nothing of Project Reboot or the Foundation. All they knew was that they were to be ready for a planned attack, details to be messaged at the last moment if it was a go."

"If they only cracked two cells, that means the kill disk probably worked," I said. "The programmer will tell his superiors what we were trying to do, but they shouldn't be able to recover any of the code itself."

Garabex leaned forward. "You fool, why didn't you eliminate the programmer?"

"That was never part of the plan," I snapped back.

"Well, nothing about the *plan* actually worked, did it? Any elementary corporal knows to cut losses and minimize damage." He directed his attention to the others. "Why are we even listening to this little girl?"

Talon, the next youngest lieutenant, spoke up. "Taylor explicitly left Zoe in charge of the glitcher unit. The plan was solid—we'd all agreed it was the best option."

"We've just never been close enough to gather intel on how

the Link programming is disseminated," I said. "The code isn't uploaded at a single port in the Central City mainframe system like we thought. Our techers were basing their assumptions on what was probably false intel circulated by the Community, as an added security measure."

"The girl is right," said Lonyi, a short-haired woman. "Now is no time to assign blame. We all agreed on the plan. It failed. Now we reassess and move on."

"Fine," said Garabex. "But we don't know how much time we have. One of our Rez spies reported about what we think is a new weapon the Chancellor has acquired. He only saw the name of a file. Something called an 'Amplifier.' He wasn't able to find any more details. We need to go back to the EMP option so we can strike first—"

"No!" I said, then pulled back and tried to mask my emotions again. "We cannot go forward with a plan that kills so many innocent people."

Garabex scoffed loudly and threw up his hands. "Will someone please remove this *child* from the council?"

I balled my hands into fists to keep myself from reacting to his words. The only way I'd earn my place at this table was by not letting myself be baited.

"We are all that's left of the Resistance," Garabex continued. "Just five command posts and a paltry amount of small scattered cells whose members are often on the run. Any one of us could be cracked at any moment. The Rez is hanging on by the thinnest of threads. We must act before it is too late and that thread snaps. I refuse to let a two-hundred-year-old movement crumble to dust on my watch!"

"The EMP option is unacceptable," I said firmly. "There's collateral damage and then there's mass murder. If we plan to rebuild a world better than this one, we better know the difference."

Talon and Sanyez nodded. Garabex and Lonyi looked un-convinced.

Sanyez addressed the rest of the council. "Nothing will be decided today on this issue. We need to regroup after today's events, recoup losses, and keep our heads down. As Colonel Garabex said, we're barely managing to survive as it is. Being too hasty at this point would only jeopardize the tenuous grip we still have. And when we *do* reach the point where we can consider new proposals on how to proceed, keep in mind the Council must agree unanimously before any action is taken."

Garabex scowled. "We *were* in unison about the EMP op-tion before this upstart showed up. It was Taylor's idea in the first place. It's her vote that should count, even from beyond the grave."

"The fact that she appointed me in her place is proof enough that she had doubts about the plan." I wasn't sure if it was true, but it sounded good. Besides, I knew some of the others had hesitations about the EMP option. They wouldn't want it back on the table unless there was absolutely nothing left to try.

Garabex looked like he was about to launch into another tirade, but Lonyi spoke up before he could. "What do we do then? The Rez is the smallest it's ever been. Underchancellor Bright is cracking safe houses right as we set them up. She always seems three steps ahead of us. We've already tried hav-ing Zoe crush the V-chips of small populations at a time, but that didn't work."

I grimaced, remembering the experiment. With my telek, I was able to reach and crush the tiny embedded chips in about a hundred people at a time. So we'd infiltrated an Academy, hoping we could add to our diminishing ranks, but Regs had quickly descended and captured all the confused teenagers right after I'd freed them from the V-chip. We'd only been able to rescue a few before having to escape ourselves.

"If we don't do something," Lonyi continued, her voice impassioned, "then there will be no Rez left to speak of soon. We have to act now before we don't have the manpower to enact any plans we come up with!"

"The Underchancellor is the problem," Talon said. "It's her we need to take out."

I nodded. He was right. Every attempt we'd made so far had failed. She was surrounded at all times by fifty Regs and an impressive band of glitchers she'd collected.

But there was still one thing we hadn't tried—sending me in alone to try to assassinate her.

It would be risky. Maybe even a suicide mission. I'd wanted to exhaust every other possibility before I suggested it, but if it was that or letting them go ahead with the EMP option . . .

Sanyez held up her hand. "We can talk about that next week when we reconvene. Right now we need to recoup, count our losses, and rest. Ali will send you the encryption pattern an hour before the next meeting as always. We must be more vigilant than ever about security protocols. Next year in freedom," she finished, the standard council salutation.

"Freedom for all," we all responded back. Everyone in the Rez had grown up with the saying. It was always *next* year, never now.

After I switched off the camera I sighed out a long breath and ran my hands through my still-wet hair. When I got up to walk to the Med Center, my steps were heavy. My whole body felt like lead. I didn't want to think about any of it, any of the responsibilities of knowing the Rez was getting smaller every day or worrying about the refugees who would no doubt come clamoring to me tomorrow with more problems I didn't have a solution to. I wished I had an off switch so I could stop caring about all of it.

In spite of how I'd just avowed how important life and

morality was, sometimes I worried that I was turning into General Taylor. I remembered when I first met her, I'd been shocked by her coldness. She seemed callous, uncaring about other people's feelings, and, in the end, unconcerned with sacrificing millions of people. But she hadn't been afraid of death either. She took on her duty as a mantle to the last moment when she'd decided to come with me against the Chancellor. Her last thought had been for the future of the Rez.

I headed into the hallway and heard other footsteps echoing down the parallel corridor. I knew even without seeing him that it was the Professor. He paced the hallways now at night, like a ghost. He must hear me too on the nights I couldn't sleep, but we kept to our separate hallways and never spoke of it. We insomniacs kept each other's secrets.

I listened to him now, aimlessly walking back and forth. I'd always thought of the General as a project of his, another person to save. But now I wondered if it wasn't the other way around. He barely functioned without her. Did that mean he loved her more than she did him? If it had been the reverse, and he'd died, I knew she'd have gone on as if nothing had happened. Seeing Henry so broken made me wonder if her way wasn't better. Maybe it was better not to love anything too much.

But that didn't stop me from walking to the darkened Med Center where Adrien lay submerged in the chamber in the corner. The sides were made of glass, and it was lit from underneath, which made the blue regrowth gel look luminescent. Otherworldly.

Adrien's slim form, wearing a tight bodysuit, seemed just as alien.

An oxygen mask covered the lower half of his face, and wired patches were placed at strategic points around his body and all over his head. His eyes were closed.

I put a hand to the side of the tank.

His head moved so quickly to look at me, I almost fell over backwards. He stared at me, but nothing registered on his face. It was as if he was staring past me at the wall. His eyes seemed focused, but nothing else from his expression would suggest he knew me. I swallowed hard and leaned forward again. It was just the heavy sedatives Jilia had given him, I tried to reassure myself. The sessions in the chamber always lasted five days, and it was better if he could sleep through most of it. I placed my hand where it had been before.

The gel inside was warm, I could feel the heat through the glass. But seeing Adrien suspended in this sensory deprivation tank still made me feel cold. Jilia believed it would help his neural patterns learn to rewire themselves if he started from a blank slate of stimulus and response, at least during periods of amygdala tissue regrowth. I'd known he was going in for another session, but I had hoped he'd be out by the time I got back.

Of course, I'd planned to be out starting a revolution right now. In my secret dreams, I'd envisioned the world free of the Link. Sure, I'd known it would be a long fight. But I'd dreamed of its end; maybe a year from now we would have captured enough strategic points to install a new government. And the regrowth therapy would have finally begun working and Adrien would stand by my side as we looked out on a new world.

I thought back to one of the times he'd visited me in the lab hideout where I'd spent several months last year.

He'd been sitting beside me, wrapping one of my long curls round and round his finger. "What would you do if the war was over and you could do anything?" he asked.

"Hmm," I said languorously, dropping my head to his shoulder and relaxing against him. "I guess we'd be working every day to help people who'd been freed from the Link.

We'd have to make sure that food production didn't waver and that basic utilities continued so everything didn't descend into chaos and—"

"Not like that," Adrien laughed. "I mean, what would you do if there was no war? Like if you lived back in the Old World and were free and there was no government telling you what you had to do. Or if we lived in some alternate universe where instead of Comm Corp coming to power, everyone was free and at peace with each other. What would you do then?"

I frowned. "I don't know." I shifted a little so that I could look up at him. "I can't imagine a world outside this one." I smiled and kissed him. "You're the dreamer. What would *you* do?"

"Okay, I'll go first," he said, relenting. "But don't think I'm not gonna come back to the question."

I laughed. "Okay. But you tell me first, so I know what kinds of things you mean."

He laid back on my bed, his hands under his head, elbows out. He looked up at the ceiling, but the way his blue-green eyes glistened with possibility, I could tell he wasn't seeing just a ceiling.

"I'd own a house by a river. A small river, not one of those big ones that boats would go down. And there would be woods nearby. Thick woods that I'd be able to see out my window when I woke up each morning."

"And what would you do in this house in the woods by a river?" I asked, half teasing. But he didn't take the bait; he just kept that goofy grin on his face.

"Well, first of all, you'd be there beside me waking up each morning." He moved so quickly I didn't have time to register, grabbing me around the waist and pulling me down so that I was lying beside him, my back to his chest. He wrapped his arms around the front of my waist and pulled me into him.

I'd never felt safer or more secure in my life. I let out a small contented sigh.

"And what would we do every day after we woke up and looked at the woods?"

"I'd spend hours reading," he said. "I'd read the great philosophers and poets, and then I'd take a transport into a small city where I would be a professor. I'd ask the students questions and get them engaged, and we'd spend hours talking about ideas from the books we'd read." He nuzzled his chin into my hair. "We'd discover new things about ideas we thought we already knew or understood. And then we'd leave class with our heads full of new thoughts and new ways of seeing the world. That would be my job. Talking about ideas all day. But only a few days a week."

"And the other days?"

He flipped me over until I was lying on my back, his body suspended over mine. The grin was gone, replaced by a shy intensity. He looked down, and his cheeks reddened a moment before meeting my eyes again. "The rest of the time we'd spend all day in bed."

It was my turn for my face to redden. We spent hours kissing whenever he came by on these rare visits, but hadn't pushed it further to discover the mysteries of what happened when all the clothes came off.

A small alarm had beeped right then, signaling it was time for him to leave again so he'd be gone in plenty of time before the rest of the lab workers came in.

He'd spent several more minutes ignoring the alarm anyway, holding me close and kissing me. But then, like always, he'd had to leave.

I lifted my other hand to the side of the tank. Leaving. He was always leaving me. Even now when he was here, it was like he was gone.

The tears I hadn't allowed earlier now slipped down both cheeks. Adrien's eyes shifted slightly to look at my hands pressed against the glass.

But he didn't even seem curious, much less engaged in anything that was happening to him. I wanted to pull him out of this stupid tank and hold him in my arms. Even if he didn't feel anything for me, *couldn't* feel anything, it would make me feel better to hold him. I pulled back, trying to tamp down my selfish impulses. I had to think of his health, his recovery.

"I miss you." I swiped at the tears on both cheeks with my forearm. "The mission failed. I seem to be doing that a lot lately. Failing, letting people down. But obviously you know that better than anyone."

I leaned my forehead against the tank. "I love you," I whispered.

He blinked and one of his hands shot out to touch the glass in the same spot my hand had been earlier.

I lifted my hand to meet his. "Adrien?"

Our hands were together, so close to touching except for the barrier of glass between us. His eyes met mine and for a second I'd swear there was a zinging flash of recognition. His eyebrows furrowed together and he looked so profoundly *sad* as he gazed out at me.

"Adrien?" My voice echoed loudly in the empty room. My heartbeat ramped up and I put my other hand up anxiously to the glass. Anything to try to grab hold of this moment of connection. "Adrien?"

But then his hand released, relaxing limply into the gel again. His gaze drifted back to the ceiling. As if I wasn't even there.

Chapter 6

THE NEXT FEW DAYS WERE calm and absurdly normal. In the mornings, I switched off between doing physical training with my old glitcher task force and having administrative meetings with either the on-site Rez soldiers or the representative who'd been appointed to speak on behalf of refugee affairs. The afternoons were similarly split between administrative duties and joining in for Gifted Training when I could afford the time.

Today, I followed the rest of my friends to lunch after a morning training session. We'd run stairs. Most days I groaned like everyone else when Tyryn announced it was a stairs day, but today I'd enjoyed the pounding physicality of it. I'd even welcomed the pain burning through my thighs. Here, finally, was something I could control, something I could do *right*.

"God, Rand," City scrunched up her nose. "Don't you know showers after training shouldn't be optional? Especially for *you*."

Rand only grinned, jogging backwards down the hall so he could face her. "It's all about the pheromones. I'm letting the Rand musk run free, so it can overwhelm all the female senses."

Xona scoffed. "The only thing it's overwhelming is the air quality." She punched Rand hard in the arm.

Saminsa smiled as she walked behind them. She'd been opening up over the past few months. She was still far from talkative, but she seemed to enjoy observing everyone else and simply being part of the group.

"Ow!" Rand said, rubbing his arm. Then he leaned in to her. "You seem riled up, Xona. Maybe the pheromones are working on you and you don't even know it."

Xona rolled her eyes and hurried down the hallway to catch up with Cole. I stared for a moment as she talked with the hulking ex-Reg. He leaned down to hear what she said and then let out a hearty laugh. I watched with surprise. It still startled me anytime he laughed. He'd always fought hard for his humanity, but in the past six months, ever since he'd saved Xona's life and she'd finally stopped hating him, he'd positively flourished.

I watched the pair of them walk down the hallway. Her laughing response echoed off the walls.

"Don't think your pheromones are gonna work on her," Ginni said with a giggle.

Rand didn't look daunted. "Well, there's still you fine ladies," he said, putting his arms around City and Ginni.

"Gross!" City shouted, pulling away from him and making a big show of gagging. "Can't you smell how much you *reek*?"

"Aw, you don't mean that," Rand said with an impish grin. "Stop trying to fight your primordial attraction to me."

"The only attraction I feel for you," City said with a falsely ingenuous smile, "is the electrical kind." She reached out a fingertip and the tiniest spiral of electricity hit Rand between the eyebrows.

"Shunting hell, Citz," Rand cried out, rubbing his forehead. "That hurt!"

City only smiled back as we came to the entrance to the Caf. I followed in beside Ginni until I looked up and saw Molla and Max at the central table with their baby son.

He was only let out of his cell for lunchtime and for Gifted

Training, because as much as everyone disliked and distrusted him, we couldn't deny that his power *was* incredibly useful. Adrien's mother always locked herself away in her room during this part of the day to keep herself from attacking him.

Most of the time I handled seeing him with a degree of equilibrium, but today I paused as sudden intense rage flooded through me. It wasn't fair. Max was a horrible person who had done horrible things, and yet here he was, free except for his ankle monitor, playing with his cooing son. Molla loved him too, in spite of everything. Her eyes were wide and adoring as she watched Max play with the baby's fingers.

Max had a family. All the while Adrien was stuck in a sensory deprivation tank trying to regrow parts of his brain. *Because* of Max.

The image of Adrien's hand meeting mine on the glass of his tank rose like a mocking ghost. Because I knew, as much as I wanted it to be otherwise, the moment had only been the illusion of connection, not the real thing.

I set my jaw and forced myself to look away from Max as I got in line for food.

The memory of Adrien in the tank last night made an icy spike of loneliness stab through me. Adrien had been my family, the only one I had after leaving my younger brother Markan behind in the Community. My parents were lost to the adult V-chip. Adrien had been the one person in the world who cared about me more than any of the other people scattered over the earth. My friends cared, sure. Even loved me. I looked over at the table where they were gathered. Rand was making some exaggerated gesture that had Ginni and City laughing. Xona just shook her head and went back to her conversation with Cole.

They cared, but I wasn't first in their consideration—they didn't put me above all others. Losing that connection made me feel so disconnected from the world around me. I could disappear or be killed and people would mourn me (or mourn the loss of my Gift, at least), but it was a wound they'd get over in time. It wouldn't tear a hole in anyone's heart like losing Adrien had done to me.

I stepped forward in line, averting my eyes from my friends. *No*, I reminded myself firmly. Adrien wasn't lost. Not yet. And neither was my brother Markan. He was years away from the adult V-chip. I made a mental note to ask Ginni to track his location for me later. Her glitcher ability let her locate anyone, anywhere on the earth. I usually asked her every week to make sure my brother was still at the Academy or my old housing unit, but I hadn't checked in on him since before leaving for the mission. It always reassured me to know he was safe, or as safe as he could be under the Chancellor's constant observation. She'd be ready to pounce if he ever started displaying glitcher traits.

I tapped my foot impatiently. The line was taking forever today. I looked around and realized the line was far longer than it had been when I'd left on the mission. But then, I knew another group of refugees had come seeking shelter. With the Chancellor's hefty increase on raids, people who'd lived free in the Rez their whole lives had suddenly found themselves with no safe place to go. Whenever she cracked a Rez safe house, she imprisoned the leaders and chipped the rest to turn them into drones.

We'd already been rationing our food stocks before the new group had even arrived. It was getting harder and harder to acquire supplies. Everyone was running scared these days.

Last month the Chancellor had captured a supplier who'd told them we were piggybacking on Comm Corp trains to move supplies, so now there were heavy inspections on all the trains. Worse, even though no one could remember the exact location of the Foundation because of the techer boy's Gift that made people forget it, the Chancellor had still figured out that our hideout was in the south. After all, the informants she turned *could* still tell her the direction the train cars full of supplies were headed. We always had them delivered several hundred miles away and then picked them up from there, but still. There was more air traffic buzzing overhead than ever before. We even had to put a stop to groups going up to the Surface to get fresh air every day. Which had, of course, become another source of complaints. I was used to being underground, but lots of the people in the Rez who'd lived out in the open found it claustrophobic inside our mountain hideout.

I finally got to the front of the line and looked at the picked-over food in the steaming bins. I reached to spear one of the few protein patties left, then paused and glanced behind me at the still-long line. A tiny girl stood at the end of the line, her eyes huge and hungry. I pulled my hand back and shoveled a small bit of sweet potato and brown rice on my tray instead. I'd tell the cook to cut the protein patties in two tomorrow so everyone could get some.

But how long could we keep this up? I rubbed my tired eyes before picking up my tray. The cafeteria was crowded. For a moment, I looked longingly at the table where my friends were all gathered. Then I headed to the table where Tyryn, Jilia, Henk, and the top platoon leader of the Rez soldiers sat.

"Where are we on getting another rations shipment?" I asked as I sat down. Henk had been laughing with Jilia as I'd approached, but now he glowered.

"It's a right trick tryin' to get anything past those sneaky bastards, but I think I got a line on a possible supplier. It's all black market, but I think I can cut a deal with a ganger boss. Sylv was always fresh on me; I think I can charm her into working a deal."

"Is she a Rez agent?" I asked.

"Nah, but she's got no great love for Comm Corp."

Community Corp was the global conglomerate that had begun implanting V-chips in people hundreds of years ago. Almost everyone who'd escaped their control or lived on the fringes hated them.

I frowned. "But can we trust her not to rat us out to the Uppers?"

Henk shrugged. "For the right price, we could persuade her to at least think twice about it."

I shook my head. "That doesn't sound safe."

"Money we got," Henk said, "at least for the moment. But food, we don't."

"How much longer will the supplies we *do* have last?" I asked.

Jilia leaned in, her voice little higher than a whisper. "Another two weeks, maximum." We'd all agreed to keep the situation of our diminishing supplies quiet. Refugees outnumbered Rez fighters two to one now. At night almost every spare inch of floor was taken up with sleeping bags. And that was just with the people we'd been able to accommodate. The latest group that had come in was the last we could take, at least until we figured out the supplies situation. The last thing we needed was a riot within the Foundation when people who'd come here for refuge realized we might not be able to feed them.

I stared at Jilia, feeling my mouth dry up. "What about the other Rez outposts? Do they have any food they could spare?"

Henk shook his head. "They're just as strapped as us. Most are worse off."

"Then I guess we'd take our chances with the ganger boss," I said. "But take Beka with you when you go to meet with the woman. At least she'll be able to tell if Sylv is lying." I hated making these decisions. I hated that if I was wrong, people might die. Beka, whose glitcher Gift made her a human lie detector, was a sweet girl. Sending her out into such a precarious situation . . .

Henk nodded. "I'll head out tomorrow."

Jilia took a small quick breath in, then reached over as if she was going to take Henk's hand, but stopped herself and pulled her hand back.

"Aw, doc," Henk gave her his characteristic side grin, "you worried about me?"

Jilia tilted her head, smiling with false sweetness. "Why would I worry? Just because a man who can't manage to eat peas without spilling half of them on the table is heading off as our one lifeline to more supplies?"

He grinned back at her and I had to look away. Whenever they bantered like this, all I felt was a yawning emptiness that cut as quick as a knife. Adrien and I used to look at each other like that. I shoveled down the rest of my food.

"I'll see you in training," I said to Jilia. She nodded, a look of concern on her face as she watched me stand. I'd debriefed them all about the failed mission the day after I got back. She'd tried to talk to me about it several times since then, asking me how I was *feeling* about it all. If there was one thing I wanted to talk about even less than our dwindling supplies, it was about my feelings.

I hurried away before she could ask me anything and headed to the Gifted Training room to get a jump start on my meditation time. Meditation was all about emptying your mind. With all the thoughts, responsibilities, and guilt swirling around my head the rest of the time, it was the one place I occasionally managed to find a few moments of peace.

But no matter how much I tried to let go of my worries, today I couldn't find any relief. Everyone else filed in. Juan began to play his cello. His Gift of manipulating emotion through music often helped push me over the edge into an iridescent blanket of peace. But even though the lull of the music calmed me, thoughts still managed to pierce through: what if Henk wasn't able to make contact with Sylv, or if it turned out that she was double-crossing us from the start? Henk and Beka could be killed or captured. And Adrien—

I was glad when Jilia rang the bell and everyone opened their eyes.

"Today we'll continue with sparring against each other, especially against the mind-workers," Jilia said. "We know the Chancellor is gathering more glitchers every day, and many of those glitchers will have mind-working skills. They can make you see things that aren't there, make you feel things you don't actually feel. More than the external powers like City's electricity or Saminsa's orbs," she glanced at the two girls, "these are the powers that are the most difficult to defend against. They are the attacks you won't be able to see coming. But what have we learned over the past two months since we've been training with the help of our own mind-workers?"

"That if you know what to look for, you can feel them in your head," Ginni said.

Jilia nodded. "Exactly. This is our most important defense."

City scoffed. "But it only gives us like a ten-second lead time. None of us have managed to actually *stop* the attack, even when we realize it's coming."

"As I mentioned before, we've only been trying for two months." Jilia's voice was patient. "But we *know* it's possible to throw off a mind-worker because it has been accomplished before, albeit under extreme circumstances."

I swallowed. She was talking about Adrien. He'd somehow found a way to break the Chancellor's compulsion power over him because his love for me was so strong. When she'd compelled him to tell her a vision that gave her the blueprints to kill me, his mind had somehow managed to repel her compulsion. That was when she'd started in on the surgical options.

"What was accomplished under duress we hope to duplicate through continued practice," Jilia said. Adrien hadn't been able to tell us how he'd done it, but the simple fact that he had managed it at all inspired Jilia to begin this new training regime. "So now let us pair up. Shaun, you'll spar with City."

City kicked at the ground. "If I wanted to take a nap, I could have just skipped class and gone to my bunk."

Shaun was a recently acquired addition who'd come in with a group of refugees a few months ago. His glitcher power was to put people to sleep. With one touch of his mind, you were unconscious within seconds.

But Shaun was approaching City with an equal wariness. She'd become adept at gauging her electricity just to stun a person. Even though Jilia had repeatedly told us not to attack back with our powers, since the point of the exercise was to learn to recognize and hopefully withstand the mind-worker's power, several of City's last sparing partners had ended up on the floor anyway.

"Ginni will be paired with . . ." Jilia paused, looking momentarily confused.

"Simin," a dark-haired boy in the corner said, looking only mildly annoyed. "My name's Simin. I'm the one who makes you forget."

"But I'm starting to remember you," Ginni piped up. "I watch the video of you explaining it every morning and sometimes I even remember you until lunch!"

It didn't sound like much to me, but Simin beamed at her. I was struck by how lonely it must be to be him. Unlike most of us, his Gift was involuntary and constantly active, even in his sleep.

Jilia went on to pair up the others. Everyone let out a

grumble when Rand got paired with Amara, who could make you feel euphoric. Of all the mind-workers, hers was the only Gift that was actually pleasant to be attacked with.

"And Zoe, you'll be paired with Max."

I glared at him, but nodded curtly. It was a good idea to pair with Max, I knew that. After all, if he managed to override the anklet and tried to disappear and escape, I was the only one who could sense him with my telek to track him down before he got far. Though I didn't think he'd be that stupid, not with the kill chip now installed at the base of his brain.

"Remember what I've told you to practice. Visualize your mind like a house. First seal up the windows, then the door, then any cracks you find. Make your mind into a fortress and focus only on its walls. When you feel the tug of an intrusion, put up another wall."

We all nodded, but it was far easier said than done.

"Hey," Max said, coming up to me as all the groups paired off around the room.

I put myself in a relaxed but alert stance. "Attack," I said.

"Zoe, wait, can't we talk at least a little about—"

"Attack!" I said through gritted teeth. "Or I'll slam you against a wall."

He hung his head, and all I wanted to do was slug him. But he didn't say anything else, he just got into a similar stance as me and closed his eyes.

I set my jaw and tried to put up the mental walls Jilia described. I could feel the telltale intrusion of his power on my mind only seconds before he disappeared from sight. This was another reason why I paired with him—he was the best. I closed my eyes and tried to concentrate on how the intrusion felt. Over the past several months, I'd begun recognizing the signs. There was a very slight pressure right behind my forehead and very occasionally I'd feel a gentle tugging pulse on my own thoughts.

I kept my telek raised the whole time. I always felt more secure when I had a concrete sense of my attacker in front of me. I concentrated on letting my mind expand as I tried to push out the intrusion and fortify my walls.

But then, for a startling second, Max disappeared from my telek-sense as well. My eyes flew open and I reached out to grab hold of where his forearm should be. My hand gripped solid flesh and my telek latched on to him again.

"What?" Max asked, becoming visible to my eyes.

"What did you just do?"

He looked at me steadily. "I didn't do anything, Zoe."

I stared hard at him another long moment. You'd think after all this time I'd be able to recognize for sure when he was lying. I thought about sending a com to Beka to have her come question him, but she was off preparing for her mission with Henk. I shook my head. I was probably being paranoid. I'd been concentrating so hard on trying to push him out, I must have let go of control on my telek for a moment.

I took a deep breath and closed my eyes. "Again."

I sat with my friends at dinner and tried to lose myself in their easy banter. But mostly I just sat silently watching them all, like an observer watching lab specimens through a window. It's how I felt a lot these days, like there was a sheet of glass between me and the rest of the world. After dinner, when we were rising to empty our trays, several of the refugees asked Cole to speak.

Cole nodded and moved to the front of the room.

Shunt, I'd forgotten it was Monday. I looked for a way I

might exit quietly before anyone noticed. I'd heard about Cole's impromptu Monday night talks, but I'd always managed to be absent from them. Tonight Ginni tugged on my arm so I was forced back down beside her.

Cole remained standing while the rest of the room quieted. He took several moments, as if gathering his thoughts.

"Though so many of us were drones," he finally began, "we've been freed. We're learning how to become human again. But we can't reclaim the lost years. We can't have our childhoods back, and," he looked down, his eyes heavy, "we can't undo the acts we performed when under the control of the hardware in our brains."

He looked back up. "It's not our fault. That's what I tell myself every morning. It wasn't my fault. But the thing is, I still have the memories of the things these hands did." He raised his metal reinforced palms. "I remember what it felt like to squeeze the life out of a man. I can still hear the screams of a woman as I hauled her off to an interrogation cell."

I found myself leaning in, interested in spite of myself.

"But what's surprised me most, in talking with so many of you here, is that this experience isn't something unique to just former Regulators." His eyes swept across the gathered crowd. "Even those of you who were never drones. I've heard your stories about the things you've had to do to survive. About the acts of desperation that hunger can drive a person to. About the ones you had to leave behind in order to save yourselves. So many of us bear a heavy guilt deep down in the marrow of our bones. It's what this world they created has made us—they would crush us until we all cease to be men."

I had to look away from him. My heart beat erratically in my chest. I knew the kind of guilt he spoke of. I dealt with it just fine. By ignoring it. Him speaking about the dark thing I kept buried in the corners of my soul made me squirm in my chair. I looked up again at the exit.

"So how then are we redeemed?" Cole's voice was passionate as he asked the question. His eyes seemed to zero in on me, as if he could somehow sense I wanted to flee. "How are we made human again, if our humanity has been stripped from us one way or another? How do we turn steel—whether fused to the body," he raised up his gleaming metal forearm, "or to the soul—back into flesh?"

He paced back and forth at the front of the room. "It's the question that's driven me to look for answers wherever I could find them. There's this one text I like. When speaking to a people who had lost their way, much like we have in our world today, God says he will give them new hearts. He says he will put a new spirit in them, that he will take away their hearts of stone and give them hearts of flesh instead.

"I wept when I read it." He paused and his voice grew soft, his eyebrows bunched together. So much emotion was on his face, it almost hurt to look at. "When I first was freed, I wanted the doctor to cut all the metal out of my body, even if it would leave me weakened and deformed."

My mouth dropped open a little. I hadn't known that.

"But God says, 'I will take away their hearts of stone and give them hearts of flesh.' It helped me realize that the metal in my body can't touch my heart. I *could* be made a man again, and the process was less about my metal exoskeleton and more about the choices I make and whether or not I will live a life full of compassion and mercy.

"But it means that we have to believe that forgiveness is still possible even if those we committed crimes against will not forgive us. It means that what matters most is how we live now. It's what redemption is all about."

I shifted uncomfortably again in my seat.

Cole planted his feet in the center of the room and raised his arms as he spoke. "If we can learn to love one another and lift each other up, then we will not fall, no matter the assault the enemy might bring." His voice was booming now. "We are human now, our hearts are flesh, I declare it! And by our strong will and by God's grace, we will not allow them to harden back into stone!"

A cry of agreement went up from the crowd. They surged to their feet, as swept up by his words as I had been. I looked at their faces, the tears running down cheeks, the looks of joy in their gleaming eyes. So many of us were longing for the forgiveness Cole promised was possible.

"Let's pray," Cole said, and the crowd quieted, but didn't sit back down. One voice spoke out in prayer, and when they finished, another rose and then another. Most people closed their eyes as they spoke. I couldn't bear to look at them anymore. I left my tray and got to my feet, slowly inching my way through the suffocating crowd until I reached the hallway. When I got to the hall, I started running. I ran all the way back to my dorm, and when inside, I bent to lean my head over my knees and took breath after breath.

Cole said forgiveness was possible. Redemption. Even for him, and he'd *killed* while under the control of the Regulators' programming. Didn't that mean that I too could be redeemed? Even in spite of calling out to the Regs and getting my older brother killed when I was a child, in spite of so many others who'd gotten hurt or captured because of me? In spite of all that had been done to Adrien?

I sat on my bed with my knees drawn up to my chin. Lately it had seemed easier to let myself be stone, but maybe Cole was right. Wasn't letting ourselves be softened by compassion and mercy at the heart of what we were fighting for in the first place?

I stared hard at the wall. I didn't want to be driven by rage or hatred anymore. I wanted a heart of flesh again.

Xona and Ginni came in a few minutes later. I saw questions in their eyes when they looked at me, probably wondering why I'd left in the middle of the prayers. I wasn't sure how to explain it, if I even wanted to, so I turned to Ginni instead.

"Hey, Ginns, can you check on my brother?"

"Sure." She smiled brightly. I leaned my head back against the wall of my bunk and closed my eyes. I'd get my weekly reassurance he was okay, and tonight, for once, I'd fall asleep easily.

But after a few moments, Ginni still hadn't said anything. My head snapped up. She was frowning, her brow furrowed.

"Ginni," I prompted, barely managing to keep my voice steady. "Where is he?"

She didn't speak for several more seconds, but then her eyes flew open. My chest went tight with dread.

Her lips trembled as she said, "He's with the Chancellor at her personal compound."

Chapter 7

I WAS RUNNING THROUGH THE woods. The sunlight was bright. It made my eyes hurt. We shouldn't be here. But someone insistently tugged me forward, and I looked down to see a young man's hand dwarfing mine. I followed the line of his arm up to his body and face. One second it was my older brother Daavd, but the next moment the face shifted slightly to become Markan. He lifted his other hand to his mouth.

"Shh, Zoe, don't make a sound."

I knew what came next. I knew it like a script I'd spoken too many times: me calling out to the Regulators, them chasing my brother to the ground in front of me, and the betrayed look on his face as he gazed at me in the last moment of his life. All my fault.

Even as the dream played out, I struggled against it. My child's mouth opened to call out to the guard. I felt my desire for all the confusing and anomalous things to stop. But then I also felt the horror of it and clamped a hand over my mouth. This was my brother! I wouldn't! I wouldn't betray him again!

But then the ground under our feet started rumbling, and the Regulators nearby found us anyway. We weren't in a forest anymore, but were surrounded by a rocky terrain with giant boulders that were slowly closing in on us from all sides.

"Markan, run!" I shouted. But the shaking ground tripped

him. He fell, letting go of my hand. And I just kept running. Even though everything in me screamed to go back for him, my feet kept moving forward. I looked behind me. The Regulators were so close now. They were almost to Markan. With a herculean effort, I forced my feet to a stop and spun around. I held out my hands as a blistering rage rose and then exploded outward through my fingertips. The Regulators' bodies were ripped into a hundred pieces, like they'd exploded from the inside out. I looked over to my brother.

And then screamed in horror. Because in the rush of power, I'd accidently killed Markan too. I dropped to my knees beside him. *No!*

I woke up to someone shaking me violently.

I sat up, barely hearing Xona's frantic voice over my own screams. She grabbed both of my shoulders in her firm grip and forced me to look at her.

"Wake the hell *up!*"

I blinked, trying to pull away from her, confused. "But Daavd! Markan!"

"Calm down, you're shunting shaking the whole compound!"

Her words finally sank in and I stopped struggling in her arms. Of course. It was just a dream. I hadn't killed my brother. At least not as directly as I had in the dream. In reality, I'd called out to the Regulators to report my eldest brother Daavd and they'd killed him. I was only four, I feverishly reminded myself. I'd been a drone, I hadn't known what I was doing.

But Markan. The Chancellor had him now. Because I hadn't gone back to save him.

A loud crash sounded close by. Ginni and the other refugees sleeping on the floor screamed. Xona and I tumbled out of our bunks. That's when I realized part of the ceiling had collapsed, a large boulder of concrete and rock breaking through the steel struts. Dust filled the room and everyone jumped out of the way with confused shouts.

I looked around and the reality of the situation settled in. Oh God, what had I done? I heard shouts from the hallway beyond our room and knew it wasn't only our dorm that was damaged.

"Is everyone okay?" I shouted.

Ginni coughed and held her arm over her face. The refugee women all looked disoriented and terrified, clutching each other. They probably thought we were being attacked. Xona cursed in the corner, punching the door open button. The door screeched in its tracks—the frame had been damaged in the quake, but it finally slid halfway open. Xona wedged herself through the small space and forced it open the rest of the way. My arm panel lit up in response when I touched it. I spoke into my wrist. "Jilia, is everyone okay?" I suddenly had a horrible thought. What if I'd ruptured Adrien's tank?

"Is Adrien okay?"

I ran out the door behind Xona. Part of the hallway had caved in too, but Xona was able to jump over the rubble to check the dorm next to ours.

"Are they okay?" I shouted to Xona. "Molla and the baby?"

A spark exploded from the ceiling and the lights went out. Several women yelped from behind me, but the backup generator made the emergency lights along the wall slowly sputter to life.

"Xona, are they okay?" My voice was panicked, verging on hysterical.

"Everyone's fine," Xona called back.

I sank against the wall in relief.

Jilia's voice sounded over the open channel in my arm com. "Everyone, try to make your way to the training room. From the readouts, it looks like it's the east wing that's most damaged. Zoe, Adrien's fine, the Med Center was barely touched."

I swallowed. Of course it was worst where I was sleeping. I'd been the epicenter of the quake.

"I'm still waiting for everyone to com me back," Jilia continued, "but so far there's only a few injuries. Tyryn's making a survey of the military level. So far, no casualties."

My hand trembled as I switched the com off.

I could have killed someone tonight. One of my friends. One of the refugees. Just because of my power. Because of what I was. The only reason the Chancellor had been watching Markan was because of me, and now I'd wrecked one of the last sanctuaries the Rez had left. I destroyed everything I touched. A sharp pang of self-loathing choked me. With great effort, I swallowed all my emotions back down. This wasn't the time to let fear and doubt choke me. I had to be orderly. Cold.

Ginni and I got to the training center where everyone was gathered in a huddle on the right side of the room. The baby wailed. Molla walked around, bouncing him up and down to quiet him. She shot me a glare when I entered, but then went back to bouncing.

I looked around. Even here, a large portion of the left wall was crumbling, huge chunks of stone and concrete strewn across the floor.

How would we ever fix all this?

Everyone was talking at once. City came forward as I entered. I could see the anger fuming off her. "How could you forget to Link yourself? Your stupid mistake could have gotten us killed!"

"I *did* Link myself!" I flung back, before remembering my resolve to stay cold and not let anything affect me.

Jilia had come up behind City. "You did?"

I nodded, my shoulders hunching over. "I Linked myself just like I always do, but somehow I started dreaming anyway and then lost control."

"Why didn't it work?" City asked.

"I don't know." I tried, unsuccessfully, to keep the frustration out of my voice.

"It's okay," Ginni said, coming forward and putting a hand on my shoulder. "You couldn't control it, it's not your fault."

I gave her a small nod, but couldn't manage a smile. "Thanks, Ginns." I turned to the others. "Now, what's the damage report?"

Tyryn came in the door with a flood of people at his back, both refugees and soldiers.

"Report," I said, hoping I sounded more confident than I felt. Tyryn strode close.

"The lower level isn't as bad," he said. "No cave-ins."

I took a deep breath. Good, that meant the floor of our level should still be solid. The air filtration system which ran through the walls must not have been ruptured either, because I didn't feel even the faintest prickle of an allergy attack.

"Won't someone from the outside come investigate?" City said. "Shouldn't we all be packing and getting the hell out of here?"

"Seismic activity is common enough in the region," the Professor said, coming forward. He looked so much older than he had six months ago and his limp seemed more pronounced. It was like grief had added fifteen years. In spite of how he looked, though, his voice came out strong. "And it probably didn't carry very far outside the mountain, maybe only a couple miles in every direction. Not enough to warrant an investigation."

"This location is the biggest of the last safe havens left,"

Jilia said, pacing beside him. She talked as if thinking out loud. "It's large enough to hold a significant population, and it's secure and untraceable because of the techer boy. We can fix the damage from the quake." She looked up at us all as if she'd come to a conclusion. "And like Henry said, the quake was small enough. It should go unnoticed."

"*This* time, maybe," City said, glaring my way.

"So you think it's safe to stay?" I asked, looking between Jilia, Henk, and the Professor. I ignored City even though her words were already worming their way through my brain. I'd put everyone at risk, and my presence would continue to endanger them.

A dark-haired guy stepped forward, nodding. For some reason he wore a name tag on his shoulder. It read SIMIN. The name sounded only vaguely familiar. "I can monitor air traffic and local coms." He looked down at a portable console in his hands. "There hasn't been anything out of the ordinary so far. We can keep on high alert. Their fliers don't have the cloaking tech like Henk developed for the Rez. If there's any trouble, we should be able to see it coming and evacuate."

I swallowed, my eyes immediately shooting to Henk's. We both knew there weren't enough escape pods for everyone. Not by half. Henk had been working on acquiring material to build more, but it had been put on the back burner compared to the need for food and other basic supplies. We still had three transports, though. The largest could seat up to forty people.

But if we tried to leave now, where would we go? There was a complex of cabins in the mountains that we'd set up as part of our evacuation plan, but it wasn't a very sustainable position. Not like here. It would be foolish to evacuate now if it turned out there was no threat. And Jilia, the Professor, and

Simin said they thought it'd be okay. I nodded, swallowing hard. "Okay, we stay then. But Jilia, is there anything you can give me to keep me from dreaming?"

Jilia drew her eyebrows together even farther. "There are some medications I have on hand that inhibit sleep cycles. They aren't good for long-term use, but will work until we can figure out a more permanent solution."

"And what happens if it doesn't work?" City's voice was shrill. "Look at this place!"

"There's no reason to think it won't work," Jilia said. She put a hand on her forehead, looking every inch as tired as I felt. "We'll start cleaning in the morning."

"I want updates every half hour," I said to the techer boy. He nodded, then jogged out of the room. I looked at everyone else. "And make sure the newest arrivals are familiar with the evacuation plan, just in case."

City threw her hands in the air, and spun, walking away from the group crowded around us.

I bit down on my cheek hard to help me keep my face a blank mask. Guilt nibbled me raw from the inside out, but I couldn't show it right now. I was supposed to be a leader. But as I watched City's retreating form, I realized that soon it might be in the best interest of everyone if someone else took charge. I swallowed hard as the realization struck me.

I needed to leave.

It was so obvious. As much as I might not want to admit it, this had been an accident waiting to happen. My power had continued increasing in the past few months. I'd hoped that eventually it would even out and I'd reach a point of equilibrium. But it hadn't. And every day that my power morphed and developed, I was putting the people around me at risk.

I stood up ramrod straight. Cole might think we needed hearts of flesh, but flesh was weak. It was not made for war.

Right now I needed to be stone. Or even better, steel. I envisioned molten steel slowly coating my spine and then radiating outward until it seeped over all of my skin, covering my body head to toe. I couldn't feel the sting of hurt at knowing the best way to keep the people I loved safe was to leave them behind. No, emotion could not touch me.

I closed my eyes for a second to steady myself, then turned to the gathered crowd. "Let's start setting up beds on the floor in here." I looked out across the wide low space of the training room. "It might be uncomfortable for a few days while we make sure the support struts in the corridors that lead to the dorms haven't been too damaged. For all we know, they could still collapse completely. Everyone must stay in the areas we know are safe until we can determine the extent of the damage."

The crowd of refugees grumbled assent. Some had cowed shoulders, as if another disaster or more promised discomfort was no less than they expected. Others looked angry, their bodies taut.

"We make the best of a bad situation," I said. "Now let's work together until everyone is settled in again for the night."

We all worked steadily for the next couple of hours. I held the ceiling up over the damaged corridors with my telek while Xona ventured through to retrieve bedding and other basic personal items. Finally, everyone was settled in.

I was tired, more in soul than in body, as I walked down the east corridor. Imagining myself as steel had gotten me through the past couple hours, but now that I was finally alone again, the reality of what had happened, and what it meant, came crashing back in.

As I passed the Caf, I saw a section of the east hallway that was almost completely caved in. I knew if I backtracked a little, I could go around and enter the Med Center from the west corridor entrance, but I went closer to inspect the damage anyway. This was because of me. The least I could do was start cleaning it up. It was four in the morning, but I certainly wasn't going to risk sleeping any more tonight. I sighed and started pulling away the collapsed steel beams with my telek.

The next day we continued cleaning up. The whole east wing was trashed. After we'd made it out last night, the other support struts had failed and caved in a long portion of hallway.

"But all my things!" Ginni cried when Jilia told us. "I was starting this new dress design; it was really going to be something special. I can't just leave it—"

"I'm sure we'll be able to get through to get your things," Jilia said, then paused. "Eventually. But in the meantime, we'll have to triple up in the dorms that are cleared. All boys in one dorm room, girls in the other."

"Max Jr. and I will not share a room with *her*."

I didn't look up. I was tired of Molla's accusing eyes, and frankly, I was afraid I'd say something I regretted if I looked back at her. It wasn't like I'd meant to bring the shunting mountain down on us! Guilt followed. It didn't matter if I meant to. I'd done it anyway.

"You and the baby can sleep in the Med Center," Jilia said, always conciliatory. I didn't know how she managed sometimes, putting up with all of us. While I was officially in charge, she was the one people looked to for internal disputes.

"Eli, Wytt, and I will start clearing the debris," said Cole.

I jumped up. "I'll help you."

"Me too," Xona said.

We both followed the three ex-Regs out of the training center and back toward the east wing. Jilia was right. About five feet in, rubble completely blocked the hallway. The ex-Regs

were surprisingly nimble in spite of their heavy metal exoskeletons. Eli and Wytt climbed up to the top of the rubble
and started handing down heavy pieces of concrete and metal.
Xona was about to join them when I held up a hand.

"Wait," I said. "I think I have a faster way to do this. Just
tell me where we're putting the debris."

"We'll have to get it out of here," Wytt said, jumping back
down, his metal feet bracings resounding with a loud *clang* as
he hit the ground. "There's an unpaved dump site along the
side of the transport bay, all still underground. It should be
a safe place for disposal."

"Has anyone checked on it yet?" I asked. "Made sure it's
still stable up there?"

"Jilia checked last night," Xona said. "All the transports are
fine and elevator's operational too."

I breathed out. "Good."

I turned toward the debris blocking the hallway in front of
us and let my telek buzz and expand under my skin. I imagined the energy passing through the bridge of my pores and
out into the hallway. I could feel the whole space now, in that
peculiar way that happened when I focused my telek. It was
as if the hall was inside me, rotating in the space of my head
like a 3-D projection cube. And in this space, little things like
weight and gravity didn't apply.

I easily lifted a large five-foot-diameter chunk of steel and
rock, carefully dislodging it as best I could from the surrounding wall and ceiling pieces. I brought it out, easily catching the
rest of the debris that threatened to tumble down now that a sup-
porting piece had been taken away. It was as easy as untangling
a pile of fallen children's blocks.

Xona whistled. "Well, if you can clear it away this quick, I
bet repairs won't be as hard as we thought. Rand can help us
melt down the steel to mold new struts and you can keep the

space stable while we rebuild." Her eyes were sharp as she calculated in her head.

I nodded. Yes. I would help them rebuild. But then I would leave. I was sure the news would make Molla and City happy, at least.

"Come on," I said, hoping my voice didn't betray any of the emotion I felt inside. "Let's get this junk out of here."

Xona and Cole walked with me while the other two ex-Regs stayed behind to keep clearing. They were chatting, but I was too wrapped up in my own thoughts to listen.

How would I leave? I'd have to tell Jilia or the Professor, at least, and the techer boy, so he could give me a safe device to communicate in case they needed me. As long as I had a med container to sleep in, I could go anywhere. The Chancellor wouldn't expect that. She still didn't know I could control my allergy now.

But Adrien. How could I leave *him*? I missed a step at the thought, barely managing to keep myself upright and not lose hold of the load that was floating along behind us. I clenched my jaw. Steel. I would be steel.

I was only able to fit half the load in the elevator at a time, so Xona and Wytt stayed up with the rest of the debris while I took a trip up to the transport bay. I tugged the load out of the elevator, glad to see that Jilia had been right: there was no damage here at all. The wide paved runway and three transports were clear of rubble. The walls of the low bay were unfinished rock, machine marks from where they'd been carved out still visible. I squinted a little at the light coming through the windows of the retractable bay door that opened to the Surface at the end of the runway. I dropped the load of twisted metal and rock in the unpaved pit we'd dug out by the far wall.

When I turned to walk back to the elevator, I paused. What was that strange high-pitched whine? It had been getting louder over the last minute. I frowned and tried to listen closer. Maybe the quake had busted a pipe nearby.

I followed the noise, walking down the runway to the wide door that opened to the Surface. *It must be coming from outside.* I looked out the small window.

Three troop transports circled above the top of the canyon, and they weren't ours. One broke out of formation.

It headed straight toward the transport bay where I stood.

Chapter 8

I BACKED AWAY FROM THE window as if, if I couldn't see it, I could pretend it wasn't real. It was impossible. Everyone had seemed so confident the quake wouldn't be a problem, and the techer had assured us he'd be able to track anything coming. Obviously we'd all been wrong.

I felt sick as I frantically touched my wrist com. "There are fliers above the canyon!" I couldn't keep the panic out of my voice. "Enact plan Emergency Exodus. Everyone get to the escape pods now!"

I ran to the elevator and rode it down, pacing in the small space. Every second counted. Why was this elevator so slow? I bypassed the allergen shower and hit the button to open the door directly into the entry hall.

When the doors opened, the small open foyer was crowded with confused people. Some of my team were there, along with Tyryn, Jilia, and the Professor. Max Jr. was crying again, but I was glad that Molla and the baby had made it here first. There were three escape pods in this room. They'd be able to get in one.

The internal alarm started going off, a loud beeping that should alert everyone to get to the pod nearest to them.

Xona ran up to me. "What's going on? Ginni just com'd the techer and he said he hasn't seen anything on the Sat Imagery."

"Then they're cloaked somehow." I strode forward. "I saw them with my own eyes. Three fliers, circling."

She swore.

I let my telek expand out beyond my body, beyond the hallway, beyond the mountain and into the air. Yes, there they were. One was landing on a small ledge right near the transport bay where I'd been standing moments ago.

"Shunt, they're landing!" I looked at Jilia, Tyryn, and the Professor. "Get to your pods and start loading people in, quick as you can." The pods would shuttle underground through to the other side of the mountain range before launching and turning into normal air transports. "Launch them as soon as they're at capacity, there's not much time."

They nodded, hearing what I didn't say. Each pod could only seat up to fifteen. There were only ten working pods, and over three hundred people crammed in the Foundation at the moment. There wouldn't be enough for everyone, but we still had to try to get as many people out of here as we could. I looked around for Henk but didn't see him. Hopefully he was helping people into pods wherever he was.

For a moment panic swallowed me. I'd failed everyone again. So many people would be left behind. But the next second, I realized there was no time for those thoughts now. I just needed to do what must be done.

More and more refugees came in, shouting to know what was going on. Tyryn and Jilia started directing them into the pods on both sides of the entryway. One pod quickly filled up. They were supposed to be filled half with refugees, half with Rez fighters, but in the chaos, the scared refugees had filled all the seats in the shuttle.

"Tyryn, get on board, then launch!" I called. Tyryn nodded. We needed at least one head Rez operative who knew the launch protocol on board each pod. He entered, taking a couple of extra people with him even though they wouldn't have harnesses to belt themselves in with. Rez fighters held back the surging crowd so he could slide the door shut behind him. Good, at least one pod was off safely.

I'd been keeping my mind's eye on the transport that landed. A flood of large bodies poured out of it, followed by a very small one. I felt the contours of the small figure. It felt like a little girl. They were approaching the entrance gate at the transport bay.

"I've got to get Adrien out," I shouted to Xona. "We'll try to get in Pod 5 by the Med Center. I'll get it filled and launched."

She nodded, grabbing Cole's hand and sprinting down the hallway to help with the other pods.

Suddenly, I couldn't see anything with my telek at all. All my energy slammed back into my body, making me stagger backward a few steps. The next second, my power was gone completely. I tried to project outward again, but there was no buzzing, no rush of power.

Rand had been rubbing his palms together, no doubt preparing to unleash his power on the intruders, but suddenly he stood up and frowned.

My blood seemed to freeze in my veins. "Rand, what is it?"

"My power," he said, staring down at his hands. "It's not working."

I turned to City. "Does yours work?"

She raised her hand, then frowned when nothing happened.

I swore. "They must have a glitcher with them who can somehow, I don't know, negate our abilities. Just get to the pods before they blast their way in!" We were no match for Regs without our powers.

"We'll go get everyone out of the Caf," Rand said, pulling City along behind him.

They took off sprinting, and I looked around at the crowd. There were only three pods in this bay and far too many people.

"The pods are filling here," I shouted into the crowd. "Head toward the other pods!" But the noise was so loud, barely anyone heard me.

A loud banging noise sounded above us, shaking the walls. The lights flickered several times and people started screaming.

When the lights came back on, I grabbed a tall refugee man holding his young daughter in his arms. "Follow me!" I shouted. I pulled on the arms of several others who were closest to me, then I took off down the west corridor toward the Med Center. We'd had compound-wide practice routes to the pods before, but the compound hadn't been nearly so full the last time we ran a drill. I passed more people crowding around pod sites. I slowed for a moment outside Pod 5. It was already stuffed to the brim.

I stopped at the Med Center, but waved the group behind me onward. "There are two more pods at the end of this hall," I shouted at them. "If those are full, the rubble's cleared enough, you should be able to follow the switchback around the Caf to get to the pods in the east corridor."

I turned back to the Med Center. Adrien's mom, Sophia, had already started draining the tank and was reaching into the gel to pull the electrode patches from his skin. I hurried over to help her. The blue gel was warm to the touch, and I focused on ripping the nodes off Adrien's forehead.

Jilia's frantic voice came shouting over my com. Screams filled the background. "They've breeched, they're inside! Pods one and two have launched, we're a minute away from launching the third. I'm enacting the emergency protocol to slow them down."

"Stay safe," I said back, my heart thumping with fear for Jilia, for all of us.

The beeping alert overhead switched to one long ear-splitting tone. The emergency protocol was triggered. The blast doors would shut every thirty seconds now. Once they closed, there was no opening them again.

"Help me lift him," Sophia shouted. We each reached under one of Adrien's arms and hefted his slim body over the side of the tank. His foot caught the side and the whole tank tipped over sideways, shattering glass and blue goo all over the floor.

"You need to stand up, honey." Sophia bent over to help him up.

Adrien tried to obey, but his legs buckled and he fell. We only barely managed to catch him before he crumpled to the ground.

"It always takes half an hour or more for him to be able to walk after he gets out of the tank," Sophia said.

Laser fire shot past the door opened to the west corridor. They were already here. Sophia's terrified eyes locked onto mine. I knew it wasn't herself she was afraid for. It was for her son.

"Drag him!" I shouted to her. "My power isn't working. We'll have to take our chances with the east corridor."

There were two entrances to the Med Center, and we grabbed Adrien by his arms and hauled him toward the far door that opened to the east corridor. It was still partially obstructed by rubble, but we should still be able to get through. The floor was slippery with gel. While it made it harder to stay on my feet, Adrien's body slid easily across the floor.

I hopped over the boulder blocking the bottom of the doorway. The door itself was still jammed so that it was only half-open. I reached back to help Adrien through when three short beeps sounded from the other side of the Med Center. The three-foot-thick metal blast doors in both corridors leading to the Med Center were closing.

Which meant we had exactly thirty seconds to get past the next blast door, and then past one more, to where the pod launch was located. Or else we'd be trapped inside. I took a quick glance out into the hallway behind me. The door was only fifteen feet away, and the path was clear of debris. We'd get there in plenty of time.

I gripped the upper half of Adrien's body and Sophia shoved from the other side. But his shoulders were so wide, he got caught.

"Sideways," Sophia shouted, "Turn him sideways."

I shifted my grip to angle his shoulders sideways through the narrow opening.

"Halt," a voice called out from behind Sophia. "Turn around!"

My heart leapt into my throat as I looked past Sophia in shock to see three Regs and a slight girl standing right inside the blast door, just feet away from the west entrance to the Med Center. *No!* They must have made it in before the last door had closed. I couldn't imagine how they could have gotten here so quickly. But then I remembered how fast the Regs had run in the arena.

A smile curved upward on the girl's cherubic face. She was a teenager, but she couldn't have weighed more than ninety pounds. She spoke into her arm com, her voice sweet and high-pitched. "We have visual confirmation on Zoel Q-24."

I held up my hand out of instinct, but no power crackled to life underneath my fingertips. The guards raised their weapons, and in the same half second, I heard the blast doors in the hallway behind me grating as they began to shut. Our thirty seconds were up.

I leapt backward, my grip on Adrien's elbow like iron. His mother must have had a similar impulse. She threw Adrien backwards with what seemed like inhuman force. Between her push and my pull, Adrien's body was finally yanked sideways through the narrow doorway. I kept our momentum going as I dragged him toward the blast door with a strength I didn't know I had. I dropped down to my knees at the last second. With our bodies still slick from the gel, Adrien and I slid under the blast door right before it shut with a loud *clang*.

I heard the dull thud of laser fire behind the door and sat stunned for a moment. Adrien's mother. Sophia, she—

"We need to hurry," Adrien said, swallowing hard as he stared at the blast door. He blinked rapidly, like he was trying to shake off the befuddling haze of the sedatives he'd been on while in the tank.

I looked over at him, full of grief. "Adrien, I'm so sorry . . ."

His jaw tightened and he looked away from me, but he didn't say anything else other than repeating in a monotone, "We need to hurry."

Bile rose in my throat, but I managed to get to my feet anyway. Sophia wouldn't sacrifice herself for nothing. I would get her son to safety.

"Try to put a little weight on your feet," I commanded Adrien, dragging him to a standing position. I pulled his arm around my shoulder and we both stumbled forward. He was so weak, he had to lean most of his weight on me. With each

step I was sure it was going to be too much and we were going to topple to the ground and miss the next door.

No. The word blared in my mind. We would not fall. *We
would not fall.* "The pod's right past the next blast door."

We got to the next door with five seconds to spare as it
slammed shut. The Regs were probably getting through the
doors behind us already. Blast doors were only a hindrance to
Regs, not an insurmountable obstacle.

I looked around. The pod door was untouched. I'd been
afraid it would have already launched without us, but there was
no one else here. I spun around and saw that farther down, part
of the hallway I'd cleared this morning had caved in again, no
doubt from all the blasts shaking the compound. No one else
had been able to make it through.

I felt a jolt of sadness mixed horribly with relief. The pod
was still clear for Adrien, but so many others would be killed
or captured. There was nothing that could be done for them,
though. Adrien, at least, I could save.

I turned back to the escape pod door and clicked it open.
The pod was a large cylinder, bare except for the seats and
belt restraints lining the circular walls, stacked two high. I
didn't speak, just dropped Adrien's gel-soaked body into one
of the chairs near the door.

"Get your belts fastened." I turned to shut and secure the
door. I clicked through a small interface near the door to start
the pod. Lights slowly glowed to life along the floor, and the
whir of the engine started.

When I finished clicking through the launch sequence, I
heard a noise. A loud banging. The Regs were getting through.
Henk had estimated when he built the blast doors it would take
a Reg at least twenty minutes to get through each one. They
must have equipment we hadn't anticipated.

I swallowed down my terror and sat in the chair beside Adrien, right by the interface. I fastened the belts across my waist and chest with trembling fingers.

I glanced over at Adrien. He looked up at me with his eyebrows furrowed together in bewildered confusion and said, "Sophia."

Something glistened on his cheek. I couldn't tell if it was a tear or leftover gel.

I started to say something, but then realized he still hadn't strapped himself in. I swore and grabbed his straps, clicking them together as best as I could. The banging noise got louder.

I held onto the control stick and said, "Launching in three, two—"

I watched through the pod's small window as a bright molten red circle appeared on the blast door out in the corridor. I didn't bother to finish counting. I hit the launch button.

Immediately the pod flew up the chute overhead like a supercharged elevator. The force pressed me down against the seat of my chair so hard it felt like I might slam right through it and out the bottom of the pod.

Several of the packs that should have been stowed securely under our chairs flew out and banged around the floor as the pod rounded a corner and began to accelerate.

After a moment, the buzzing burst to life in my head again. I was too confused by the speed at first, but I finally realized: I had my telek back. We must have gotten far enough away from the glitcher who muted my powers.

I let it expand outward and suddenly the speed and force of the module didn't seem so daunting. I always felt more in control when my telek was active, like the too-fast world of action and reaction was slowed to an acceptable speed. I felt forward down the tunnel we hurtled down until I could see the whole of it in the projection cube in my mind; it looked like a long worm burrowed under the ground and we were a tiny light traveling through its stomach.

And that's when I felt the obstruction a couple miles ahead. The whole tunnel was caved in.

Chapter 9

MY EYES WIDENED AND MY heartbeat sped up. I swore under my breath. At the speed we were going, we'd crash into the caved-in section in less than two minutes. I pulled back my telek from the length of the tunnel and surrounded our pod like a net. I imagined the cords of energy wrapping around it, slowing our speed as gently as I could.

Adrien's head still pitched forward with the sudden deceleration.

I bit my lip hard as I concentrated, trying to transition to lower speeds more gracefully. It would be easier to just bring our pod to an immediate stop, like putting a hand over a rolling marble, but I couldn't be sure that Adrien and I wouldn't end up with concussions, or worse.

Finally we slowed and stopped. And not a moment too soon. I projected outward. The cave-in was only fifty paces ahead. The pod cylinder was on its side at this point in the track. Adrien and I hung suspended from what was now the ceiling, held in only by our buckles. When I released the straps belting me in, I tumbled down to the floor. At least my fall was broken by several of the packs that had become dislodged. I clicked the door-release button, but an error message popped up: ERROR: DESTINATION NOT ACHIEVED. AUTO-LOCKS REMAIN ENGAGED.

I impatiently hit the override button, but when the door finally opened, I was met with a wall of rock.

Shunt. I'd hoped there'd be enough space for us to slip around the sides, but the tunnel around the pod was carved with only inches of clearance. We didn't have time for this. I was sure the Regs had climbed up onto the pod's track and were sprinting down the tunnel toward us this very second. I wasn't sure how far we'd made it—maybe five or ten miles? If it was five, they could cover that distance in ten minutes, maybe less.

I unstrapped Adrien, lowering him gently to the ground with my telek. Then I turned and put out my arm again, ripping out the ceiling of the pod that faced the collapsed tunnel. It was melded steel alloy, but with my power, the top popped off with no more resistance than the lid on a food canister.

I grabbed two of the loose packs from the ground, pulled the small rectangular med kit off the wall, and climbed out through the new exit. I looked back. Adrien was slumped against the wall.

"I'm going to lift you out now."

He nodded.

"Good." I climbed out through the top of the pod. My mast cells immediately reacted to allergens in the damp tunnel air, but I was practiced enough at deflecting it that I could still lift Adrien's body out, in addition to keeping the cells under control. Splitting my focus like this used to be difficult. But after months of intense practice, now I didn't even break a sweat.

It was pitch black in the tunnel. I must have busted the circuitry on the pod's emergency lights when I took the top off.

In spite of my resolve to stay calm, panic bubbled up in my chest at the darkness. I hastily touched the panel on my arm for light, but it was paltry and only illuminated a small sphere around me. At least Adrien looked a little more alert. I set him down on his feet and he managed to stand on his own, but he still had to lean against the tunnel wall. It was clear that we'd never be able to outrun the Regs.

We were trapped in the dark underneath a mountain, with murderous machine men headed straight toward us. And I had absolutely no idea what to do next.

I tried not to think of the Regs coming down the tunnel behind us. I tried not to think about the fact that, back in the compound behind us, Adrien's mother was probably dead. Too many things not to think about, and that wasn't including the collapsed tunnel in front of us. My body started to tremble.

Stop. Focus. I squeezed my eyes shut for one long second and took several deep breaths. First one thing and then another.

I needed to clear the tunnel. With my eyes still closed, I lifted an arm to move the largest chunks of rock and steel to the sides of the tunnel. The rocks scraped against each other as I moved them and the steel beams screeched.

I could already feel the rest of the mountain threatening to crash in from the weak spot above. Dirt sifted down, so I held up my other arm and kept the rest of the rock back. Sweat began to bead on my forehead. Splitting my focus on two objects was one thing, but holding this much mass back while also keeping my mast cells in check was far more taxing.

I looked at the small hole I'd made and realized there was no way I'd be able to get the pod through. Even if I cleared enough of the fallen rock out of the way, the walls were too close. Wherever I moved the pieces of rock, they'd only cause another obstruction.

Adrien finally spoke up. "We should fly out of the mountain."

"We can't." I knew it wasn't his fault, but I couldn't help how sharply my words came out. "The tunnel's too tight. The pod isn't flying anywhere. And we're still at least fifteen miles from the Surface."

He just stared straight at me, his translucent gray eyes uncanny in the dim light. "We should fly out."

"I can't fly!" I said. He was obviously still not able to think straight.

"Why not?" he asked. "You just made me fly out of the pod."

I was about to respond back that he was being ludicrous, that of course I hadn't made him fly. I was simply using my telek to make him occupy another space where gravity didn't matter and—

Oh.

Right. Wow. I blinked in surprise.

I'd only ever lifted other objects. I'd never really thought about lifting myself. A distant repetitive *thunk*ing noise echoed down the long tunnel behind us. It must be the Regs. They were gaining on us.

I raised Adrien up behind me and tugged him forward on an invisible leash. He floated along until we were well past the rubble. I released my hold on the ceiling, and more rock crumbled in and sealed off the tunnel behind us. It wouldn't keep the Regs back for long, but it might help.

"Now," Adrien said. "Fly."

The absurdity of what he was asking struck me all over again. I couldn't *fly*. But I also realized I didn't have any choice except to try. I'd never be able to outrun the Regs on foot.

I closed my eyes and let the telek buzz in my ears until it was a steady drone, then I pulled out of myself and felt the shape of my own body in the tunnel. It was such a small thing to lift myself off the ground. Easy, even.

What I hadn't expected was the disorientation. I tried to steady myself with my feet, but there was nothing but air. I lost focus and plummeted back the two feet to the ground, landing unceremoniously on my backside.

Adrien laughed, then stopped, looking as surprised at the sound as I felt. I stared a moment longer than I should have. Had I imagined the sound of his laugh? It had sounded so normal, so *Adrien*. Which was doubly absurd considering our position.

I closed my eyes again and lifted my body off the ground. I tried to focus only on the projection cube in my mind. Tried to ignore the rest of my senses that were screaming *Oh-shunting-hell-I'm-not-touching-the-ground!*

I took Adrien's hand, as if holding on to another floating object would make the fact that *I* was floating seem less bizarre. It didn't.

"We should accelerate," Adrien said, looking down at our connected hands with an expression I couldn't read.

"Right," I said. Accelerate. Just like that.

More noise sounded behind us in the distance. Watching the ground, even in such dim light, would only get me cracked. If I was going to do this, I had to rely only on my telek sense alone. I closed my eyes and propelled us forward again. I tried not to think about the air brushing against my face or the smell of the dusty rock surrounding us. Weight didn't matter. Objects occupying space, that's all we were.

I visualized the long skinny tunnel and us as a tiny object zooming through it.

I felt out the curves of the tunnel far before we came to them. After a few minutes, the terror that I might accidently fly us full speed into a wall dimmed. The tunnel around us was just like those old virtual exercises they used to train us with in nanobio-engineering. We'd put on the goggles and then zoom past minuscule cell walls as if they were huge hallways. I could do the same here. Accelerate, adjust left, slight right. The only difference was here I could feel my hair blowing backward with our speed.

I kept my telek projected down the entire tunnel, and we were quickly approaching the end. The sudden vastness of the open air beyond the tunnel almost choked me as we got near. I could navigate the slim contours of the narrow walls with a fair amount of precision, but how could I even begin to wrap my head around that much awful open *space*? The Surface and the sky were still the stuff of nightmares to me.

I slowed us down as we came to the lip of the tunnel. I dropped us to our feet again in front of the tree- and brush-covered entrance. The rock that had been hewn in a perfect circle now grew wider, with more natural jagged edges as it opened to the Surface.

If we'd still been in the escape pod, we would have burst through the slight barrier of tree branches and scrub brush that covered the entrance with little problem. Then the propulsion thrusters would have kicked in as it turned from a launch pod into a regular air transport.

As it was, we had to make our way through the thick brush and brambles, earning several scratches for the effort. Finally we reached a small ledge overlooking the mountains. The smell of sharp pine filled my nose. I could feel my mast cells threatening to kick into overdrive with the amount of allergens suddenly being introduced to my body. I ground my teeth together to keep them all in check.

Adrien seemed to have gained more strength back. He'd opened his pack and pulled out a new pair of pants and tunic. Two pairs of clothes came standard in each pack, along with other basic supplies like food, blankets, lamps, and coolant harnesses to avoid Infrared Sat Cams when traveling at night. As I watched, he pulled his gel-soaked top off over his head. He reached for his pants next.

I spun around so that my back was to him. "What are you doing? We've got to get going."

"I don't like the feel of the gel."

"There are more important things to be focusing on right now!" Like the fact that his mother was probably lying dead in the Med Center all those miles behind us. Did it mean *any-thing* to him?

"Maybe we can contact one of the other escape pods," I said, trying to push away all my worries about those who hadn't been able to make it out. All I could do now was problem-solve what came next. "See if one of the other groups can come pick us up?"

"I thought about that, but we can't talk to them." Adrien held up the external com that was tucked in the side of the rations pack. He held it out toward me.

On the readout, it said ERROR 8. I looked up at him. We knew what that meant: the channel wasn't clear. It must have been compromised. If we tried to use it, the enemy could trace it back to us and we'd be cracked.

I looked out into the landscape. "What do we do now?" There was a slightly hysterical note in my voice, but I couldn't help it.

Adrien didn't answer me. He just clicked the com unit apart until the inside was exposed and flipped a switch. The device started smoking in his hand and he dropped it. It was the protocol, I knew. But as I watched our only way of communicating with the rest of the Rez go up in smoke, my heart dropped. Only a week ago I'd believed we'd be able to take down the Community, and now here we were with no home, fleeing for our lives.

"We head to the rendezvous site," he said. "You know the destination, right?"

I nodded. Each pod leader had memorized the location.

I looked out again at the landscape. It was beautiful, but I didn't see the beauty. I just saw terrain to be crossed. Satellite cameras were so developed these days they could make out your fingerprints if your palms happened to be faced up. Just because no one was around didn't mean no one was watching.

"We'll have to stay under the tree cover," I said.

"Then fly us under the tree cover."

"I can't just—" I sputtered.

He interrupted me. "Why not? It's the only way we can move without leaving tracks." His face was calm, like all this was just another math theorem he could methodically problem-solve his way through.

I closed my eyes and tried to sense outward with my telek. Immediately I felt the open space above us, the lack of contour. My heartbeat sped up at the very thought of all that space, so I directed my attention back toward the land. But that was almost as overwhelming.

There were so many trees, bushes, leaves, and branches swaying in the wind. Birds even, and a hundred other things I couldn't identify. Usually I captured the space in my mental projection cube before I tried to move objects, but there was simply too much moving around me. If this was going to work, I was going to have to change my method and abandon the level of control I was used to. I swallowed hard at the thought.

A banging noise echoed down the tunnel behind us. Had the Regs already made it to the collapsed portion? That meant they were moving faster than I thought.

Adrien looked back with me and frowned. "It doesn't seem wise to stay here."

"I know, I know," I muttered, pacing as I tried to figure out what to do.

"So fly us out of here. I bet you could move us fast. Maybe as fast as a transport if you tried."

"And which direction would we go? I have no cracking idea

where we even *are!*" I rubbed my forehead. "I know where the rendezvous site is, but have no idea where we're starting from. That techer boy's power made it so I never knew."

"Then how was anyone going to find their way there?"

"The pods had programmed coordinates for satellite sites that would be recognizable. From there we would all switch vehicles and go to the memorized rendezvous point. We never anticipated one of the pods not making it out of the mountain in the first place!"

"I can find out where we are," Adrien said.

I looked up at him in surprise. He'd pulled a long rectangular box out of the pack, then clicked it open. A row of tiny chips was secured inside. "Standard in every rations pack."

"Can we use one as another com?" I asked hopefully.

"No, I bet all com channels are cracked," he said. "But this one," he pulled out the fingernail-sized chip and inserted it into the slot on his arm panel, "is a maps application. Now that the techer is gone and his power isn't affecting me, I should be able to read it just fine and see where we are. Then I can help you navigate as you fly. Where's the rendezvous site?"

"It's right outside New Presinal. It's a big trade city."

He tapped through a few screens, then looked out at the horizon and pointed. "We head north. That way."

"How far away is it?"

"Four hundred miles," he said calmly.

"Four hundred miles!" I grabbed his forearm to see the map better. Willing it to show something different.

"We're in Sector Five now," he said, "and we'll have to get back to Six."

I stared at him, shocked. This whole time, the Foundation had been in a different *country* and I'd never even known. Meanwhile Adrien was staying so calm I wanted to scream. "Don't you see the one little problem with that?" I threw my hands up in frustration. "It's four hundred miles away, and we don't have a vehicle."

He watched me, unmoved. "But we have you, and you can fly."

Chapter 10

I TOOK HIS ARM, CLOSING my eyes as I projected my telek outward again to get a better sense of the landscape. There were just so many trees, and they all felt identical. I didn't know how to differentiate one from another, much less how to find and hold a clear path through them.

Not to mention, I was already exhausted from everything that had happened and by the focus it took to constantly keep the allergies at bay. It hadn't been this hard when Max and I had been with the Uppers at Central City. The city had been on the Surface and didn't have a tight air-filtration system or anything. But we'd been inside at least, out of the sunlight. Right now, the assaulting allergens were overwhelming. I'd just have to concentrate that much harder.

I lifted us up a few inches off the ground. We dipped in the air and I held out my hands to steady myself—which was ridiculous because there was nothing to actually brace myself against, only air. It felt just as unnatural as earlier when I'd done it in the tunnel, but worse now without the comforting confines of walls surrounding us.

I flew us into the forest, side by side, with our feet inches above the ground. Fallen brown needles carpeted the forest floor. The trees themselves were tall and spindly—so different from the last forest I'd been in where the tree trunks were thicker than I was tall. These trees weren't wide, but about five feet up thousands of tiny needle-laden branches sprouted from the trunks. They swayed in the wind like they were dancing. The wind itself felt unnatural against my skin, like a giant was blowing a cold breath over me.

"Ow!" Adrien said, and I paused, looking over at him. I'd run him straight into a row of scratchy branches. Brown needles rained to the ground where he'd smacked into them.

"Sorry!" I said, losing concentration. Both of us dropped out of the air. I landed on my feet, but Adrien fell on his backside. "Sorry again!"

He didn't say anything, just frowned as he stood up and brushed the pine needles off his shoulders. As bad as I felt for running him into a tree, it was nice to see anything other than his normally monotonous expression of calm.

"There's just so much to concentrate on," I said.

"Yeah, but you're breaking branches everywhere," he said. "Any tracking bot could find you from a mile away like this."

"Well, what do you suggest?" Irrational anger surged through me. I felt like shoving him in the chest. I felt like screaming at him. I felt like curling into a ball and pulling my tunic over my head to shut out the world.

It was myself I really wanted to scream at. How many people were lying broken or dead back at the Foundation? All because of me. I was familiar enough with failure, but never on such a colossal scale. It was my worst nightmare made real.

I closed my eyes and put my hands on my head with my elbows together in front of my face to create a small cocoon to block out the world so I could try to calm down. None of this

was Adrien's fault. And he was right, of course. They'd be tracking us. The Regs would have reported about the tunnel already.
We didn't have time for me to behave like an irate little kid.

I dropped my arms. "Maybe we should, I don't know, hold
hands?"

He paused a moment as if considering. "It'll be easier if
you're only moving one object instead of two, right?" He
didn't wait for me to respond. He just stepped behind me, his
chest to my back, and looped his arms around my waist. I
stiffened at the touch, feeling a burst of too many emotions to
count. I hadn't been this close to him since . . .

I shook off the thought. *Steel*, I thought to myself, *I will be
steel*. I put my arms through my rations pack. Instead of sling-
ing it over my back, I kept it on my front like a pouch. The
truth was Adrien's touch, even if it meant nothing to him,
made me feel better. More confident, like I wasn't alone,
and I needed every bit of strength, wherever I could draw it
from.

I closed my eyes and let the projection cube expand in my
mind. Gently, I lifted us off the ground again. Adrien was
right. It was easier not having to worry about the surface area
of two separate individuals. But the pressure of him against
my back was distracting.

As I flew us forward, navigating around the branches, Adrien
reached up several times to tug at my hair. His fingers tickled
my neck and I only narrowly missed flying us into a tree trunk.

"What are you *doing*?" I snapped.

"Your hair keeps getting in my face," he said.

I grabbed for the tie I always kept around my wrist and
tried to reach back to tie my hair up, which was awkward
since I was flying with Adrien basically hanging off my back.
Not to mention I continued being distracted by the awareness
of every inch of his body where it made contact with mine.

"Maybe we should fly with our bodies horizontal to the ground," Adrien said after a few more minutes. "We would move faster."

I bit down on my cheek hard to keep myself from snapping at him again. I was having a difficult enough time keeping us moving forward without him distracting me every other minute.

"It's just that it would be far more aerodynamic and—"

A metallic grinding noise echoed from behind us in the forest. I swiveled my head around to look. "What was that?" I whispered.

"Maybe they got past the blockage."

My eyes widened, and then I closed them back tight again, pouring all of my energy into my telek sense. I tipped us forward until we were horizontal with the ground. I had to admit, we were smacking into fewer tree branches this way, and we were able to move faster.

Flying entailed a strange balance of calculating carefully where we were aiming and ignoring the inner stream of logic screaming that flying at all should be impossible. For a few moments here and there I was able to find the equilibrium where I kept us moving forward instinctually rather than intellectually. Dip, adjust to the left, avoid the split branch hanging down. I kept my telek focused spatially forward and down. If I let myself think about the unending expanse of sky above the trees or the Regulators on our heels, I wouldn't be able to keep it up.

Every so often Adrien checked his arm panel and told me to aim left or right, but other than that, we stayed silent. The amount of concentration necessary to keep us in the air and keep my allergens at bay at the same time became quickly tiresome, but I managed to keep us going for several hours before finally dropping us back to the ground.

"I need a break," I said to Adrien. I was tired. The passage between trees had been so narrow at times that we were both covered in scrapes and stray brown needles. I'd had my eyes closed to stay better focused on what I felt with my telek, but now that I opened them, I saw it was almost dark. I leaned my back against a tree and stretched my neck.

The forest at twilight was full of unfamiliar sounds. You'd think being out here all alone in the middle of nowhere, it would be quiet. Instead it was loud, but not like noises I was used to—the groan of steel settling or the steady mechanic whir of machines. No, the noise around us now didn't seem to come from any one place. Insead it came from everywhere, from the wind in the trees, to the scratch of rustling bushes, to the weird high-pitched clicking noise that had to be some kind of animal or insect.

Then I frowned. Wait, it was nighttime, that meant . . .

"Oh no, we haven't put on the coolant harnesses." I looked up as if I could sense the Infrared Satellite Cams overhead. They switched from normal Sat Cams to IR Cams at night.

Adrien waved a hand dismissively from where he walked nearby, stretching his legs. "We're safe from IR cameras as long as we're under the trees. They cover our heat signature. Besides, there are enough things living in this forest that even if they catch a glimpse of us, they'll just think we're a deer or a bear or something."

I let out a sigh of relief. Then I frowned, "Wait, did you just say there are bears out here?"

Adrien ignored my question and looked up, even though any vision of the darkening sky was encumbered by the treetops. A breeze blew in that twisted and shook the leaves on all sides. I closed my eyes for a moment, enjoying the cool breeze. I'd felt hot and sticky all day, but now that the sun was going down, it was cooling off rapidly.

I touched my forearm panel for light and watched Adrien

gazing up at the sky. He was so tall and skinny, you'd almost mistake his shadow for just another trunk.

The trees were taller here than they'd been when we left the mountain tunnel. I'd followed the direction Adrien had pointed out as closely as I could, but I'd had to divert my path so often to avoid low-lying branches, I couldn't be sure if we'd continued going north like we were supposed to.

Adrien took a few steps forward and broke off a bit of bark. "Coniferous." He sniffed it. "Pine trees. When I was a kid, Sophia and I used to move through the forests around here if a situation got too hot in Sector Six." He dropped down and rubbed a small shrub plant between his fingers. "She always knew which foods were good to eat and which weren't."

I couldn't be sure, but it seemed like his voice got quieter when he mentioned his mother. The scene I'd been trying to keep at bay suddenly resurfaced—her shoving Adrien through the door. She'd had no thought for herself. When I'd first met her, I couldn't understand her animosity toward me. She had visions like Adrien used to, but, unlike his, hers only happened every few years and were vague and sometimes unintelligible. But she'd known I was trouble the first moment she met me. She told me she'd foreseen that I would do harm to her son. Why hadn't I listened?

I went over and put a hand on Adrien's shoulder, guilt weighing heavily. "I'm so sorry about what happened to her."

He didn't respond, just stared blankly ahead like he couldn't hear me. Or was pretending he couldn't. I could never tell what was going on in his head anymore. I used to be able to read him so easily before he was taken by the Chancellor.

I shook my head and sat down. Several of the needle-leaves poked me, but with a few readjustments, I could sit comfortably. I would get Adrien to safety, that was all that mattered now.

"Let's check the map," I said.

He nodded and touched his arm panel, pulling up the section of map that showed both southern Sector Six and northern Sector Five. He settled himself beside me, his forearm glowing in the dim evening light.

"So are we somewhere around here?" I pointed at the bottom of the small screen embedded in his arm.

He leaned his head closer and nodded. Even though we'd been close all day, him holding on to me as we flew, I hadn't allowed myself to focus on it. But now with him crouched beside me, his face only a half foot from mine as he leaned in to see the map, my heartbeat started to quicken.

I couldn't stop staring at him as his eyes searched the map. His eyes had changed colors while he'd been captured. The bright blue-green had become a translucent gray. Now they were strange, even eerie to look at, but still beautiful in their own way.

"You should get the blanket out of your pack too, and have something to eat," I said, a lump forming in my throat. How could a person be so close, and yet so far away?

He nodded and opened his pack. First he pulled out a small lamp and set it up between us. I blinked at the brightness of the lamp after getting so used to the darkness. It created a small penumbra of light in the circle between several tall trees where we'd settled.

"How much farther till we hit the border fence?"

"Half a day, maybe more."

I dragged the blanket out of my own pack and wrapped it closer around myself, wishing I was comforted. My teeth chattered.

Adrien frowned, looking down at his pack. "Aren't there supposed to be twenty protein bars per pack?"

I nodded. He laid the bars in an orderly line, then looked back up at me. "I only count nine."

"That can't be right." I emptied my own pack on the ground, sorting through the contents. I only counted seven bars.

"Shunt," I swore loudly. "It must have been the refugees. We caught them breaking into the pantry last week. They must have realized the escape pods would have rations too. Idiots!" I kicked at the empty pack. "Didn't they realize they might have to survive on these packs one day?"

"When you're living life on the run, you tend to just worry about today, not tomorrow. Besides," Adrien said, his voice calm and reasonable, "if we ration ourselves, we should be able to survive on two bars a day. Even if it takes us three days to get to the Rendezvous site, we'll be fine."

I tried to let go of my frustration as I looked through the rest of the contents to see if they'd stolen anything else. The heat lamp, blankets, extra change of clothes, and the coolant harnesses were still there, at least. I turned on the small lamp so I could see better in the darkness.

"They took the external tablet and the small laser weapon too." I tossed over the rest of the objects. "Even the water bottles!" I sat back, suddenly feeling inordinately thirsty now that I knew there was no water.

"My pack's got one bottle, at least," he said. "We can share it till we find some more fresh water. There are streams all over these mountains." He took a quick drink and then handed the bottle to me. I tried not to sip too much, but ended up taking out a quarter of the bottle anyway. I replaced the cap and handed it back to him.

"At least the info chips were stored in a side pocket," he said. "They must not have seen them. And we've got the arm panels, so we don't need the external tablet to use them."

His confidence and calm about everything did make me feel better. He'd done this kind of thing all his life. We'd made it out of the mountain and gotten far enough away that we were safe. The rest of the pods were probably already at the rendezvous site by now.

But then I thought about all those who hadn't been able to make it out of the Foundation. I remembered the screams as the lights flickered. What had happened once the Regulators had reached the main level? Did they take everyone prisoner, or had they just opened fire on the crowd? And then there was my brother. What was the Chancellor doing to him? Did she have him under her compulsion, or something worse? I rubbed my temple as if I could erase the images that had suddenly popped up in my head. There was nothing I could do about it right now. Not till we met up with the others.

"Let's get some sleep," I finally said. "A few hours would do us both good."

But then I looked back at the contents of the pack and my heart sank. No, surely they wouldn't have . . .

My hands became more frantic as I lifted every object and tossed it aside.

No, no, no, this couldn't be happening.

It wasn't there. Every pack was supposed to include a biosuit for me and two oxygen reserves. But they were gone.

"Is there a biosuit in your pack?" I asked, standing up and running over to Adrien's pack. I unceremoniously dumped it all out and began sorting through items, but his was the same. No suit.

"Why the hell would they take my biosuits?" I shouted, throwing the empty pack to the ground as hard as I could.

Adrien looked down at the strewn contents in dismay. "Reg armadas use chemical weapons sometimes. Suits like that are valuable, either to use themselves or to sell on the black market." He flipped over a few more objects from his pack. "Whoever took it probably didn't think it'd do any harm because there were suits in every other pack. So if they took a few things here and there, maybe they thought it wouldn't be missed."

I had another thought. "At least we still have the epi infusers," I said, trying to reassure myself. Then at least I could revive myself if I started having an allergy attack, and it would afford me twelve hours of safe breathing time. "Each pod should have two of them in the med kit." I searched through the supplies. "Where *is* the med kit?"

"Here," Adrien pulled out the small metal box from where he'd stowed it in a side pocket of his pack. He clicked it open and then his eyes widened. He turned the box toward me. The two epi injections that should have been stowed in little latches on the lid were gone.

"Medicines are also big sellers on the black market," he said quietly.

All of a sudden, I felt like laughing hysterically. Of course they were.

I sat back on my heels and rubbed my eyes, conscious of how tired I already was. I'd barely slept at all last night. We had prepped three redundancies with every pod in consideration of my condition—one collapsible med container, a biosuit in every pack, and epi infusions in the med kit. And yet here I was, without any of them. Everything had been so hectic in the tunnel, I hadn't even bothered with the med container since I'd been confident that there would be a suit in my pack. Stupid. I should have known something was wrong when I first saw that the packs were unsecured.

"Look, we'll get to the safe house in a few more days," he said. "They'll have all the medicines we need . . ." Then his eyes narrowed. "Oh," he finally said, my predicament apparently sinking in.

"Yeah. Oh. The second I fall asleep and stop controlling my allergies, I'll go into anaphylactic shock." I looked up at him. "I'll die within minutes."

Chapter 11

I SWALLOWED HARD AT THE thought, trying not to wallow in the memories of how it felt for my throat to close up and to gasp for breaths that wouldn't come. Even though we'd stopped in an area where the needle-carpeted ground was clear, the thick tree trunks surrounding us seemed to suddenly close in. I doubled my grip on my mast cells and took several long, deep breaths to calm myself down. It helped, sort of.

Adrien frowned, still crouched by his pack. "Your allergens do make you a liability."

"A liability . . ." I repeated slowly, feeling punched in the gut. I looked to see if he was joking, but no, his face was intent and serious.

"Why are you even bothering to stay with me if you feel that way?"

He stared at me a moment, as if genuinely considering the question. "Instinct, I guess," he finally said, sitting down by the mess I'd made. He sifted through the objects I'd tossed and began to align them in orderly rows. "I care about your survival."

"You do?" I asked hesitantly. Was this a sign that Adrien was finally starting to be himself again? Now that I thought about it, he'd been far more communicative ever since we'd left the Foundation. Maybe this last regrowth session had finally done it.

"Your assets make you valuable in spite of your liabilities. I have a far better chance of surviving if you do." He nodded to himself, as if pleased with his reasoning.

I stood up, suddenly furious. "You say that like I'm just . . . a thing or a tool or something. Like when I start to become more of a *liability* than an asset you'll leave me behind."

"I'm only being logical." He examined the food bars from the overturned pack, picking up each one and examining the label. "Survival instincts," he said, like he was the Professor leading a lesson. "We all have assets and liabilities—it's why people have been working together in tribes and communities since the beginning of history. One person with a particular strength can make up for another who's weak in that area and vice versa."

He finally found the protein bar he wanted and unwrapped it, taking a big bite and staring thoughtfully into the distance before continuing. "Your assets in this particular situation, for instance, are that you can fly and protect us from anything that attacks. Your liabilities are that you are physically weak and now might die because of your allergies."

"Thanks, I wasn't aware enough of my deficiencies." I tried not to show him how much his words hurt, but my sarcasm was lost on him.

"I'm happy to help," he said.

"So what are *your* liabilities and assets then?" I shot back.

He chewed on his protein bar. "That's fair to ask. Well," he leaned back against a tree trunk, "I'm very smart. I've survived in woods like these before, and if we run out of rations, I'll be able to provide food for myself."

"Just yourself?" I asked.

"And those in my group or tribe." He inclined his head toward me. "As long as they have assets to trade."

I rolled my eyes, trying to ignore how much it stung to hear him say these things. "Of course, only then. What else do you have to offer?"

"I'm good in a fight. There's a firearm tucked away in my rations pack. I'm a better shot than you. And I'm a good techer." His face darkened for a moment. "Or at least I will be again, once the doctor's poisons get out of my system. Besides, in the wilderness, two are always better than one."

"So what if my allergies become too much of a liability? Then you'd just pack up your things, and, well . . ." I paused as I tried to wrap my head around his way of thinking, "I guess you'd take my things too at that point and leave me to die?"

He blinked a few times, a slight frown on his face. "I guess there wouldn't be any logical reason for me to stay . . ." He looked conflicted, and for a moment I hoped he'd realized the absurdity of what he was saying. But then he continued, "I guess . . . hypothetically, yes."

"Oh, really?" I scoffed. "Gonna dump me off the first cliff-side you see, then?"

He shook his head. "Of course not. Haven't you been listening? Your assets are valuable to me. As long as there continues to be an even exchange, we should both be able to make it to the rendezvous site just fine."

I'd been trying to harden myself against his demeanor, to pretend the things he was saying didn't hurt. But suddenly I tired of the effort. I rubbed my eyes, then looked up at the tree branches that made a dense ceiling overhead.

"You called it poison. Is that what you really think of Jilia's treatments?"

He nodded. "They made me sick, and I could never do any intricate coding work afterwards." I remembered he spent a lot of time in the Security Hub where he liked to work on multiple consoles. At least he had before Jilia had upped his meds so he was getting injections every day.

"We were only trying to *help* you. Your mother and I—" I stopped again at the mention of his mom. The image of the closing blast door flashed in my mind. "I'm sorry. You know, she might have found another way out. Or they could be holding her for questioning. That's probably what they are doing—"

Something sparked in his eyes, but it wasn't sorrow or grief. He jumped to his feet. "That is exactly why I don't want any more of the poisons. You say you were trying to heal me but all you wanted was to make me weak."

"What?" I asked.

"You all delude yourselves constantly, but *I'm* the one who's broken and sick? You can't even tell the truth when it's obvious to both of us. Sophia is dead. You know it and I know it. I don't have to hide behind pretty delusions. It's all lies, all of you trying to shape the world the way you want it to be, instead of seeing it like it really is. And you treat me the same way."

"What do you mean? We all just want you to get better—"

"No." He held up a finger sharply, advancing toward me. "That's another lie. You want me to be him."

"What?" I put my hands on my waist. "We want you to be you."

"No." He shook his head. "You want me to be *him*. Sophia wanted me to be him too," he said, seeming agitated. He spun and walked away from me. He cast a long dark shadow as he passed in front of the lamp. "She barely knew me. It was him she wanted. All of you are the same, trying to pressure me into pretending to be someone I'm not."

He turned again to look at me. "I may have his face, but I'm not him. None of you are willing to see it. Not you, not the doctor, and most of all, not the woman who called herself my mother. You kept dunking me in that shunting chamber for weeks at a time, hoping I'd turn back into him, when I'm perfectly healthy as I am."

"How can you say that?" Angry heat rose in my cheeks. "Your mother sacrificed herself for you because she loved you. If you can't see that, then you obviously *are* still broken. You're cold and emotionless. You're not a whole human being."

"Emotionless?" His voice rose an octave. "Then what do you call this?" He threw his hands out wide, then brought them back and hit his chest with his palms. "I'm a human being. I feel anger. You're just upset because I don't feel what you consider the right emotions—I don't feel what you *want* me to feel. You all walk around ignoring your most basic human instincts."

"And what are those?"

"The instinct to survive!" he yelled. "That woman, sacrificing herself for us? She was a fool. All we have is this life and she just threw it away."

"She was your mother—"

"She should have been trying to save herself!"

I was shocked and taken aback at all the emotion showing so clearly on his face.

"Instead she wasted her life for nothing—for a memory of someone who's not even here anymore. She didn't love me. She didn't even *know* me, and she died for nothing."

"Don't you dare say that," I said, stepping toe to toe with him. "She died for *you.* You grew in her body and she birthed you and she'd die for you no matter what you've turned into."

"She was a fool," he repeated, his face red. "And I used to be a fool too, back when I thought lumps of flesh had souls." He threw his hands up in the air. "It's so obviously the opposite. We are organisms, and like all organisms who are threatened, we adapted to survive. That's all."

He moved to turn away from me again, but I grabbed his arm. "No, that's not all," I said, even though once I had thought the same thing. When we'd first met, we'd had this argument backward. I didn't know now if I'd said it because I actually believed it, or if I'd wanted to believe it. "You always said there was more to it. That we matter. That relationships between even just two human beings—that love—can change the world."

He shook his head. "What you call love is the ultimate lie. It means putting someone else's needs above your own. Which can get you killed. It got Sophia killed." He paused and looked straight at me with a burning intensity. "And it got me tortured and lobotomized."

A lump rose in my throat. All my anger dried up in an instant. I knew what he was saying. It was my fault. Loving me had gotten him tortured within an inch of his life. All that pain and anguish, when it would have been so much easier to relent and give into the Chancellor's compulsion. He was right. He'd already suffered enough on my account. It would serve me right to be left behind here to die.

I let go of his arm. "I'm so sorry," I finally managed to whisper, barely able to find my voice. I knew my apology wasn't enough, would never be near enough. The chasm of all I owed to him, of all he'd gone through, because of me—

"Don't be," he said. He closed his eyes, and his heaving chest stilled. "It was my own fault for being weak enough to fall in love in the first place. I know better now. You shouldn't let useless guilt weigh you down either."

I stared at him, wanting to pull him close and rest my head on his chest, to listen to his heartbeat. Anything to try to reassure myself that the boy I had loved was still inside the person in front of me somewhere. Instead, I stayed rooted where I stood.

"Why didn't you say any of this before?"

He pinched his lips together before speaking. "You never asked."

I took a step toward him involuntarily. "I asked you every day how you were feeling."

"Exactly," he shook his head. "How I was *feeling*. You asked about emotions. You wanted some evidence so you could pretend I was starting to become him again. You didn't want to know about the things I was interested in. I tried telling you about my coding projects. I showed you the exciting math theorems I was working on. But you didn't want to hear it. All you wanted to talk about was love and souls and emotions, or worse," he grimaced, "memories of the past."

"Why is talking about memories a bad thing?" My voice broke and I couldn't help it. "I was only trying to help you remember who you are."

"Who I *was*," he corrected. He'd calmed down some, but his eyes were still lit with intensity in the blue light of the lamp. "I've been trying to make you see who I am *now*."

I stepped back, stunned. He talked about the old Adrien as if he was gone for good. As if that's the way he wanted it.

I stared at him as he organized and restuffed the packs. It was so obvious he was different. I must have been willingly blinding myself not to see it. The way he ordered things into neat rows, everything in its place, when the old Adrien had been messy. How he read complex math texts for fun when my Adrien would have wanted to go look at the sunset or read a book of poems. Maybe it wasn't fair of me to keep trying to pretend he was someone else.

No, I tried to tell myself. I looked down at the brown crumpled leaves under my feet. He was still sick. That was all. When he got better . . .

I squeezed my hands into fists at my sides. I couldn't think about any of this right now. Right now it was time to push all this emotion under a shadowed stone somewhere deep in my soul and face the situation in front of us. We needed to get to the safe house. That was all.

Adrien finished closing up his pack. I took a moment to steady my voice. "We should get moving."

Chapter 12

BY LATE AFTERNOON OF THE next day, we still hadn't hit the border fence between Sectors Five and Six. We'd flown all morning and hadn't spoken much. All the words that mattered had been slung last night.

I set us down on the ground. The crunch of our feet on fallen leaves as we walked sounded extraordinarily loud. After a few steps on my weak legs, I barely managed to stay standing. I'd never felt such an allover achy soreness like this before. My shoulder blades felt like they were slicing through my back, and even my eyes felt bruised. It had been over thirty-six hours since I'd last slept.

The afternoon sun was like a spike in my eyes when I opened them. I immediately backed away into the shadow of a tree and rolled my shoulders to stretch them out. I was beyond exhausted. I'd left exhaustion behind hours ago. I felt like I was about to collapse.

I slumped to the ground with my back to a tree. We'd both agreed earlier it would be safer to cross the fence at night and figured we should take the opportunity to rest now during the day. Which meant we had a few hours of rest, or at least as much as I could rest without falling asleep.

Soon it would be over, I reminded myself. We'd get past the border, then into Sector Six. We'd make our way slowly to the rendezvous site. Everyone would be safe and together again. Except for my brother. He was with the Chancellor, under her compulsion. Was she treating him well? If he had a useful enough glitcher Gift, she would, but there was no way to know.

And then there was everyone who hadn't been able to make it into the pods. I selfishly hoped my friends had all made it to safety and it was the refugees who'd been left behind. I pushed my palms against my eyes as if I could scrub the horrible thought away. I just needed to get Adrien safely there, get some sleep, and then I'd take off on my own so whoever was left could stay protected.

Adrien refilled our bottle with water from the stream we'd been following. It had been an easy way to orient myself and make sure I was headed up the mountain so we'd hit the border fence at a deserted area. I'd flown underneath the overhanging branches of the trees along the shore to avoid detection. Without bushes and brambles snagging at us from below, we'd been able to fly faster.

Adrien handed me the bottle of water and sat down nearby. "I drank at the river, so have as much as you want."

He pulled out a protein bar he'd halved earlier and began munching. I took a long swallow of the cold water and let out a sigh of pleasure at how good it tasted.

He sat on a large rock and looked outward, his elbows on his knees. I followed his gaze.

We'd come halfway up the nearest mountain. At times it had been so steep we'd almost been flying vertically. We were high enough up that other peaks spread out before us, sloping rises stacked against each other in the late-afternoon sun.

"It's strange not to see the peaks covered by snow," he said, looking out. "This one time when Sophia and I spent half a year hiding out in the mountains, the peaks were all covered in white." A small smile tugged at the edges of his mouth.

"She told me the white caps were the mountains' hats, so they could stay warm all winter." His smile faltered. "Completely illogical, of course, but at the time it amused me."

I stared at him, tracing the lines of his face as if I could memorize what it had looked like when he'd smiled. But as quickly as the smile had come, it was gone again. I looked away from him and pulled my hair out of its tie to run my fingers through it and rebraid it.

Now that we'd stopped, the noise I'd been hearing in the background for the past few hours suddenly seemed extremely piercing, a high-pitched chirping sound. It wasn't anything mechanical, I could tell that much. "What *is* that?"

"What?"

"That constant screeching noise."

The smile was back. "Cicadas. There's millions of them out there, all singing to each other. Don't worry, you'll get so used to it you won't even hear it anymore."

"You really should get some sleep," I said, my voice abrupt. Seeing him smile pained me in a strange way. It was more evidence that even though he could feel emotion now, he still felt none for me. "No reason for both of us to be sleep deprived."

I ground my back against the rough bark of the tree to keep myself awake. I was so tired, all I wanted to do was close my eyes. A day and a half might not seem like a long time to be awake, but I'd also been using my powers at maximum. That alone without the sleep deprivation would have exhausted me on a normal day.

I blinked my eyes and forced them open wider. Going to sleep would get me killed. I'd just have to remind myself of that every 0.3 seconds when my eyes started getting heavy again.

Adrien nodded and laid on his side beside the rock, his arms curled up for a pillow. He closed his eyes without another word.

After a few more breaths, he was asleep. I watched his rising and falling chest, the way his mouth slackened slightly in sleep, and the long angles of his face in the soft afternoon light. I wanted so badly to curl up beside him and relax against his wiry frame.

Instead, I took off my outer shirt so I'd feel the cool breeze of the afternoon wind more sharply to keep me from dozing off. At least I didn't have to worry about another overload like what happened with the earthquake back at the Foundation. It only occurred when I had too much power stored up inside me. I was using it constantly now so that wouldn't be a problem. I focused my telek senses on the continuous task of keeping my mast cells in check. When even that became a repetitive lull teasing me toward sleep, I paced a path under the tree cover. My steps slowed with each pass.

I sat down, putting several sharp rocks underneath me so I wouldn't get comfortable. I tried to think of my training with Jilia. She said people could meditate quietly for hours, even days. I had to think like that. That I was just training my body. I wondered if there was a way to meditate where I could go into a restful state without actually falling asleep. Now probably wasn't the best time to be experimenting though, considering it could cost me my life.

I looked at the ferns and shrubs all over the ground, then up at the tree trunks, then finally to the dots of sky visible through the tree tops. The leaves undulated and shook in the wind. There was so much life all around me. And noise, especially the continuous screech of the cicadas and the musiclike trill of what I assumed was a bird—I'd never seen or heard one up close before. Occasionally another bird would respond with a low guttural call that ended in a squawk. It made the hairs on my arms stand up. I wondered what other living things were out there hidden among the trees—I remembered Adrien's comment about bears and shuddered.

But eventually, not even my worry about hungry forest animals could keep me awake. It had been easier when we were moving, but sitting still like this, staying awake was becoming impossible. I'd find my eyes slowly closing, only blinking them rapidly before they dropped shut completely. So I tried closing one eye at a time, hoping that would help. Instead, it only made me more aware of how *good* it would feel to close both my eyes.

I jumped to my feet to avoid the temptation of letting my eyes fall shut. At this point I don't think even lying on a bed of nails would keep me awake for long. Nothing was going to really help except actual sleep. I paced again. I just had to keep moving, that was the trick.

I didn't know how long I'd been at it, a few hours maybe, when Adrien suddenly cried out.

I hurried over to him in the dim light of the setting sun. He sat straight up and gasped as if he couldn't get a breath. An animal-like noise came from his throat.

I dropped down beside him. "What's wrong?"

He didn't answer. Had something bitten him? An insect or snake? I did a quick survey of his body, examining each limb, then his torso and head. But there was nothing. He just kept rocking back and forth, clutching his arms to his chest. Finally I realized he wasn't hurt.

He was crying. Adrien was crying.

"Adrien." I hurriedly wrapped my arms around his shaking shoulders. "Shh, it's okay, it was only a dream."

I couldn't be sure, but I thought he moved his head a tiny bit so that it rested on my shoulder as his sobs slowed.

"It's okay," I kept murmuring. I gently stroked his hair, clutching him closer. "It's okay now. You're safe."

"I dreamed of Sophia dying." His voice was barely a whisper. "The Regulators smashed her face in. I saw her head explode like a melon and there was so much blood . . ."

"Shhhhh," I said. "Shh, it's gonna be okay. We're going to be okay." The mumbled words were all I could think to say. It was the first time I'd seen Adrien cry since the lobotomy. Over the past few months, I'd assumed that he wasn't capable of emotions anymore, but maybe that was only because he hadn't let me see. When had he started being able to *feel* again? It was a month ago that he'd stopped letting me take his hand when I visited in the afternoons. Had it been that long?

"I hate it when I cry." The way he said it made it sound like this wasn't the first time. He pulled away from me finally and swiped angrily at his eyes. "It's completely illogical."

"Not everything is about logic. You're crying because you loved her," I said.

"Impossible," he said vehemently. "I barely even knew her."

"You said you had your memories. You remember what it felt like when she held you as a child. You remember what it felt like when you were scared and she was there to comfort you."

"That's just it." He pursed his lips tightly together. "That's what none of you understand. I have the memories you talk about, but thinking about them is like watching strangers in a projection vid. It doesn't feel like they happened to *me*. I never loved her. *He* loved her. She meant nothing to me."

"Then why are you crying?" My voice went high-pitched as my emotions bubbled up in spite of my determination to stay patient. I was tired of his cold reasoning. "She obviously does mean something to you. You have emotions even if you don't want them. You can feel love and hate and sadness and passion. Even if you've changed, your soul is still the same—"

"Souls don't exist!" His eerily translucent eyes flashed up at me. "The entire notion is ridiculous. The body is a machine, that is all."

"Then what's the point of living?" I cried. I took a deep

breath to calm myself down before continuing. "I'm explaining it badly. The soul is just a word you always used to describe that part of us that is something more than just our flesh and bones and the electrical synapses in our brains. It's the part of us that makes us human."

"Well, that's one more thing he was a fool about," Adrien said, his voice turning bitter. He swiped at his eyes one last time. "If souls were located somewhere other than the flesh, then mine couldn't have been cut out of me when they hacked into my brain. But it was. I felt nothing, *nothing*," he repeated vehemently, "for months. And when I did begin to feel things again, it was all sadness and pain and the realization that I wasn't the person everyone wanted me to be. I was better off beforehand."

He looked away. "The sun is down. We should get going so we can make it to the fence tonight."

"But Adrien—"

He grabbed his pack and stood with his back to me. "We should get moving."

I sighed and rubbed my tired eyes. A headache was blooming across my skull. Like a fool, I'd gotten my hopes up when I saw his tears—thought for a second maybe there was a way he could find his way back to who he had been. Back to me. Instead, like always, I was just seeing what I wanted to see. I looked back at him before quickly averting my eyes again. I was terrified that someday soon, I was going to have to stop pretending to see the light of the Adrien I'd loved in the eyes of the stranger in front of me.

Chapter 13

I LOOKED OVER AT ADRIEN when we next stopped, right before we got to the border fence. I was so exhausted, my vision was getting blurry. In the light of Adrien's arm panel, it looked like he had two heads. I blinked several times until the two overlapping images settled back into one. I slumped against a nearby tree, ignoring the bark stabbing at my back as I slid down to the ground. It was the middle of the night now and the fight to stay awake was getting more and more impossible. It felt like every cell in my body was screaming at me to sleep.

"Get your coolant harness out," Adrien said. His voice was cold, mechanical almost. He'd been like this all day, the few times he was forced to speak to me. Almost as if, by becoming completely robotic now, he could erase the memory of his earlier emotional outburst. "We'll be exposed to the Infrared Sat Cams while we're crossing the fence."

My hands felt thick and clumsy as I sorted through my pack. The headache from earlier had only gotten worse. I swallowed another couple of pain pills from the med kit and rubbed my temple.

"Actually we'll be fine with just my harness," Adrien said, frowning as he watched me swallow the medicine. "It'll cover our heat signatures for a four-foot radius as long as we stay close." He put his arms through the harness and clasped it around his stomach. Then he clicked the button and the straps of the harness began to inflate. Luminescent nano-infused coolant gel began flowing through the inflated straps like water through pipes.

Adrien craned his head to look up. "There's no moon out tonight. That should help us cross without detection."

I closed my eyes for a long moment, then jerked them open again right as I felt myself start nodding off. My arms began to prickle from the momentary lapse in concentration controlling my mast cells. I swallowed hard as I focused my telek again. I couldn't afford to let my attention slip. Not now.

He checked the map on his arm panel. "Perfect. The fence is right past those trees. We'll have to fly over it," Adrien said.

"I already know that," I snapped, the exhaustion making me irritable.

"I meant that we'll have to fly far up and over it. It's not just electrified, there are motion sensors on every inch of it, eyes without eyes."

"So?" My befuddled mind wasn't following whatever point he was trying to make.

"So I'm saying we'll have to fly *far* overhead to avoid triggering it. Motion detectors can usually sense anything in a hundred-foot radius."

"Oh." I got his meaning now. It wouldn't be just a quick hop over the fence. We'd have to fly up high into the sky. I sighed, tired even thinking about it. I was only getting the hang of flying *because* of all the things surrounding us. Having objects on all four sides meant I had a lot of solid points of references I could then maneuver us through. But the open sky?

Adrien came near and I stumbled as I tried to get to my feet. He held out a hand to help me, but again my vision blurred and it looked like two hands. I shook my head and held on to the tree instead as I finally got my feet under me. Adrien didn't say anything, just wrapped his arms around me from behind. I took a deep breath, then I raised us up off the ground again.

Or rather, I tried. Each time I lifted off now, it took longer and longer for my power to buzz to life. I used to be able to easily split my concentration between focusing on my mast cells and on external objects, but it was getting more and more difficult with each passing hour. Not to mention that without sleep, I was running through my supply of telek energy. We could only hope that I was able to get us to the rendezvous site before I was totally depleted.

We rose in the air, higher and higher. The solid shape of the ground beneath us got farther away. My heart beat faster with every foot we rose. The sudden adrenaline sharpened my focus and cleared away some of the fog in my brain.

"Just a little farther," Adrien said, "then we should be clear."

But the ground was already so far away. I struggled to find something to hold on to, some shape or object I could use as a guide to steady us.

All I felt was emptiness, all around.

I lost my grip.

We tumbled forward suddenly, then dropped like a stone.

"Find the ground," Adrien shouted in my ear. "Use that to focus your telek!"

I cast outward again and finally found the floor beneath us. The trees swayed in the wind, but they were firm. I tried to feel all the way down to their roots planted in the unmoving earth.

I finally caught us again and held us steady. I could feel the pumping of Adrien's chest behind me as he tried to catch his breath. Neither of us said anything though, and we began to rise again. I kept my concentration firmly rooted in the ground with the trees.

After a few more seconds, Adrien said, his voice still unsteady, "We're high enough. Now go north."

"Which way is north?"

He lifted his arm panel, looking over my shoulder to see it. His breath was hot on my neck and I shivered. "To your left."

I nodded, closing my eyes. The stars were bright and I didn't think I could handle seeing just how far we had to drop if I faltered. I gritted my teeth, then pushed us forward in the direction Adrien had indicated.

We flew fast. Far faster than we had when we stayed below the tree line. Up here there were no obstructions, nothing to block my path and nothing I had to be careful to maneuver around. It seemed like only a second later when Adrien said we'd cleared the fence without any problem.

I nodded my head but didn't say anything else. In my determination to fight through my exhaustion, I'd pierced my bottom lip with my teeth. I tasted blood, but I wasn't about to stop now. This was the only way we'd have a hope of making up the distance to the rendezvous site before I collapsed from exhaustion.

I pressed forward through the night sky. The wind got louder and louder in my ears as we gathered speed until it was all I could hear. The contours of the trees below blurred together as I pushed faster still. I cut out all other thought and feeling and sensation. I was an arrow in the wind.

"It's almost morning," Adrien said in my ear after a long while.

I opened my eyes in surprise and saw the sky around us had turned from solid black to a murky gray. A heavy morning fog coated the ground below us. I'd gone into almost a trance as I flew, thinking of nothing except pushing forward.

Our forward motion hiccupped, and I lost control again.

Adrien's body was ripped away from mine and we both plummeted down through the foggy clouds, end over end. I had no idea which was up and which was down.

"Zoe!" Adrien shouted.

I cast outward to where I thought the ground should be, but it was only more air. I tried another direction—still just the endless sky. I must have drifted up far higher than I'd meant to without realizing it.

"Zoe!"

There! I felt the ground. I threw all my telek force at it and managed to catch hold again. Our bodies were yanked up roughly like we'd been attached to the end of a rope that had suddenly run out.

The ground was only a few feet below. I shuddered. If we'd tumbled out of the sky over the treetops instead of a small open field, we'd have been—

I cut off the thought and gently set us down the last few feet, then promptly collapsed. I laid flat on my stomach, panting for several long moments with my face against the grass.

"If you're trying to deactivate us," Adrien said as he lay beside me, breathing heavily, "there are more pleasant ways to die than plummeting to the earth." Then he laughed. The noise echoed oddly in the air. "When I was a kid I always dreamed about flying. I think I'm cured of it now."

If I hadn't been so exhausted, I'd have been surprised at the laugh. As it was, all I could do was giggle in response. I was so deliriously tired, it seemed like the funniest thing I'd ever heard. His laugh sounded so . . . so *Adrien*.

"Yeah," I said. "I'll have to work on the landings." I rolled over onto my back. My body felt so heavy, like rocks had been sewn into my skin. The sun was rising. Everything around me seemed to glow, indistinct and blurry around the edges because of the early morning fog. It was hard to tell where the light ended and the trees began.

I giggled again at how pretty it all was. I put a hand over my mouth but couldn't stifle the high-pitched laughter, even though Adrien was looking at me strangely. Part of me knew this was just the sleep deprivation getting to me, but I was too distracted to care.

"The light," I said, pointing. "It's so beautiful."

The fog tumbled along the ground. I reached out to touch it, imagining it would feel like cotton. But my fingers passed right through. I looked over at Adrien. The fog curled around him, and suddenly I had the strangest fear that he was a ghost. Adrien had read to me about them once, a long time ago. Intangible spirits who took the shape of people you'd loved and lost.

And then suddenly, instead of laughing, I wanted to cry. Because that was what Adrien felt like to me now. A hollow echo who took the shape of the boy I'd loved, the boy who'd died all those months ago. I reached out for him, terrified my fingers would pass through him like they had the fog.

But he was solid. I almost choked with relief. He wasn't a ghost. He was still here. He was my Adrien, and he always would be. I didn't care what he said.

I rolled myself toward him and kissed his lips. He blinked in surprise, but didn't pull away. I kissed him harder, pressing my lips against his. Then, almost without thinking, I wrapped my arms around his body, pulling him into me. For a moment, just a moment, I could pretend that he was my Adrien.

With my hand on his chest, I could feel his heart starting to beat faster. After a long moment, his lips responded to mine.

I was delirious with joy or lack of sleep, I didn't care which. Adrien was kissing me again. Adrien loved me. Some small part of my brain registered that his kisses felt strange. Even though they were the same lips, he used them differently. His mouth was clumsy, as if he'd never done this before.

I pushed him back so that he was on the ground, but kept my mouth connected to his, always connected. He moved beneath me and my body responded. Matching his perfectly. I'd always thought we were two parts of a puzzle that only clicked into place when we were with each other. Even though he responded slightly differently now, it was still the only thing that felt right on this entire earth.

But then he broke away, panting hard. His eyes were wide, wild even. He stared at me several long moments before lifting me by the waist and depositing me on the ground beside him. "You're exhausted. You're forgetting I'm not him."

He bolted to his feet and walked away a few steps, lacing his fingers behind his head and hiding his face in his elbows for several long seconds.

When he turned back to me, his face was a hard mask. "We should check the map. See how close we are." He started tapping away at his arm panel.

I stared at him in disbelief, and the illusion was instantly broken.

I tried to get to my feet, wanting to shove him or punch him or do something to make him remember who he was. But I tripped on a bush when I tried to stand up and managed to catch myself on my elbows when I fell, only narrowly avoiding slamming my face into the ground.

When I looked over at him, my exhausted eyes were seeing doubles again. It looked like there were two Adriens standing side by side—the old and the new. The old Adrien would have caught me when I stumbled a moment earlier, would have thrown himself underneath me to break my fall. He would have wanted to kiss me for hours until our lips were numb and our bodies flushed.

But the new Adrien didn't even ask if I was okay. He just moved away from me and promptly clicked through the maps on his arm panel. Tears leaked out of my eyes. The two images before me settled back into one, and I finally understood for certain that it was not my Adrien left standing.

"Look," he said, pointing at his arm and coming over to show me. I didn't want to look. I wanted to curl up into a ball and sob. Even if the person standing in front of me wasn't a ghost, my Adrien was dead. A thick wave of grief slammed into me.

"It's what I thought," he continued, as if nothing was wrong, as if my entire world wasn't crashing to pieces. "We're very close. I've been watching the map on my arm panel, calculating our speed. I think we're right here."

I still wouldn't look.

"Zoe," he said softly, his voice pitched low. He reached out to touch my arm, but I yanked it away.

"Look, Zoe, we're less than a mile away from the safe house. We made it to the rendezvous site."

I looked at him in confusion. That couldn't be right.

"Just a mile?" I finally looked at the map. Indeed, the tiny beacon that indicated our position was blinking right beside the location for the rendezvous site. "But we were hundreds of miles away a few hours ago. It doesn't make any sense—" I tried to wrap my befuddled mind around it.

"You flew much faster in the open air. We'll be there soon, and you can finally sleep."

I blinked and then blinked again. My eyes felt like sandpaper in their sockets. Sleep. Yes, that would be very good. I could shut my eyes and forget the sharp grief that was tearing its way through my stomach.

I got to my feet and lurched awkwardly, the mix of adrenaline and exhaustion tipping me one way, then the next. I held my arms out and the breeze seemed to lift me up, like I was as light as a leaf, and I'd be carried along easily instead of having to work so hard. I'd lift right up out of this world with all its sadness and pain.

"I don't think you should be flying anymore," Adrien said. "Not in your condition."

I dropped my arms to my sides and they felt extremely heavy again. I looked around in confusion. I tried to focus on what Adrien was saying. "It will take forever if we don't fly," I finally managed to say, though my words came out a little garbled. "We don't have forever. We need to get there now."

He put a restraining hand on my arm right as I lifted off the ground. "If by forever you mean about fifteen minutes."

I tugged my arm away, but landed back on the ground. And stumbled again. Why was the earth all tilted funny? It was impossible to stand straight. Gravity was really a ridiculous thing. The world would be far better off without it. Objects shouldn't be tethered to the ground. It wasn't fair.

"Yeah, you definitely shouldn't be flying," Adrien said, holding me upright. "I'm not even sure you should be standing. Here, take my arm." He held out his arm.

"Oh, what do you care?" I asked, choked again by a dark mixture of anger and sadness. "I'm just a *liability*." I lurched forward again on the word.

He held out a hand to steady me.

"I don't need your help." I pushed away from him.

And then I ran into a tree.

"Clearly," he said, taking my arm and putting it around his waist to help stabilize me.

My legs felt rubbery, but with his support I was able to walk, only tripping occasionally on logs and brush. I couldn't tell how long we walked. It took all my energy to stay upright and keep my telek loosely focused on stemming my mast cells from an allergy attack. Adrien checked the map again, squinting at his arm as we neared a rise in the forest. The fog was thick overhead. The air smelled a little funny, but I couldn't quite put my finger on where I'd smelled it before.

"Zoe," he said, sounding excited, "we made it. The rendezvous site is right over that rise."

I grinned and felt a wave of adrenaline pour through my body. I grabbed his hand and started to run with a sudden burst of energy. Adrien easily kept pace beside me. We topped the rise and looked down at the valley below.

And then my legs dropped out from under me. Because the cabin was gone. It wasn't just more fog ahead I'd seen, and the funny smell suddenly made sense too.

It was smoke.

All that was left of the place where all my friends and everyone else at the Foundation were supposed to be waiting for us was the smoking remains of a building that had been blasted to bits.

Chapter 14

ADRIEN IMMEDIATELY PULLED ME BACKWARD. "We've got to get out of here," he whispered, dragging me back farther into the forest, away from the ridge.

But I could only stare ahead, unseeing. No, it couldn't be. I tried to fight off Adrien's hold for a moment so I could go look again. I had to have seen wrong. There was no way the rendezvous site could have been cracked. No one knew the coordinates other than those who had been in the pods . . . a wave of nausea hit and I grabbed my stomach. They must have tracked one of the pods itself somehow, in spite of Henk's cloaking tech.

All those people. I thought of everyone who'd made it in the first pod that launched. Tyryn. All the refugees. Molla and the baby.

"No, they can't be dead," I whispered, stumbling back from Adrien's grip. "It can't be."

"We don't know anything," Adrien said, coming up to me again. "Except that we need to get out of here. They probably know it's a rendezvous site, so they'll be watching to see if anyone else shows."

My eyes strayed back to the ridge as a sob choked its way out of me. I'd urged everyone to get in the pods thinking it would save them, when really I'd been sending them straight to their deaths. Over a hundred people. Dead because of me.

"It can't be, I just need to look again." I tried to lurch back toward the top of the hill, but Adrien grabbed my arms again.

"We saw it wrong." I wrestled to get out of his grasp. "We saw it wrong!"

"Stop it, Zoe." Adrien took my face in both hands and forced me to look at him. His eyes searched back and forth between mine. "You need to focus and fly us out of here. Right now. I know you're tired. But you have to do this. They'll kill us if they find us. Do you understand? You'll die."

I shook my head. No. I didn't understand anything. None of this made sense. I ground my palms into my eyes.

"Fine, if you don't care about saving yourself, then think about me." Adrien's voice was sharp like a slap. "If you don't get me out of here, they'll find us and kill me. Is that what you want, to get me killed?"

My head snapped up. Of course. I was his only escape route. It stung, but he was right. I couldn't let him get hurt anymore because of me.

I breathed out. *Empty mind, empty mind,* I intoned to myself. Just like back in meditation practice. I couldn't think about what might have happened to everyone. I was the reason Adrien was a shell of his former self. I owed it to him to get him safely away from here. The thought sharpened my mind to a single focus. There was nothing else in the world except this moment right now: objects filling space and the feel of the wind against our faces as I lifted us off the ground. Somehow I managed to pull from wells of energy reserves I didn't know I had.

We flew up, up, up until we were right below the tops of the trees. And then I propelled us forward. For once, I succeeded at clearing my mind of any thoughts. I was truly emptied out. But it didn't feel a thing like being at peace.

We flew until I simply couldn't anymore. We continued heading north, trying to put as much distance between ourselves and the safe house as possible. Adrien checked his arm panel every so often to tell me which way to turn and by how many degrees so that we'd stay in the mountains. I had no idea where we were, or where we were going. I didn't let my thoughts stray from the task at hand. The trees remained thick, that was all that mattered. We wouldn't be seen. Adrien would be safe.

But I'd been awake going on two and a half days now, and suddenly I just couldn't do it any longer. All the other thoughts I'd been keeping at bay suddenly rushed back in. The smoking cabin. Wondering if all that was left of my friends were charred bones. The trees started swirling around me again, and the air seemed like liquid, like the edges of everything seeped into one another. I slowed down and dropped us to the ground.

Adrien checked his arm panel the moment his feet touched the earth. "Good," he said. "We're near a city. I can probably slip inside without any problem."

I noticed he said *I*, not *we*. He was going to leave me.

I was too tired to even feel hurt by it. All chance of me getting to an allergen-safe chamber in time was gone now. I was dead weight, just like the broken bodies of everyone who'd been in the safe house.

So of course Adrien was going to leave and save himself. What had he called it? Survival instincts? I swallowed hard with the realization. When I leaned over, it felt like my ribs were knifing into my lungs. My shoulders ached raw in their sockets.

At least he'd be safe. At least I'd gotten him this far. I closed my eyes for a long blink, until the itchiness biting its way up my arms woke me abruptly a second later. I immediately got hold of my mast cells again with my telek. But when I finally got the allergy attack under control and opened my eyes, Adrien was gone.

He'd left without even saying good-bye.

Chapter 15

I PROPPED MYSELF UP AGAINST a tree. I grabbed a sharp rock and ground it into my thigh in an attempt to keep myself awake. I looked out at the forest. The sounds seemed inordinately loud to my exhausted ears. Above every other noise was the weirdly rhythmic high-pitched screech of cicadas. I put my hands on my ears to try to block out the sound, but it was no use. This was how I was going to die then. All alone with a million insects screaming out my death knell.

I knew the world was so much larger than this, so much bigger than my personal tragedy. I wasn't the first to lose a loved one in this war and certainly wasn't the first to lose my own life. I thought again of the smoking remains of the cabin.

All year I'd worried about bad things happening to faceless Rez operatives and the nameless families who hadn't been able to flee the cities in time. But now it was happening to me. I couldn't hold off sleep much longer, and the allergies would descend the moment I closed my eyes.

It would be a quick but painful way to die. I was sure I'd wake up every few seconds and use my telek to fight against the allergy attack, then inevitably grow weary with exhaustion and fall back asleep again. I wondered how many times I'd wake up again and push it back before not even my Gift would be able to stop the onslaught of released histamines.

A sob shook my chest. I looked at the now empty spot where Adrien had stood.

Had it all really been for nothing then? I'd believed so passionately that the Resistance had a destiny and that, in the end, good would overcome evil. Even if the road was difficult and the sacrifices severe. Maybe they still would go on and manage to win the war, without me.

Or did this new Adrien have it right? Were hope and love merely lies we told ourselves to try to create meaning where there was none? And if we were brave, we'd just look in the face of it and call hope what it truly was: a delusion to make the cold nothingness of life seem less dark and futile.

Surely that was the lesson of this moment. I'd failed everyone. My power, which was supposed to save people, had led instead to the destruction of the Rez's last safe haven. If it hadn't been for the earthquake I'd caused, the Foundation never would have been discovered. From both my brothers to Adrien, to the people dead at the burned-out cabin, to all the others who hadn't made it out of the Foundation in the first place—my presence had been nothing but a beacon leading straight to the destruction of the people I cared for most.

I hugged my arms hard to my stomach. I'd hoped so hard that I'd have a chance to atone for it all. That if I could just manage to free the drones from the power of the Link, or take down the Chancellor once and for all, then it would have all had some twisted kind of *meaning*.

But it didn't. It had all been for nothing.

Bitterness and sorrow were thick on my tongue like ash. I swallowed hard and stared up at the sky through the tree branches. Thick clouds hid the light of the sun.

I wanted it to end quickly now. Could I have that last, small mercy? Blocking my mast cells was second nature now, almost instinct. But maybe I could purposefully let the allergy attack take me the first time I fell asleep. Maybe it was possible to stop myself from fighting against it. A quick death.

I breathed in and out rapidly, trying to psych myself up to it. I looked around me, feeling half-delirious as I watched the strange world dip and spin around me through my exhausted eyes.

I couldn't do it.

I'd fight until the bitter end no matter what. Survival instincts, right? I could probably manage to keep the allergies at bay for another few hours, even if I was only prolonging the inevitable. I dug the rock in harder to my thigh.

Hours later, I used some thin brambly vines to tie several sharp rocks to a stick that I grated over my skin like a torture device whenever my heavy eyes dropped shut for too long. The sky darkened above. I blinked, confused. Was it night already? I couldn't see much through the treetops—just the blue slowly replaced by gray.

Gray. It was how I'd lived most of my life as a drone, and it was how I was going to die. No one would know that a girl named Zoe had once loved a boy named Adrien. No one would know about the beauty of all the conversations we'd had and the zinging electricity his touch sent through my limbs. We'd been a brief flame that had sputtered out like the now darkening day.

Another blink, and I'd be gone.

I walked up a staircase. It was completely dark. I swiveled my head back and forth but couldn't see anything, not even my own hand. I kept going upwards because I couldn't stand the thought of going back. I'd already come this far. Surely I was almost there. My thighs felt leaden with the effort and my throat burned. When was the last time I'd had a drink of water? Why was my body so heavy? It seemed like every footstep got heavier, and the slower I went, the further away I was from ever getting to the top.

And then, in the middle of the darkest black, a crack of light appeared. It grew wider and wider like a door opening above me. I stumbled toward it, now barely able to breathe at all. I reached out my hand, trying to touch the light.

Someone shouted my name, and it echoed out from the blinding light. I still couldn't get close enough. I couldn't breathe. I collapsed, my hands at my throat.

"Zoe! Wake up!" The voice was louder than before.

I blinked my swollen eyes and tried to sit up, but I could barely move. The realization hit all at once. I was still in the forest.

I must have fallen asleep, and I was in the middle of an allergy attack. It had been going on for at least a few minutes already, because when I frantically wheezed in trying to get a breath, no air made it through the closed-up passage of my throat.

The buzzing of my telek burned to life in my brain. But when I reached inward to flood the cells of my body with my power, the cells felt different. They were all wrong. The mast cells were swollen, spewing histamines like tiny geysers. I tried desperately to use my power to plug them, but I was too tired and confused. I couldn't repair the damage already done.

I dropped sideways to the ground from where I'd been sitting against a tree. Crunchy leaves and pine needles stabbed my face. My body spasmed. Every inch of my skin felt on fire, and my lungs squeezed in on themselves, unable to get that next lifesaving breath.

I wasn't so far gone though that I couldn't feel hands gripping my arms. Someone had flipped me onto my back. My eyes were so swollen I could barely see through tiny slits, and I could only make out the vague outline of a figure standing over me. The pain was so excruciating now, I could barely tell what was going on.

But I did feel the sharp bite of the needle being shoved into my thigh. I thrashed against the figure straddling my body, but the held me down. A jolting spike of adrenaline shuddered throughout my body. I sat up with the suddenness of it and cracked the person on top of me straight in the forehead, then fell backwards again.

I blinked in shock and was even more stunned to be able to open my eyes wider than I had before. I gasped in another desperate breath and air finally flooded my lungs.

When I looked up again, I could see a person who was rubbing their forehead and looking down at me anxiously.

It was Adrien. An opened med kit sat on the ground beside him, along with a used epi infuser.

He'd come back for me.

Chapter 16

ADRIEN WRAPPED ONE OF THE silver med blankets from the pack around me, but I shrugged it off after a few minutes. I was still sweating from all the exertion my body had just gone through, even though the air had a chill to it now. The wind blew harder, making an eerie whistling sound through the tree branches.

With the shot of epi, I was breathing fine now. Other than the leftover rash on some of my skin, I felt better too. But none of that mattered.

Adrien had come back. I couldn't stop staring at him.

He was still leaning over me, one hand on my cheek as he pushed back the matted hair from my face. "Are you sure you're okay?"

I nodded, befuddled. I reached up my hand to cover his, but he suddenly sat back and started rifling through his rations pack. "You should eat something."

"You came back," I whispered, still not believing it.

"Of course I came back." His eyebrows furrowed as he held my gaze a moment, then he looked away again. "It was easy. We're close to Driward. A couple hours down the mountain I was able to hack and steal a transport to get me closer to the city. It's a big factory town, and I know it pretty well. There's a quick way in and out through one of the off-site packaging facilities. I thought one of the other factories might have what we needed."

"Needed for what?" My mind was still swimming from exhaustion, and nothing he said made sense.

He frowned down at me as if *I* was the one not making any sense. "For your allergy. So you can sleep. Then when I got the epi, I snuck back out of the city and put the transport back where I found it. They probably won't even know it was missing. Well, except for my muddy footprints all over it."

I continued staring at him. He'd gone to get help for me?

"The inside of the factories are almost all automated," he went on, "so there weren't many people on the floor to see me. But I knew that all of them have fully stocked med kits near the offices. So I snuck in between drone shift changes and grabbed the kit. There was only one epi infuser, but look what else I found." A smile lit his face. It looked simultaneously foreign and so achingly familiar. "I had to almost empty out my pack to make it fit."

He pulled out a bunch of crinkling, bulky material. I'd seen something like this before.

"You found a biosuit!" It was one of the bulky kind, not the slim tribound polysutrate that had been designed for me, but it would still work fine.

Adrien grinned. "Complete with a four-hour oxy tank. The factory works with dangerous chemicals. I knew they always keep these around in case of spills. But right now you'll be fine with just the long-release epi shot. You've got twelve free hours without going into an attack."

I shook my head, dizzy and delirious and not able to think much beyond the happy thought of: *he came back for me*. I tried to focus on what he was saying.

"Wait, so you mean, I can sleep? Right now?"

"Right now." He smiled back. He seemed to be smiling a lot all of a sudden. I shook my head. I really was still delirious.

"Okay, then." I laughed. "Let's find some place for me to curl up and sleep."

A loud booming rumble suddenly sounded overhead. I let out a surprised scream and looked up. "What was that?"

Maybe they'd found us, and it was one of the propulsion-fueled transports roaring closer. My heartbeat ratcheted up several notches.

"It's only thunder." Adrien said as a fat raindrop plopped on my nose. "The storm's been rolling in all aftern—" Suddenly Adrien clutched his head and fell to his knees.

"Adrien!" I stumbled over to him.

He curled up in a ball on the ground. His eyes bulged wildly, like he was in excruciating pain.

"Adrien, what's wrong?" I grabbed his shoulders, trying to get him to look at me. "Talk to me!" But he stayed in the same position, shaking violently. I held on to him tighter, wishing I'd had more classes on med assistance. Maybe he was having a seizure because of what the Chancellor had done to his brain?

But then, as suddenly as it had hit, his shaking stilled. He blinked his eyes and they seemed to come back into focus. Another couple of raindrops splattered on his face.

"Are you okay?" I helped him sit up. His eyes wide, he lifted a hand to his forehead.

"I had a vision." His voice was low, terrified.

"But." I frowned. "You don't have visions anymore." That part of him was broken, never to return. Jilia had said so.

But then, Jilia had never dealt with anyone with as extensive brain damage, much less a glitcher receiving experimental tissue regrowth treatments.

"Like, a *vision* vision?" I'd watched him have plenty of visions in the past, and they'd never ended up with him on the ground clutching his head.

He shook his head, his face pale. "It wasn't like they used

to be. This was different. It was fractured." His troubled gaze finally met mine. "I saw two separate futures."

I frowned. "Like two separate events that happen in the future?"

He shook his head, slowly running his hand through his hair. It was such an Adrien thing to do. "I don't think so. It was like . . . like I saw things that were happening at the same time, but I saw it two different ways. As if the future could diverge into two paths, and I saw each one."

"What happened in the visions?" I asked. My voice was small. It seemed nothing was simple anymore, not even his visions of the future.

"I saw us. In the first vision, you and I are in a cave." He frowned. "When I used to get visions, it was just images, but this . . ."

"What?"

He looked back up at me. "This time it was like I was jumping into my future body for a few moments. I could smell the damp air inside the cave, and I could tell that we'd been there at least a few days. We were alone and scared."

"Then what?"

"Then nothing. It switched to the other vision."

"We were back in the cave again," he started. "But this time we left it. I skipped in and out of my body as the days passed. We made a run into a city together, I don't know which one. But we were caught. The Regs grabbed you and then . . ."

He stopped.

"And then what?" I prodded.

"And then I watched you die." His words came out only as a whisper. A drop of water rolled down his face. At first I thought it was a tear, but then I realized it was only the rain dripping off the tree branches overhead. It was coming down harder now. "And I wasn't just watching it happen as a bystander like my visions used to be. I was in my own body, I could *feel* everything." His voice broke. "Feel the anguish of losing you."

I paused for a moment as my exhausted mind tried to soak in everything he was saying. "So which one is the real vision?" My voice was quiet. He'd foreseen my death. I didn't know what to say to that. "Or are they both possible?"

"Maybe," he said, frowning and chewing on his bottom lip as he thought, "they hinge on some decision someone makes. Even how we decide to respond to the foreknowledge from the vision."

"But in both visions we end up in some cave?"

He nodded. "I don't know where it is though. If we find it, then it's clear we should stay there." The raindrops fell faster and heavier. He stood up and held out a hand to help me up. "Come on, let's start looking for it. Maybe it's nearby."

"No," I responded immediately, getting clumsily to my feet.

He scrunched his eyebrows. "Why not?"

"Because if we do, we're just making the vision come true," I said. "Both visions start in the cave. If we go there, that means the other vision where I die becomes possible. I'm not walking into a trap like that." I shook my head. "We should go somewhere else, get out of the mountains. Now we know I can fly faster at night; we could go to one of the cities after I get some sleep, try to track down some Rez operatives. You said yourself it was easy getting into Driwald."

"Easy for an in-and-out supply run, maybe," he said. "But just because we don't go to the cave doesn't mean the rest of the vision won't come true. We can't risk taking you into a city. Besides, we don't know where any of the Rez operatives are. Half the safe houses have been cracked in the last six months. We'd be in enemy territory without any idea where to go. Our safest bet is out here where no one can find us."

"I'm not going in a cave!" I said, all but stomping my foot. "I've seen people do things because your visions said it would happen. Commander Taylor *died* because of it. You got lobotomized. No, I'm not going anywhere near—"

The rain fell in sheets now and it was harder to hear our voices.

"Fine, but we've got to at least get somewhere dry." Adrien took my hand and led me through the woods. I didn't know where he was taking me, but I did know that no matter how exhausted I was, I'd rather soak through to the bone than voluntarily go in a cave. But then Adrien stopped at a copse of dense trees near a small lake's edge, where one huge tree dominated the others. The long leafy green branches hung over one another in layers like a waterfall of leaves, all the way to the ground.

Adrien pushed aside some of the soft branches and ushered me in. The wind from the rainstorm made the branches swing back and forth lightly, but it was completely dry near the fat inner tree trunk. It got dim as soon as Adrien let the branches we'd entered through settle back down, shutting us inside like it was a little room.

"I saw this tree when I hiked back in," he said. "Sophia and I used to always sleep under weeping willows whenever we traveled and it rained, especially if we found a big old one like this where the branches reach all the way to the ground."

I leaned against the trunk. It was freezing, but I was still so tired my eyes were already dropping closed.

"We should both get some sleep," he said, coming over to me. "We'll be warmer if we sleep close together. You know, just to keep our vital organs warm."

I nodded and lay down, too tired to even be excited about the thought of him letting me get that close. He lay down too, facing me and settling a blanket from his pack over us.

He pulled out the blanket from my pack too, but instead of adding it to the first, he bundled it up and slipped it under my head like a pillow.

My eyes were so heavy I was asleep within seconds, but for a brief fuzzy moment before I lost consciousness, I could have sworn Adrien wrapped one arm around my waist, pulling me close.

I woke to Adrien shaking my shoulder. I blearily opened my eyes, coming out of my deep sleep to find wind wailing around us. The branches of the willow blew and twisted crazily. Several of the long leafy vines snapped loose and flew toward us, smacking Adrien so hard in the chest he winced. I'd been sleeping so heavily, I hadn't even heard the thunder that was now booming all around us.

"We've got to get out of here," Adrien shouted over the wind. "It's not safe!"

I nodded and let him pull me to my feet. We stumbled out from under the willow. The rain lashed at our faces. Severed tree branches and other debris flew through the air. The sky was a strange sickly green color and the wind, which I'd barely noticed before except for the pleasant noise it made when it blew gently through the tree branches, was now howling like a freight train around us.

Chapter 17

THE THUNDER BOOMED AGAIN, so loud it seemed to shake the ground beneath us. The wind roared even louder, and the next time it thundered, lightning split the air at almost the same moment.

Adrien grabbed my arm and pulled me forward. "We've gotta go," he shouted. "Now!"

"Where?" I yelled back, but let him drag me forward anyway.

"There's a clearing just a little farther around the lake," he called over his shoulder. I could barely make out his words. "There was a ditch there where we might be safe."

I nodded, abandoning trying to talk anymore.

Thunder boomed overhead, several loud rumbling punches, followed by lightning. The rain was harder after we burst out from under the tree coverage. It pelted us in diagonal sheets. I could barely see a foot in front of me. The only other time I'd seen a storm anything like this was back in the Community when I'd been in one of the few Sublevel 0 rooms that had thick triple-paned windows to the Surface. The growling thunder and splattering rain had given me nightmares for weeks.

Now there was no glass separating me from it, no elevator to take back underground to safety. And that storm hadn't been nearly as powerful as this.

"Put your arm over your face," Adrien yelled. I tried, but it barely mattered. The rain and wind blew so hard that I had a hard time staying on my feet. My hair whipped around me until I felt sure it would be yanked out by the roots. Adrien, tall and thin, bent his head into the wind and tried trudging forward, but he was having as much difficulty as I was.

"Shunting hell, it's a tornado!" he suddenly yelled, looking off to the left. I followed his gaze, my hand cupped above my eyes so I could see.

I'd never heard of a tornado, but I saw what he meant. The sky seemed to drop down until a portion of dark gray-green cloud touched the ground in a wide funnel. The wind around us whipped even harder, and the noise of the storm became a monstrous roar.

Adrien screamed something I couldn't hear and we ran across the clearing as the storm continued gathering force behind us.

The clearing rose and then dipped, and Adrien dropped down into a natural trench. He pulled me down beside him. I put both hands over my head to keep away the rain and flying debris. Adrien popped his head up to look back, and then before I even knew what was going on, he'd hauled me back to my feet.

"It's coming this way!" he yelled. I was barely able to make out his voice amid the howling winds.

I clenched his hand as we ran down the field, perpendicular to the path the tornado was heading. Debris flew in the air around us and a quick glance behind me showed the funnel was even closer than before. I saw the truth of the matter. If it turned this direction, there was no way we'd be able to outrun it.

I cast outward with my telek to see if I could sense any kind of shelter. But all I could feel was the massive shape of the funnel and the mounds of debris circling in it. I wrenched my attention away from it and cast out in front of us instead. There were just more and more trees, no protected place.

But then my quick telek survey paused. There! I felt an outcropping of rocks ahead. Adrien was pulling me away from the lake, but I stopped him. "No," I shouted. "This way!"

I grabbed his hand and headed to the left, running along the edge of the churning lake.

"Zoe, getting in the water won't make us any safer—"

"Look!" I cut him off, and pointed down a small hill to the edge of the lake where the terrain turned rocky. I sprinted toward it right as the tornado roared closer behind us.

If I was wrong, this would be the end of us.

We jumped down the rocky embankment. I didn't even pause to breathe out in relief. When I saw some overhanging rock that looked like it would give shelter, I just launched toward it, pulling Adrien after me.

What I'd thought was just a bunch of rocks actually opened inward into a dark open space. We tumbled inside. The sudden dry and quiet was startling. We clambered farther and farther into the narrow opening until the growling wind outside sounded like only a mute whimper. We could still see it through the opening though—the raging twister passed in front of us, flinging debris and tree branches into the first few feet of our safe haven. We huddled behind some natural boulders in the darkness, and waited.

Then, only minutes later, all the noise abated. The rain still spattered gently at the mouth of the opening, but sunlight began filtering down too. We waited, shivering and not speaking for another five minutes, until we were sure that the storm had truly gone.

Then Adrien raised his head and froze. "Zoe, this is the cave from my vision."

Chapter 18

I SCRAMBLED UP OUT OF my hiding place and ran for the entrance. But it was too late. I'd already been inside. Coming out now could just be the beginning of Adrien's second vision. "Shunt!" I shouted in frustration.

The ground was churned up and trees were uprooted for a half-mile stretch where the tornado had landed. But the sky was a ridiculous bright blue with only a tufting of light gray clouds now.

Adrien followed me out and looked around with me.

Across the lake, bright colors lit the sky. Not like sunsets I'd seen before where purples and pinks splashed across the entire horizon. These colors were all lined up together, like someone had taken a paintbrush to put them there. It was absurdly beautiful.

"It's a rainbow," Adrien said. He was quiet for a long moment before speaking again. "Sophia read me a story once about a terrible storm that made the earth flood for forty days and nights. And afterward, there was a rainbow—it was their god's promise that the world would never be destroyed by flood again. She said rainbows have been symbols of hope ever since then."

"Hope?" I couldn't help scoffing. "It seems like the god could have just prevented it from raining in the first place."

He laughed, a deep hearty noise that jolted me out of my frustration. "If I remember right, that's what I said too."

I couldn't help grinning. Then I took a deep breath, feeling calmer finally. "Okay, so what do we do now?"

"First you should probably sleep some more. The epi infusion will keep working for another few hours. Better to get sleep now so we can save the tank for later."

I nodded, then glared behind me at the cave. "I guess it's dry in there, at least."

I blinked my eyes open after several blissful hours of heavy sleep.

There had been no dreams at all—my favorite kind of sleep. When Adrien shook my shoulders to wake me, at first I pushed him off. Sleep was so easy. Empty. Nothing was asked of me there. Waking meant entering back into the world of struggle and strife, and I didn't want that, not yet.

Finally I gave in to the inevitable and opened my eyes. I sat up, every muscle in my body sore. Adrien had turned on the small portable heat lamp in the center of the chamber where the cave widened out. Our soaked clothing was mostly dry, and in spite of everything, I felt about a thousand times better than I had in days.

Adrien leaned over me, staring at me with his eyebrows knit in concern. The previous day came rushing in. The details about everything that had happened were fuzzy because I'd been so exhausted and half-delirious, but I remembered him leaving.

And him coming back.

I stared up at him in confusion. The way he was looking at me now, as if he was concerned about me, as if he cared—

But, as if he could sense where my thoughts were starting to go, he pulled back and made his face an impassive mask.

I sat up, pushing off the two thermal blankets on top of me. I looked down at them. I'd had only one blanket when I went to sleep.

"I didn't want you to get cold," he explained, as if reading the question on my face.

"What about yourself? Aren't you cold?"

He shook his head. "I stayed by the lamp."

I blinked again and looked around us. I shivered in spite of the fact that I was warm. We were in the cave from Adrien's vision. "What time is it?"

"Nine at night."

That was good. I'd slept almost nine hours altogether today.

I rubbed my eyes and looked around. The cave walls were moist, almost slimy. The ceiling was mostly hidden in shadow. But in the dim light provided by the heat lamp, I could see a bunch of long fingerlike structures dropping down from above. Moisture gathered at the pink-brown tips and occasionally dripped. I watched one drip, drip, drip, and listened for the resounding *plink* on the slick mound that had grown up below it.

"How long till we outwait the other vision?" I asked Adrien. "Four or five days? Then we can get moving again."

"I've been thinking about it a lot while you were sleeping." He handed me half a protein bar and then stood up, pacing back and forth on a path between the pinkish mounds lining the ground. "I'm not sure it'll be safe to leave."

"Why not?" I took a bite. Even though I'd been eating the same bars for days, this one tasted amazing, probably because I was so starved after all the exertion yesterday.

"I've never had visions like this before." Adrien ran a hand through his hair. "What if I was wrong about the timing?

What if they didn't happen at the same time like I first thought? Maybe I just had two visions together, and the second one could still happen whenever we leave the cave, even if we do wait a few days."

I choked on the bite of bar I'd swallowed. Adrien quickly handed me the water bottle and I took a long drink before turning back to him. "We can't just stay here indefinitely. We'll avoid cities to make sure the other one doesn't happen."

He shook his head with his lips pursed. "You know I've tried to avoid visions in the past. Whenever I did, I'd just end up causing them instead. We said we wouldn't look for the cave, but then the storm drove us here. What if the same thing happens with the second vision?"

"So there's no way to escape it?" I scoffed, putting the cap back on the water bottle and standing up. "I'm just supposed to accept that if I step outside of this cave then I'm doomed to die in a city somewhere?"

"No, no, no," he said quickly, still pacing. "That's not what I mean. I'm still hoping that I was right about the visions being simultaneous moments on two separate forked futures. But look at the facts." He ticked them off on his fingers. "We don't have any more epi infusions. The anti-infrared harnesses have enough coolant for maybe two more nights, at most. Then what? We have shelter here. The lake outside is spring-fed so we have fresh water. You've got the biosuit and I can head into the city by myself to steal you some more oxy tanks."

"But we have to try to get in contact with the Rez as soon as we can," I argued.

"Do you think Rez cells advertise with a sign outside their door? They're impossible to find, and you more than anyone know that being with the Rez is probably the least safe place to be these days. The Chancellor turns all the Rez agents she captures with her compulsion. Whoever she captured at the Foundation will have told her about the last few cells." He shook his head and finally stopped pacing. "No, the safest place is out here, off the grid. Besides I'm good at slipping in and out of cities. I can get us the supplies we need."

"So, what?" I asked slowly, trying to wrap my head around all he was saying. "You mean we just *live* out here?"

"Yeah. For a while anyway."

"But," I sputtered. "We can't. We have to—"

"What?" he interrupted, his voice hard. "Go start a revolution? Fight against the Chancellor? We're beat, Zoe. When are you gonna see that? The Rez is cracked, done for. Maybe there are a few cells left here or there, but they'll have scattered once news of what happened at the Foundation gets out. We'll never be able to find them."

"But you're a techer," I said. "I know you all have a secret signal you put out if something like this happens. If we could get the right equipment, then you could—"

"And what if no one's left out there?" His jaw was tight. "What then?"

"The Chancellor has my brother," I barreled on. "And there were plenty of people who couldn't get on the escape pods out of the Foundation. Some of them have valuable Gifts. The Chancellor would have imprisoned them. If I take her out, then everyone under her compulsion will be free. I could gather all the glitchers together—"

"Do you even hear yourself?" he scoffed, his voice raising an octave. "You're going to go up against thousands of Regs just by yourself? And what if she has that power-blocking girl there?"

I waved a hand dismissively. "The Chancellor would never risk keeping the girl around her. All of her control over others depends on being able to compel them, and the girl's presence would make her impotent. Besides, if I save up my strength, I could take on the Regs—"

"You've got a death wish then," he said, throwing up his hands. "That's what this is. You're letting that ridiculous guilt you carry with you everywhere drive you to an early grave. When are you gonna see that guilt's nothing more than the repression of your genuine desires? You've created this net of morals around you to strangle your most basic instincts. To *survive*."

"Some things are more important than survival," I shot back. "Like making your life count. Sacrifice for a worthy cause *means* something. It's the best of what makes us human. You used to understand that."

"Well, then I'm triply glad I'm not that shunting idiot anymore!" he yelled, his face red. His voice echoed throughout the cave. "I don't even know why I bothered coming back for you if you're so bound and determined to die."

"So why did you?" I asked, pushing closer until our chests were almost touching. "Why come back for me if you're only supposed to think about your own survival?"

His jaw tensed, but he didn't say anything. He just pulled away and stomped away farther into the dark depths of the cave.

"I thought so!" I yelled after him and kicked my blanket against the wall, not even knowing what I meant. All the peace I'd felt on waking was shattered.

We went the entire day without speaking. He slept through the night, which I spent pacing and feeling caged. I was so frustrated at him, but the farthest we could get from each other was only the twenty feet or so that we'd explored of the cave.

Half of me knew I was getting angry at him for things that weren't his fault. It was how his mind worked now—logically, not emotionally. And I was finally beginning to see him as himself instead of searching for the old Adrien in his every act and expression.

But he still baffled me. Because as different as he was now, sometimes I'd swear he still cared for me. He claimed he looked at the world with a strictly logical lens, but coming back for me . . . and then planning to risk his life to go back into the city to try to find me an oxygen tank—none of that was logical.

Or maybe to him it was. If he could keep me alive, then he'd still have use for me. I could fly us out of a bad situation. Then again, he'd already proven he could steal a vehicle without problem. So why had he come back? Why? The question kept pinging in my brain throughout the long night.

I looked down at Adrien. Even in sleep he looked different than the old Adrien had. As if his features weren't quite relaxed. Was he having a bad dream? The scars across his head gave him a slightly menacing look. Maybe he was only here because he'd seen himself present in the vision of the cave, so he was staying in order to fulfill it? But he'd had that vision *after* coming back for me.

I suddenly felt inordinately tired again. I had a feeling the boy on the ground in front of me was a mystery I might never truly figure out.

My clothes felt crunchy, having dried on my body after the storm. I tried running my fingers through my hair to rebraid it, but it was dirty with clumps of mud from dropping into the ditch yesterday. I picked out the dried mud for half an hour before I gave up and sat back against one of the mounded cave formations on the ground.

No matter what Adrien said, I wasn't going to stay here forever. I wasn't going to just wait around safe and sound while my brother was still caught in the Chancellor's snare. I should have gotten him out of the Community before she moved him to her personal estate.

At the same time, I wasn't foolish enough to leave yet in case Adrien was right about the second vision still possibly coming true. I'd just have to trust that his first instinct about his new visions happening simultaneously had been right. I'd give it two weeks at the most to make sure we averted the second vision.

Adrien finally woke up a few hours later. He glanced in my direction, but didn't say anything. After the hours of quiet throughout the night, though, I'd had enough silence. I went over and plunked myself beside him while he reached for half of a protein bar for breakfast.

"So if we're going to be stuck here, we might as well talk to help the hours pass."

He looked over the water bottle at me, as if suspicious of how nice I was being after our fight. "Talk about what?"

I shrugged. "Anything."

He just stared at me.

"How'd you sleep?" I finally prodded.

"Fine."

"Now you ask me something."

He raised an eyebrow and gave me a half smirk. "Trying to teach me to converse like a normal human?"

I rolled my eyes. "I'm only trying to fill the silence. It'll help the time pass quicker."

"I didn't notice the time was passing slowly."

"You're going to make this difficult, aren't you?"

The smirk was in full force now. "It's my style."

I laughed and sat back with my elbows on my knees. "Okay, I'll try another tactic. How about a hypothetical? What would you do if the war was over and you could do anything?"

His jaw tightened. "You know I have his memories. He played this little game with you before."

"I know," I said softly. "That's why I'm asking. I know what his answer was. But now I want to know *yours*."

"Oh." His face softened lightly in surprise. "Well, um. You go first. You never did tell him yours."

I looked out the cave entrance at the bright midmorning sunlight sparkling on the lake. "I've thought about it sometimes since then. I'd want a really big house."

"Really?" He sounded surprised. "I didn't figure you for the materialistic sort."

"If you'd let me finish, I was going to say that I'd want a big house where all my family and closest friends would live. Markan would be there with me." I swallowed hard at the mention of my brother's name, then went on. "Kind of like the Foundation, but everyone would be there because they wanted to be. They'd all go out to their separate jobs every day, but we'd all meet together for dinner every night. There'd be this huge table and we'd all sit together with mounds of good food and talk and laugh for hours every night."

"And what about the rest of the day?" he asked. His voice had lost its mocking tone. "What would you do?"

I smiled and closed my eyes, imagining it. "I'd buy a hundred canvases and fill each one. There would be academies just for artists, and I'd go and learn to paint all day."

"So what about you?" I opened my eyes. "What would you do?"

His voice was hesitant at first. "I'd be a mathematician. But we'd be doing the kind of math that leaves numbers behind. That happens when you get deep enough into studying it. It's more about theories than facts. Actually, it starts becoming a little like philosophy."

"Really?"

"Both math and philosophy are asking the same question. Why? Then they use reasoning to try to discover the answers." He nodded to himself. "They make sense when so little else does."

"Is that why you've spent so much time studying them?"

He looked up at me, then down at his folded hands again. "Partly. After what the Chancellor did . . ." He swallowed. "Everything felt alien. All the people around me, you all felt . . . not just like strangers . . ." He paused as if looking for the right way to explain it. I was suprised he was actually opening up and didn't say anything in case it made him clam up again. "It was like you were all a different species. You and Sophia were always crying whenever you visited me. You asked me questions I never knew the answers to. I didn't know how to communicate with you. I genuinely didn't understand what was going on around me at a very basic level."

His face contorted. "And on top of it all, I was being put through those strange and painful treatments. It was all so confusing. But around the second month, I started reading. I began with philosophy because I had that memory of you calling me a philosopher. At the beginning, you see," he looked up at me, his eyes both searching and sad, "I genuinely wanted to go back to being him. It's what you all told me I should be trying for, so I did."

Wow. I sat a little stunned. I hadn't known any of that was going on in his head. I'd been so desperate for him to go back to being normal during those afternoon visits, I hadn't seen how much he'd been struggling.

He shrugged his shoulders. "But I never could. When I started working my way through the philosophy texts, though, I felt this rush of recognition because here, *finally*, were people speaking a language I could understand."

"What do you mean?" I asked, genuinely curious. I hadn't listened closely enough back then, but I could now. I accepted he was different, I just still didn't understand why or how deeply the differences went.

He looked upwards, as if sorting through his memory.

"They were asking questions like: how do you know what you think you know? Is it because you trust in the power of reason to work your way to an answer? Or can you only know the things you personally experience through your five senses? And even if you trust in only what you yourself experience, aren't those experiences filtered by the mind anyway? So is reality merely what you *think* it is?"

My brain seemed to twist in on itself as I tried to follow him. "That all seems really complicated. I'm not sure I understand."

A half smile tugged at his lips. "I didn't either, not at first, but slowly the puzzle pieces started falling into place. It was like the philosophers were turning life into math problems. With enough time, I could start breaking each one down into manageable chunks to start solving some of the equations."

"So what did you find out?" I leaned in. "What's the answer to *why*?"

His face clouded over a little. "That's the thing. At a certain point, it gets beyond logic, or at least the human ability to reason it out. It's true of both math and philosophy. Like I said earlier, there's always a point where things stop being facts and start to become theories about the way the world works. Like this." He reached in his pocket and rummaged around for a moment, then pulled out a tiny object.

"It's a snail shell I found by the lake when I was gathering water last night." He slid over closer until he was sitting beside me. He held up the shell closer. "See these tiny spirals all over the shell?" He traced the spiraling line with the tip of his forefinger.

I nodded.

"This shell and others all throughout the world follow the same mathematical sequence. Flower petals and pinecones and shells all grow according to this identical pattern. Even the ratios of the bones in the human body are related." He held up his hand. "We see these patterns everywhere, but we don't know *why* they happen."

He looked back up at me, his gray eyes bright. It was a surreal sight. I'd seen Adrien excited about ideas like this in the past, but it was different now, and not just because the blue-green color was gone from his eyes.

He continued, oblivious to my scrutiny. "I mean, it's an efficient growth pattern. But how do the plants *know* it's the most efficient? Millions of years of evolution, of trial and error, I guess. But still. Why, across multiple species and multiple millennia, do they all follow the exact same pattern? And that's not even getting into humankind's most recent adaptation with all these powers we glitchers have developed. The smartest minds throughout history haven't been able to even make a dent at solving some of the great whys of the universe." He shook his head, looking out toward the cave entrance. "It's all this insane mixture of order and chaos. The more I understand, the less I understand."

I stared at him, watching his long fingers as he rubbed his chin thoughtfully. There was such spark and life in his eyes as he'd spoken. I didn't know how to say it in a way that wouldn't make him angry, but he was wrong. The old Adrien wasn't gone completely. Maybe there wasn't even an "old" or "new" like I'd been categorizing him in my mind. It was more like parts of him that had always been there were simply more dominant now.

I looked at him closer, frowning slightly as I tried to puzzle out how to fit the old and new into the single amalgam that was simply *Adrien*.

He'd always been good with numbers. It was why he was such a good techer. He could fly through code because he understood mathematical structure and relationships in a way I never could. He'd been amazed at the complexity of the universe before the lobotomy too—one of our first conversations had been about the limits of science, back when he was trying to convince me human beings had souls. It was the same impulse as I'd seen when he was talking about the shells. He used different methods and came to different conclusions now. He got just as excited when talking about ideas, but he was less likely to make sweeping statements about what those unexplained mysteries meant. He didn't communicate as easily as he used to. He was slower to become emotional. But that didn't mean he didn't feel things, and maybe even feel them very deeply.

I reached out to put my hand on his. After letting it linger a moment, his eyes half-dropping closed, he suddenly pulled away and jumped to his feet.

"I wanted to get an early start today heading toward the city to find some more oxy tanks," he said. He threw a few objects in his almost empty pack and then pulled on his boots.

I frowned deeper, staring after him. Why did he always do that? Every time I was on the cusp of connection with him, he'd sever it.

"I should be back in about a day," he mumbled. "Two at most." He headed out of the cave, keeping low until he got to the tree line. His clothes and pack were still so caked with mud from the storm, he blended in perfectly with the ground.

A sad ache settled in my chest and I leaned back against the cave wall. I stared after him long after he'd disappeared into the forest. As much as I saw similarities with the boy I'd loved, maybe the differences were still too insurmountable for love to translate.

Chapter 19

I STOOD AT THE BASE of the cave with my hand over my eyes, searching the horizon for any sight of Adrien. He said he'd be back within a day or two.

That had been four days ago.

Last night I'd put on the coolant harness and bathed in the lake, but not even the wonderful feeling of finally being clean had been able to dislodge the icy fear about Adrien that had settled in my stomach. At about midnight I'd been forced to give in to exhaustion and put on the biosuit so I could sleep. I'd set the alarm on my arm panel for just two hours, wanting to use up as little of the air supply as possible. But the loud clanging of the alarm only finally woke me after an extra hour and a half.

I looked over at the tank leaning against the wall. Only thirty minutes of air left. Enough for a short nap, and I was already reeling from exhaustion again. Three and a half hours hadn't been nearly enough after another three days without sleep.

My eyes were weary and gritty as I squinted to look past the lake, willing Adrien to appear. My head pounded from the headache that had lodged itself behind my eyeballs two days ago. It had been a little better after the few hours of sleep last night, but now it was back in full force.

Finally I pulled back in frustration and paced a well-worn path around the cave. I was so stupid. How could I have allowed him to risk his life *yet again* for me? Since he'd seen himself with me in the vision, I'd taken it for granted that he'd make it back fine. But we didn't know how these new visions worked. I should never have let him go.

What if someone saw him sneaking into the city or trying to steal the oxy tanks? Oxy tanks were bulky. What if they slowed him down so much he couldn't escape? What if cameras caught his face and the recognition software set off an alarm? The city's Regulators would be on him in seconds. There were a hundred other things that could have gone wrong too—

"Zoe."

I whipped around, sure it was just my imagination playing tricks.

But no, it was really him.

He stood right inside the entrance of the cave, so dirty I barely recognized him. I ran toward him and threw my arms around him, ignoring the crusted-over grime that coated his entire body. Pressing my head to his chest, I listened to his heartbeat as if to reassure myself he was real.

His arms slowly curled around me. I clutched him tight and willed him not to pull away. Not this time.

He didn't. Instead, his arms tightened ever so slightly, pulling me in closer. The feel of his arms so secure and warm around me made all my fears finally begin to subside. He was here. He was safe. I whispered the two phrases inside my head like a mantra. *He was here. He was safe.*

He finally pulled back from me. There were deep shadows under his eyes. "I couldn't get any oxy tanks, Zoe. I'm so sorry."

"What happened? Why did it take so long? And what on earth is that *smell*?" I wrinkled my nose in distaste.

He cracked a grin at my last comment, but it was gone quickly as he sat down by the wall near the entrance.

"I snuck into the steel foundry because I knew they'd have

oxy tanks. But once I got inside, I realized they were all too big for me to carry, much less sneak out of the city. So I spent the day sleeping in a maintenance closet and then tried to break into a medical facility the next night."

"Adrien," I hissed, "you promised you wouldn't try anything so risky!"

He shrugged off my worry and massaged his temple. "I had trouble getting in. I could have hacked the security codes if I'd just had the right equipment!" The frustration was clear on his face. "I kept thinking of the oxy tanks that were stored *right* behind the flimsy clinic walls. So I took an ax I'd brought from the foundry—"

"You didn't!"

"—and hacked through the door," he continued, ignoring me. "The alarms went off, of course. I thought I might still have enough time to get in and grab a couple oxy tanks or epi infusers at least, but the clinic was in a more densely populated area. Regs were there in half a minute. I barely managed to slip out through the back door. I had to spend the next couple days hiding in the sewers until they stopped patrolling and I was clear to come back. I just went about it all wrong." He shook his head. "But I had to come back and make sure you're okay. When I go back in, I'll be more careful."

"No," I said firmly.

He looked up, obviously confused. "No, I shouldn't be more careful?"

"No, as in, you are *not* going back."

"Of course I'm going back. I didn't get any oxy tanks, and you still need—"

"What I *need*," I interrupted, "is for you to stay alive and safe. I won't let you risk your life for me. I shouldn't have let you go in the first place."

"But you have to sleep." He looked at me as if I was making no sense. "And to sleep you need oxy tanks."

"We'll figure it out in the morning," I said. I had a feeling he'd just fight me on it if I told him what I really thought. Tomorrow, one way or another, we were leaving this cave. He looked like he might say something else, so I held up a protein bar, the second to last one left. "I bet you're hungry. And," I said, scrunching up my face, "maybe you could use a bath in the lake."

He laughed. "Judging by the look on your face, it must be bad. After the first night in the sewer I got kind of immune to it all."

I smiled and said sarcastically, "Well, not all of us have had such luxury."

"Okay." He held up his hands. "Bath first. Food second."

I handed him the coolant harness and the tube of soap.

When he came back in a fresh tunic, I couldn't stop looking at him. Having him back again after the long, seemingly endless past few days was like a gift.

I watched his hands as he snapped off a quarter section of protein bar and rewrapped the rest. I wished I had drawing supplies. I wanted to capture on paper what his hands looked like in motion. So careful in their every movement, artful almost.

After a while, he noticed me staring.

"Are you tired?" I asked. "Do you want to sleep?"

He shook his head. "I'm rested enough." He squinted his eyes, as if scrutinizing me. "But you look really tired."

I put a hand up to rub my aching temple. "I used up most of the oxy tank last night and got a few hours of sleep."

"It doesn't look like it did much good." A deep worried crease settled in his forehead. "I'll stay up with you tonight to make sure you don't accidentally fall asleep."

His eyes were locked on mine. I couldn't read what I saw there. He looked at me like . . . like . . . I swallowed and forced myself to look away. No. He'd made it abundantly clear that he didn't feel that way about me. Not anymore.

"Why don't I read something?" I turned away abruptly and reached for the small rectangular box of tech chips from his pack. A couple of days ago after fiddling around with all the different chips, several of which I couldn't figure out the function of, I'd discovered that one was loaded with texts of all kinds: history, scientific treatises, even fiction. There were so many archived on it, I'd had a hard time knowing where to start. If Ginni had been with me, she would have pointed me toward some melodramatic romance, but on my own, I had no clue. Thinking about Ginni had brought on another wave of worry. I could only hope she hadn't been able to make it in the pods and was safe somewhere in the Chancellor's holding cells. In the end, I'd settled on rereading a book we'd read in Humanities last year.

"Sure, if it'll help keep you awake," Adrien said.

We didn't say much for the next few hours. He moved to the blanket across from mine, separated by the small pod light in between us. Every so often, I'd glance up and find him staring at me. His eyes were almost iridescent as they reflected the light, and his expression was so . . . intense. Each time I dropped my eyes quickly again. He was probably just interested in what I was reading. I'd chosen a philosophy text because I thought he might like it, but it was pretty incomprehensible to me.

Sometime in the middle of the night, the pod light flickered and beeped. "Cracking hell," I swore. It was about to lose its charge. The light from my arm panel would be tiresome to read from without it. "I forgot to put it in the sun to charge today."

I didn't tell him why. That I was so sick with worry about

something happening to him, the rest of the world had seemed to drop away.

He frowned. "It'll be harder for you to stay awake in the dark. Are you sure you don't want to get in the biosuit? Then at least you could get a thirty-minute nap, and I'll wake you up when it runs out."

I rubbed a hand over my face. I was exhausted, there was no denying it. Still, the precious oxygen left in that tank felt like a symbol of hope. As long as I didn't use it, there was still a chance . . .

The pod light went out and the cave was enveloped in darkness so thick, I couldn't even see my hand in front of my face. If I touched my arm panel, it would light up for a minute, but what was the point?

The light going out suddenly sapped my optimism. I tried to fight back against the heavy cloud of dread that threatened to douse me. Tomorrow we'd go find more oxygen, I tried to reassure myself. We'd find a way.

Or . . . was this how the second vision happened? What if Adrien saw us leave the cave because we had no other choice? Because if I didn't find more oxy tanks, I'd die. The security in the city Adrien had just raided would be doubly tight. I'd need to fly us somewhere far away, but what if . . . I blinked hard several times as a thought I'd been trying to avoid finally settled in.

Adrien's visions used to *always* come true.

Were we just lying to ourselves by trying to pretend they were different now? The storm had driven us here, and now my need for another oxy tank would somehow drive us into a city, bringing about exactly what he'd seen.

I couldn't help the tears that leaked down my cheeks. All year, I'd been so good at keeping it together, I'd cried maybe twice. But sleep deprivation turned me into a perpetually dripping faucet. All my emotions were so close to the surface.

"Is there anything I can do to help?" Adrien's voice seemed doubly loud in the dark. "Anything that will help you stay awake?"

I shivered, drying my eyes on my tunic sleeve. "Well, at least the cold helps." The pod light had doubled as a heat lamp, and the cold night air quickly invaded the small space. "But you should get under the blanket so you can keep warm."

"I'm fine." It was so strange hearing his voice coming out of the darkness without being able to see him. "Maybe if we keep talking, that will help?"

I didn't say anything for several long moments. My heavy eyelids were already drooping. If we couldn't read, I didn't know how I was going to stay awake. Unless . . .

The darkness made me feel a strange recklessness. As if, when I couldn't see him, barriers between us were suddenly broken down.

"Well, there is one thing," I started, then stopped, feeling foolish.

"What?"

"Whenever you touch me . . ." I stopped again.

His voice responded without any hesitation, a silken whisper in the dark. "What happens when I touch you?"

"It makes me feel, um . . ." My face went hot, and I was glad he couldn't see my blush. "The opposite of sleepy."

I didn't hear a response, and I clenched my hands into fists. Stupid. I knew talking like that would just drive him away.

There was absolute silence for a few terribly long moments, and then I heard a slight crinkling as he shifted off his thermo blanket. I couldn't be sure, but I thought he was moving toward me.

His hand brushed my arm, groping in the dark. Finally he found my hand. I froze, and let him make contact. He flipped my hand over and then used the tip of his finger to outline the lines on my palm. His touch sent an electric *ping* throughout my body.

One thing was sure. I was no longer sleepy.

"Yeah," I said, my throat suddenly dry, "like that."

He shifted until he was sitting so close, I could feel the warmth of his body beside me.

"Like this?" His fingers left my hand and touched my hair, then moved up to my forehead and cheek.

My breath caught in my throat, and I turned my face into his hand. Even though my muscles all relaxed against him, a zinging awareness ricocheted through my body.

His touch was so gentle. After ten minutes hovering along my hairline, he took my shoulders firmly and arranged me so that I was lying down, facing away from him. Then he lay behind me, his body separated from mine by mere inches. The lightest whisper of fingers traced down my arm, down the sloping dip of my waist and then over the curve of my hip. Even though my cloth tunic was between us, his touch still seared straight through to my sinew.

I didn't say anything. I didn't want to scare him away. I wanted him to keep touching me like this forever. I knew he was only doing it to help keep me awake. That it meant nothing to him. He was probably moving his hands across my body according to some mechanical pattern in his head. Cold and scientific.

But for the moment, I couldn't be bothered to care. Long minutes stretched out as he continued the tortuous path up and down my body. Always along the outermost edge, never venturing inland.

Finally I couldn't help but let out the slightest whimper, but again, he didn't pull away. Instead, his touch became heavier until he was caressing the side of my body with his entire hand. He pulled up the side of my tunic with agonizing slowness, just far enough to expose my waist, and then he brushed the tips of his fingers against my skin. I shuddered under his touch. My breathing was loud and erratic in the quiet cave.

Did he know what he was doing to me? Did he not care, as long as it accomplished the goal of keeping me awake?

My fingers itched to touch him back, to caress the jaw line of the face that I loved and then to stroke down his broad shoulders. But I kept my hands in place, balling them into fists at my side to keep them still.

After another half hour, though, my skin was on fire and the reckless impulse took over again. What was holding me back from reaching toward him in the dark? These might be my last few days on earth. Was I really going to allow my fear of rejection to keep me from living them to the fullest?

No. No, I wouldn't. I suddenly flipped over so that I was facing Adrien, though I still couldn't see anything. If he was surprised, he gave no indication. He didn't speak or shift his position at all. I stretched a trembling hand out in front of me and bumped into his chest. I flattened my hand and then followed the line of his sternum up to his neck and then to his face. I closed my eyes and sank into the sensation of finally being able to touch him again after all these months. I knew he was different now. I knew this wasn't exactly the same boy as when he'd last allowed such intimate contact. But here, in the darkness at what might be the end of my life, I realized it didn't make a difference.

I would love him forever. No matter how he changed. No matter if he didn't love me back. It might be tragic, but it was true.

I cupped his face in my hand, brushing my thumb back

and forth across the bristling hair growing along his jaw. Then I moved my forefinger to trace the outline of his full lips. They parted suddenly as he let in a quick intake of breath.

I smiled. So I *was* affecting him after all. The knowledge made me bolder. I shifted so that I was closer to him, still not touching my chest to his, but close enough that the infinitesimal space between us was afire with heat.

We didn't speak. It was as if speaking would break the spell. As if, in the darkness, here in the middle of nowhere, all the normal rules of the world were bent. Anything and everything was permitted in the dark.

His hands had been slack at his sides, but he finally lifted them again. He pulled back the wide neck of my tunic and ran his strong hands across my shoulder, massaging up my neck and then behind my head, tangling in my hair. For a brief heady moment, I thought he was going to tug me closer and kiss me, but he didn't. Instead, he kneaded my scalp at the base of my neck and then worked his way slowly upward, all across my skull. I bent my head down against his chest as he continued and breathed in the cool clean scent of him.

Eventually, he finally dropped his hand back down to my shoulder and then continued the well-worn path up and down the side of my body. I lost all sense of time. Every moment he touched me seemed to both stretch out forever and pass all too quickly. But finally, the question that had been haunting me for days popped out, a whisper that sounded inordinately loud after the heavy silence. "Why did you come back for me?"

His hand paused and I cringed. I shouldn't have said anything. I knew speaking would shatter the moment.

But to my surprise, he responded. "To be honest," his voice was hesitant, "I came back because it never occurred to me *not* to. Not once. All I knew was that you were in danger and I had to do something right away. The whole time I was gone, all I could think about was getting back to you. I couldn't imagine living in a world without you in it."

My heart stuttered, and impulsively I decided to take one last reckless chance. I lifted my hand to his face again and stretched my head forward until my lips gently brushed his. A shudder rocked through his body and I moved my lips against his more firmly.

After just a moment of hesitation, he responded. His hands on my bare waist tightened until he was gripping me hard, pulling me closer still against him. His mouth opened ever so slightly and he kissed me deeper. Every other thought flew from my head except the earth-shattering joy at finally being able to kiss the boy I loved.

I dug my hands into his hair, and he suddenly flipped me so that I was on my back. He hovered over me, bracing himself with one hand on either side of my body. He dipped down and kissed me deeply again. Then he moved from my lips and kissed his way down my neck. I arched up into him.

And then the worst possible thing happened.

A shaft of morning sunlight broke over the mountains behind us, straight into the cave. Adrien pulled back as if he'd been stung. For a brief moment, our eyes locked together, both of us breathing raggedly. But when I reached out a hand toward his face, he suddenly jumped back before I could make contact. He leapt to his feet and turned his back to me. I could tell he was still breathing hard because his back heaved violently up and down.

"Adrien, I—"

"I need to refill the water bottle," he interrupted before I could say anything more. He grabbed the bottle from his pack and then all but ran out of the cave.

I tried to talk to him all day, but he always cut me off with short, curt answers. He kept his eyes on the ground and refused to look at me. He took a long nap in the afternoon and the rest of the time kept busy unpacking and then repacking the supply bag. Anything to keep his twitching hands moving.

I was bewildered, and too tired to try to make sense of his behavior. What he'd said last night—that it had never occurred to him not to come back for me, that he didn't want to live in a world without me. Didn't that mean he cared for me?

As the sunlight finally began to dim again, announcing the start of another evening, what had happened the night before seemed like more and more of a dream. Maybe I *had* been hallucinating again. It had been days since I'd really gotten enough sleep. Maybe I'd entered some half-dream state where I was still awake enough to control my mast cells, but so rested that I'd actually had a dream.

But then I glanced up at Adrien's stiff shoulders. No, it *had* happened. Otherwise, why had he been acting like this all day? I sighed, slumping over to sit with my back against the damp cave wall. I was so tired I felt it down to the marrow in my bones.

Maybe Adrien had done and said those things just to keep me awake, and for him there'd never been any feeling behind it. Could he be so cold and calculating? I could have sworn I'd felt his desire in response to me when we'd kissed.

I shook my head. My befuddled mind was too tired to make any sense out of it. My heavy eyelids fluttered, wanting so badly to close. I snapped them open, feeling weary and defeated.

This was it then. I had no more fight left. "I want to sleep," I announced. "Let's use up the last of the oxygen." Afterwards, we'd both leave the cave and go looking for more. I didn't care how much he argued with me. I wasn't going to just sit around waiting anymore.

He gave a quick nod but didn't say a word. He stooped to gather up the equipment we'd need.

But right as I stood up, a sudden noise came from outside. It was just a slight buzz, different from the sounds of the leaves blowing in the trees or the trilling of birds. Adrien froze too.

"What is it?" he whispered.

For a second I just looked at him in tired confusion. I had no idea what it was. But then I realized he meant for me to look with my telek sense. I immediately closed my eyes and felt outward past the entrance of the cave.

"It's a transport." We both scrambled to the wall of the cave. "It's landing."

"Is it an attack transport?"

"I don't *know*," I whispered back, trying frantically to calm my racing heart so I could focus on the two bodies inside the vehicle.

"They don't feel big enough to be Regs," I said, "but I can't be sure."

Then the side of the transport opened up and a familiar lanky form stepped out. "It's Henk!" I ran forward to the front of the cave, awash with happiness. Henk was alive! That meant some of the others might be too.

"Well, where are they?" I heard Xona's voice ask. She must have been the second person I'd felt in the transport.

"I don't bloody know," Henk said. "Ginni just said they're at these coordinates. Gotta be a close pace nearby."

"Over here," I called from the mouth of the cave, waving my arms over my head. There was only the barest sliver of moon out, and I could see the outline of the transport thirty feet away, hovering near the lake's edge.

"Zoe!" Xona said. "Look, over by those rocks." She pointed my way and they hurried over.

She crushed me into a tight embrace, lifting me up off the ground. "We got here as soon as we could. Everything was so crazy."

"I thought you were dead!" I said. "I saw the rendezvous site. How'd you get away?"

Henk had come up behind Xona, more subdued. He cuffed Adrien on the back and then made his way into the cave where we'd set up camp. "This place ain't half bad."

"How did you escape?" I asked. "And what about the others?"

Xona and Henk exchanged a look, then she took a deep breath. "We loaded as many refugees as we could into the pods, but there was no more room for us. Cole and I took off for the military level right when the blast doors started closing.

"Henk and most of the rest of our task force were there. A bunch of people had been eating in the Caf and Rand rounded them up and headed down after Henk messaged him. Cole and I just barely slipped under a blast door and met up with them.

"All the pods were gone by then. But Henk said there was another tunnel that was still under construction and was mostly dug out. We raced down it, then drove the digger the last half mile through to the Surface. We thought for sure the Regs would be on our tail, but none even bothered to follow us."

I thought of the swarm of Regs who'd been chasing behind me in our tunnel. "They were probably too busy coming after me once I was sighted," I said. At least it had let my friends get away unharmed.

"Well, thank God for that then," Xona said. "The digger was slow, and the whole time we were sure they'd be on us any second. But we made it to the Surface just fine, and then to a transport Henk had stashed close by." She looked over at Henk with a nod of admiration. "The guy's got contingency plans on top of contingency plans."

"So you got out of there okay?" I asked.

"At first everything was fine." Xona blinked hard. "But

when we got closer to the rendezvous site, suddenly one of the telepathic twins who was with us, Jare, started screaming that they'd found us."

"Thought we were right cracked for sure," Henk said quietly. "I took us outta there as quick as I could."

"But they'd already seen you?" I asked.

Xona shook her head. "No, the twins had gotten separated. The other boy was in one of the other pods that had been launched. Through their telepathy, Jare saw what Jone was seeing. The rendezvous site had been compromised and Jone was trying to warn his brother. Jare said later he'd seen through his brother's eyes that one of the other pods had opened fire and then was shot down right over the main cabin. It was only because of Jone's warning while we were far enough out that we were able to escape in time."

I felt like all the breath had been knocked out of my lungs. "How many— I mean, do we know if . . ." I couldn't bring myself to finish the thought.

"From what Ginni can tell with her power," Henk said, "Jone is still alive. When his pod leader saw the armada of transports waiting, they surrendered and landed without a fight. They were taken prisoner. Tyryn's pod too."

Xona looked away at this. I reached out and put a hand on her arm, but she kept staring stonily at the ground.

"What about the rest?" I squeezed my hands into fists, trying to prepare myself for the worst.

"There were a lot who never made it out of the Foundation." Xona looked back up. "Ginni did an inventory of the survivors who were transferred to the Chancellor's personal prison. Jilia, Saminsa, and Molla and the baby were captured. Cole was with us, but the other two ex-Regs, Wytt and Eli, were killed in the fighting at the Foundation."

"Who else?" I knew Ginni's power would show her who'd died—they'd blink out from her vision.

"The Professor didn't make it. Beka and Shaun either," Xona said quietly. "But the rest of our team came with us. City, Ginni, Rand, Juan, Amara, the techer; they're all safe, along with a half dozen Rez fighters."

In spite of the list of those who were safe, I still felt sick to my stomach. Professor Henry had been such a kind and good man. I hadn't known Beka and Shaun well other than seeing them use their Gifts in training. But still, they were both so young. Far too young to die.

Henk looked over at Adrien, his eyebrows heavy. "And I'm so sorry 'bout your mother."

Adrien looked down, his face contorting as if he was trying hard not to cry. In spite of all he'd said, had some part of him harbored hope that she'd survived the attack? I wanted to go hug him, but I wasn't sure he would welcome it.

My lip trembled. The tears I'd been managing to keep back so far finally brimmed to the surface. Jilia had been like a second mom to us. And Tyryn was Xona's brother and my friend. I hugged her hard again. She didn't cry, but she held me while I did.

"What now?" Adrien asked several long moments later, running his forearm roughly across his eyes.

"Now we regroup," Henk said. His jaw was tight. "And then we go to that prison and get 'em back."

Chapter 20

WE PACKED UP THE FEW bits of our unused supplies and followed Henk and Xona back out of the cave.

It was nighttime, but I could still see the outline of the impressive vehicle in the moonlight. It was even bigger than the large group transport we'd had at the Foundation.

"Where did you get this?" I asked.

"It's why we couldn't come sooner," Henk said. "I stashed this baby away right before my cover at the transport factory got cracked last year. It's got all the newest tech, designs I kept just for the Rez—antigravity hover based, complete day and nighttime cloaking tech, and solar-celled engines. We can fly for days before we gotta stop and let the engine cells refuel."

"So why didn't you come earlier?" I asked. Adrien stood beside me, but was silent, staring at the ground.

"Because genius here stashed it halfway across the country," Xona said, cuffing Henk on the shoulder.

"Hey, how was I supposed to know when the time came, I'd be in a transport meant for four that we had to stuff sixteen people into?" Henk looked back at me.

"Seventeen," Xona said darkly. "Don't forget the traitor stowaway."

I looked at both of them in confusion. "Who?"

"That crafty little shape-shifting bastard," Henk said. "He knew we'd 'a left him behind if we could *see* him. But he made himself invisible and must've run with us down the tunnel, then he stuffed himself in with everybody else on the transport. It was so tight and we were all so cracked with everything happenin', we didn't even realize."

It sounded exactly like something Max would do. It was horribly unfair that he of all people was safe when the Professor was *dead*. But, weasel that he was, he always managed to survive.

"With so much weight, we had a right hard time liftin' off and stayin' in the air. Engine trouble stalled us out after we escaped from the rendezvous site. I'd pushed it too hard trying to get us out of there as fast as possible. We were grounded for days before I figured out how to rig some power cells to get her up in the air again."

"And we could still only manage short hops and then had to stop for half a day to let the solar cells refuel," Xona said. "Ginni told us you and Adrien were alive and hadn't been captured, so we didn't worry. We figured you'd found out that the rendezvous site was a trap and were hiding out." Then she frowned, looking around the cave. "Where'd you hide your escape pod transport?"

"We didn't have one. Long story." I waved a hand. "I'll tell you about it later."

"I was so worried about you." Xona's eyes were uncharacteristically soft, her eyebrows drawn together. "Ginni said you'd stopped moving and I was afraid you'd been hurt. After Tyryn and Jilia . . ." She looked away.

"I'm fine now." I squeezed her hand back. "I'm okay."

Henk had already jogged over to the jet and pulled open a door on the side. It released with a hiss, and a small stepladder dropped out.

Adrien shouldered our packs, and I climbed up and stepped

inside. Everything was pristine and white. A short aisle ran between four rows of plush white seats.

"The Uppers thought I was designing 'em a luxury flier." Henk smirked.

"Where are the others?" I asked. I'd half expected to find them inside.

"Left 'em at the bunker where I hid the jet," Henk said, climbing up into the front navigation chair. "They're all safe and sound. I never told a livin' soul 'bout that place. Not even Taylor knew."

Adrien joined him in the front seat. I watched the back of his head. Everything that had happened over the last week seemed suddenly surreal. Now it was back to real life.

Adrien asked Henk questions about the bunker. His voice was calm and even, but I could hear how the words caught in his throat every so often. Was he just asking questions to distract himself from thinking about his mom? Xona strapped herself into one of the overstuffed chairs and tilted her head back against the headrest. She let out a slow sigh. Her eyes were puffy and red, and there were bruiselike shadows underneath her eyes.

She looked as tired as I felt. I sat up suddenly in my seat. "Wait, so if you guys didn't leave in a pod transport, you don't have the supply packs." My entire body slumped with exhaustion. "That means you don't have any spare biosuits. Our packs didn't have any and I've barely slept this week."

Xona's eyes widened, but Henk looked back at us. "I stocked a med container at the bunker," he said. "You'll be able to sleep right when we get there."

I laughed with delirious relief. Finally! I'd be able to sleep! I looked back at Xona. "When was the last time *you* slept?" I asked.

She cracked a tired smile. "A while," she said. "But you're safe now."

"I'm sure we'll be able to rescue Tyryn and Jilia and all the rest of them too." I meant it to be comforting, but Xona frowned deeply.

She looked up at Henk. "That's what Henk wants." The way she said it made it sound like she didn't.

"Don't you too?" I asked, confused.

"Tyryn made me swear," her eyes dropped, "that I would never try to come for him if he got captured. He made me swear it on our mom and dad. Said they would want one of us to survive if it came down to it."

"But still, if we could contact some of the other Rez cells—"

"There's no one left," she said, her voice distant. She stared out the window, even though it was too dark to see anything. "We haven't been able to contact any of the other Rez cells. Some of the Rez fighters at the Foundation knew where a couple of the other Rez command posts were located. The Chancellor must have compelled them to tell her. We don't know what happened to the rest. From everything we can tell, there's no one left but us."

I swallowed hard, trying to absorb the news. It was exactly what Adrien had guessed, even without a vision. I hadn't realized just how thin a thread we'd all been hanging by. Hadn't wanted to realize. Or maybe Xona was wrong. Maybe she didn't have all the information.

Xona looked back at me, her dark brown eyes intense on mine. "And I *swore*, Zoe. Swore I wouldn't try to rescue him." She sighed. "It's been a long night, I'm gonna catch some sleep, if you don't mind."

I nodded, trying to process what she'd just told me. "Get some rest."

In a few minutes, she was asleep. I unstrapped myself and

made my way to the front of the jet. I leaned in over Henk's and Adrien's shoulders. "How bad is it, Henk? Xona said we're the only ones left. But that can't be true, can it?"

"It's bad," he said. He adjusted the driving stick and we dipped gently to the left. "I'm sure some of the folks went to ground and hid. We've all been at it so long. We know the deal when we're cracked. But from what Ginni reports, not many escaped the last round of raids. Not nearly enough."

"But the Rez has bounced back before, right? We can come back from this."

Henk's eyes met mine briefly. "Zoe, there's no Rez left to speak of."

My mouth dropped open. I still couldn't believe it. "But the Rez has been operating for over two centuries. It can't just have—"

"We never had an enemy like Chancellor Bright before," Henk said. "Don't know how she cracked all the cells, but she did, first in the northern quadrant, then in the south. They're all gone."

"But how?" I asked, still flabbergasted. "No one knew about the location of the cells led by Garabex and Sanyez." I bit my lip as I thought. "Maybe that new weapon the other Colonels were talking about helped her find them all. The Amplifier. Or maybe somehow they were able to crack all our com codes?"

"The techer boy says it shouldn'ta been possible."

"Yeah, but he didn't think they had cloaking tech that could fool his equipment either. He was wrong about that." But then I stopped talking. There was no use guessing what might have happened, at least not right now.

I gave Adrien a quick glance. He'd been watching our exchange, but looked away out the window when I turned to him. I wished so bad he'd tell me what he was thinking. I sighed and went back to my seat.

Adrien didn't say anything to me for the entire ride, but he did glance back my way a couple times. Not that I could read the expression on his face. Was he upset about his mom? Or was he just glad now that he didn't have to be saddled with my liabilities anymore? After all we'd been through together . . . after last night . . .

"How fast are we going, anyway?" I called back up to the cabin. Anything to distract myself from thinking about last night.

"This baby can go up to a steady fifteen hundred miles an hour," Henk said. "I'm just keeping it slower while we maneuver around the more populated areas. We're cloaked, but I don't want to take any chances."

I sat back and tried to relax without getting *too* relaxed and going to sleep. I'd had enough practice over the past few days that I was able to calm every muscle of my body and let myself sink into the plush seat completely without falling asleep. I kept my eyes wide open and my mind calmly concentrated on my mast cells. I could almost do it without specifically focusing anymore. It was becoming instinctual, like the way people don't notice breathing or blinking because it's something they just *do*.

A couple hours later, the jet decreased speed and started to drop altitude. I looked out the windows even though I still couldn't see much in the nighttime. We'd passed by lit-up cities occasionally, but there hadn't been any lights below for at least half an hour.

I leaned forward in my seat restraints. "Where are we?"

"Southwest part of the Sector," Henk said.

Our forward motion stopped, and then we dropped directly down. "Don't need runways with this dove." Henk patted the console deck appreciatively.

He held his hands back from the controls completely as we touched down gently to the ground.

"She self-parks too," Henk said.

"We get it." Adrien managed a half smile. "You built a good transport, Henk."

Henk stared at him for a moment. He seemed as surprised to see the smile on Adrien's face as I had been a week and a half ago.

The outer door released and slid up in its tracks.

Xona woke up the moment the door opened. "Don't forget coolant harnesses," she said, stopping me from stepping out of the open hatch. "Out here there's nothing to cover you. Can't take any chances."

We all draped the harnesses around our shoulders and waists without bothering to clip them in, then headed down the short ladder one by one.

I jumped down the few steps and landed on the ground. Adrien was waiting there for me, his mouth tensed and his gray eyes dark. For one tiny second his mask slipped and I could see the grief written on his face. He *was* thinking about his mom. I stepped as close to him as I could without touching him. He might push me away if I reached for him, but maybe if I just stood by him he could soak up some comfort anyway.

Henk clicked a button on a remote thumb–sized device, and a tarp lifted out and over, slowly covering the jet.

The morning sun peaked over the horizon and I could see for what felt like forever in every direction. The landscape was so *flat* and, other than a few giant rock formations jutting up out of the ground, almost nothing seemed to grow in the arid plane. Just a few scrub plants here and there that looked like they barely managed to eke out an existence. The earth underneath our feet was strange too. The ground was dry and cracked, a sandy red orange color I'd never seen before. Out of everywhere I'd been on the Surface, this felt the most alien.

"What is this place?"

Henk laughed. "Welcome to the desert." He led us to a small outcropping of rocks. I frowned, having no idea where he was going. I stayed close to Adrien as we walked. There didn't seem to be any structures for miles around. But I did notice that my mast cells weren't as active. In such a dry climate, there were far fewer allergens to set them off.

Henk kicked at the ground in a few places. I didn't know what he was doing until he kicked at a slightly different spot and I heard a hollow *thunk*.

He reached down and cleared away the dust and sand with his hand until I could see a small circular hunk of metal with a handle in the middle. Henk grabbed hold and twisted. With a few grunting tugs, he got it to twist open.

"This bloomin' thing was near impossible to open when we first got here, but we been workin' her in."

After a few more twists, the metal plate came off completely. Henk dropped it to the ground and gestured toward the hole. "Ladies first."

Xona dropped down inside, nimbly climbing down the ladder through what looked like a long tube. I looked down after her but couldn't see anything below.

"What's down here?" I asked Henk.

He grinned. "Generations of us Kioleskis have been paranoid bastards. My great-great-great-great-great grandpappy had this place built. Said he'd survive the end of the world down here if he had to. Everyone thought he was crazy," Henk turned his head sideways, "till D-Day happened and some of the big cities got hit. Him and his kin hunkered down here for years during the takeover and the first waves of drone implants. Eventually he hooked up with some other survivors and they were the first generation of Rez fighters. Me mum thought it was crazy when she married into the family and heard all the stories. Took me to live with her family across the ocean in Sector One when dad died, but I lit out back here just as soon as I turned eighteen."

I looked down at the dark hole. "So was this place like a headquarters or something?"

Henk laughed again. "Naw, great-grandpappy didn't trust anyone, not even his new freedom fighter mates. Never showed this place to anyone 'cept his family and made his kids swear to do the same with each new generation. No matter what, he wanted his line to survive."

"But you brought us here?"

He shrugged. "Eh, great-grandpappy was a crazy ol' bastard. And I'm the last of us, so it's my legacy now. It's the only place I could think of that the Chancellor won't be able to compel someone to tell about, 'cause no one but me knows."

I nodded. "Thank you."

He waved a hand. "It's nothin'. Now get yourself on down there. I can already hear Ginni shrieking about you getting back."

I listened and he was right, I could dimly hear Ginni's unique high-pitched squeal. I smiled and started down the ladder. In spite of all that had happened, so many of my friends were still safe. I would take the moment to enjoy it before letting all the other worries settle back in.

Ginni all but tackled me when I finally stepped off the ladder. She half strangled me, her arms were so tight around my neck.

"I was so worried!" she said.

"It's okay, Ginns. I'm safe."

I looked around at the other familiar faces packed into the small six-by-six-foot chamber that made up the entryway.

Rand clapped Adrien hard on the back, pulling him into a half hug. "Good to see ya, man."

Juan gave me a hug too. "Glad you're safe," he said when he pulled back. He used to be so ready with a smile, but even though he looked glad to see me, his face was subdued.

I looked around. The concrete walls looked like they hadn't been scrubbed down in a very long time. A layer of orange Surface dirt coated them, heavier along the bottom near the floor. We set our coolant harnesses on a hook in the entryway, then Ginni ushered me through an arched concrete doorway into a larger room. It was about twenty feet wide and maybe fifty long. The walls were also curved, like a giant animal had burrowed a large tunnel through the ground.

Cots hung from the walls all the way up to the ceiling on the right side of the room, stacked four high. Lots of people were sitting or lying on their cots. Others milled around the room. Some I recognized: City, Rand, a dark-haired boy who seemed vaguely familiar, Cole, and Amara. Max sat alone in the corner. He stood when I came in, but I looked away from him. The rest wore the distinctive Rez fighter garb.

"You must be exhausted," Ginni said. "Juan and I set up your med container." She pointed to a plastic rectanglar box set up under a cot at the farthest side of the room. Just seeing it made me feel better. I could barely imagine cobbling together more than a few hours of sleep at a time, and I all but ran toward the thing. Ginni giggled as she followed behind me.

Max met me at the container. "Zoe, I'm so glad you're safe. I was so worried—"

"Don't." I held up a hand, my voice harsh. "I don't want to hear it." He was the last person on earth I wanted to talk to right now.

"Ginni, please wake me in eight hours. And," I leaned closer, "keep an eye on Adrien. He just found out about his mom."

She nodded solemnly, and I sat down in the container and pulled the lid overhead.

Ginni woke me in time for dinner. I knew I needed more sleep, but I was also eager to catch up with everyone.

I stood up and stretched my sore body. I rolled my head slowly, stretching out the aching muscles in my neck. When I stepped out of the pod, my legs felt extremely weak. I'd probably need to sleep for a couple days before I felt back to my old self. At the same time, having used up so much of my power over the past week meant I'd be safe from another eruption of power like what happened with the earthquake. At least for a few days until my telek renewed itself.

I looked around for the first time without sleep-befuddled eyes. On the side of the room opposite the beds was a small kitchen setup with a sink and tiny square countertop. A food cooling unit was crowded in between the sink and another wide cabinet in the corner. There were a few boxes of protein bars and a stack of blankets piled up beside the cabinet.

In spite of the fact that it was all situated in an orderly way, the room felt cluttered. There was just so much stuff, not to mention people, for such a relatively small space.

I joined everyone huddled around the kitchen area. Max looked up but thankfully stayed where he was on his cot, separate from everyone else. I went to stand by Adrien, but he took one look at me and his face hardened. He walked out of the room toward the bathroom while Rand pulled a ladle up out of a pot filled with red sauce and smelled it suspiciously. I watched Adrien's receding back with an aching heart.

"Xona cooked this, right?" Rand asked. "Should I be afraid?"

Xona glared at him.

"What?" Rand dropped the ladle and put up his hands defensively. "Do we or do we not all remember the catastrophe of the protein patty casserole she tried to cook a few months ago at the Foundation?" He looked around at the rest of us for confirmation, but we wisely kept our mouths closed.

In spite of my worry about Adrien, I couldn't help smiling when I remembered Xona's attempt to cook us all a meal her mother used to make growing up. It had turned out rubbery and burned.

"Maybe Amara could bliss us all out with her power so we wouldn't care how bad it is," Rand went on, poking the ladle around suspiciously.

"I helped this time," Cole said, putting a hand to the small of Xona's back. Rand visibly relaxed. Cooking had been another pastime Cole had taken up in his quest to understand what it meant to be human again and he was good at it.

But the smile dimmed on my face as I watched how Xona turned into his chest and grinned. I knew that look. It made something deep in my stomach twist even though I was happy for her. She was in love. With the ex-Reg she'd always sworn she'd hate. I shook my head at the irony of it.

"Ha!" Amara spoke up. "Last time I used my power on you in training, Rand, you kept grinning like a fool for days afterwards, even though I'd gone easy on you and only blissed you for an hour. I don't think you could handle it full force."

"Oh, I could handle it," Rand said with a grin, shoveling a pile of rice on his place and then covering it with copious amounts of the red sauce.

"Go easy," Cole said. "We only had a couple of slightly out-of-date jars of sauce left, so I added a lot of dried hot pepper to help the flavor."

Rand added another dollop of sauce and smirked. "Heat doesn't bother me."

Cole only raised an eyebrow.

There were a few folding chairs and a small table, but most of us sat on the ground with our plates in our lap. I stirred the red sauce into the rice. Whatever it was, it smelled good. My stomach growled and I dipped my fork in.

It was delicious. Maybe it was because I'd spent the past week eating nothing but bland protein bars, but right now this tasted like the best thing I'd ever eaten in my life. It was sweeter than I expected, and the spice seemed to explode on my tongue. I was sweating within moments, and I'd only added a small bit of the sauce. There was enough rice with it that it wasn't too overwhelming.

I glanced over at Rand and couldn't help laughing. His face was bright red and he suddenly dropped the plate to the ground dramatically and sprinted to the sink, where he gulped water right from the faucet.

We all laughed. I swallowed the bit I was eating and took a long swig of water. Ginni had informed me earlier that the compound was hooked up to a deep well, so we didn't have to limit water consumption. After the last week of worrying about finding fresh water, it was a relief.

"So what happened to you guys while you were gone?" Ginni asked, gesturing at me and Adrien, who'd returned and gotten a plate of food. She grinned and leaned in. "Xona said the cave where she found you was cozy."

I choked a little on my rice, but then swallowed it down. "Um . . ." I looked over at Adrien, but he'd ducked his head and was staring at the floor. Apparently he was going back into barely speaking mode now that we were surrounded by other people again.

I related what had happened to us at the Foundation and how Adrien helped me realize that I could use my power to fly. Several people's eyes widened at that. Then I explained about the storm and the cave and Adrien's visions. I tried to catch his eye before I mentioned the last part, to see if he minded me talking about it, but his face was impassive. I glossed over it as briefly as I could. And I didn't mention anything about the dreamlike night in the dark.

Before Ginni could ask anything else more probing, I turned the questions back on her. "So tell me more about your group's escape. I just got the bare details from Xona on the way here."

In true Ginni style, what had taken Xona five minutes to tell, Ginni told in forty-five. The familiar-looking dark-haired boy sat beside her, interjecting every so often some bit of tech input. I looked at him and frowned. I'd swear I knew him, but I couldn't put my finger on where I'd met him.

Everyone finished eating but few people moved. Instead, smaller conversations broke out. The techer left to go work at his console and Ginni, Xona, and I scooted closer together.

"So what's going on with you and Cole?" I asked Xona. Any jealousy I had at their connection was far overwhelmed by happiness for my friend. Xona'd had a hard few years, losing her parents, and now her brother. That she was able to find a modicum of peace or happiness was a miracle.

She looked startled by my question, but a slow smile spread over her lips as she glanced over at Cole. He was talking to Rand and laughing about something.

"We like hanging out," Xona said simply.

Ginni rolled her eyes. "What she means to say is that they're in *love*. It's so romantic, previous mortal enemies falling for each other."

Xona punched Ginni on the shoulder. "Ow!" Ginni pulled back but was still grinning. "What? It's true."

"He's a good man," Xona said. "And a good friend."

"Who you occasionally make out with." Ginni moved out of the way this time before Xona could smack her again.

"I thought you'd given up on your spying ways," Xona said.

"It was just once," Ginni said hurriedly. "You were in the supply closet and I happened to peek—"

"Okay." Xona held up her hands. "We get the idea. Now why don't we talk about the boy who was sitting beside *you* at dinner."

Ginni frowned for a moment in confusion. I didn't know who Xona was referring to either, but then Ginni raised her arm panel and read something. Her face relaxed. "Oh, right. It's Simin. He's the techer." She looked over to where he was working on a complex console setup in the corner. She looked back at us and giggled. "I'm not positive, but I think we've kissed too!"

I smiled at her. It was both strange and wonderful that even here, at what felt like the end of the world, life went on. People fell in love. We were still able to laugh with friends. Even after all that each of us had lost.

I looked around at each face, as if I could memorize this moment. Adrien wasn't speaking, but he was sitting back and watching the others with a look that seemed contented enough. He didn't look blank anymore. As if he could feel my eyes on him, he looked my way. Our gazes locked, and then he looked down, his face darkening. My breath caught as an unexpected rush of sadness flushed through me. I diverted my gaze back toward the group, but Ginni had caught the exchange.

"So Adrien seems . . . different," she said. "I watched him all through dinner and he kept staring at you. It looked like," she paused as if searching for the right words, "like he's woken up or something. Did something happen when you guys were away?"

I forced myself not to look back in his direction. I fidgeted with the bottom hem of my tunic, torn between not wanting to talk about it and longing to open up to my friends about all the confused feelings I'd had over the past week. "He is different," I said slowly. "He can feel emotion again, but he doesn't like to. There were a few moments where I'd think we were connecting again." I allowed my gaze to stray back in Adrien's direction. "But it was probably nothing."

I looked down so I wouldn't have to see the hopeful look on her face. Ginni was the kind of person who always wanted to believe there could be a happy ending to any story.

When we all finally stood up to put away our plates, Max came up to me. "Zoe, can we please talk?"

Xona and Ginni stepped in front of me to block him, shoulder to shoulder. "She doesn't want to talk to you," Xona said.

"Zoe, please, I just want to talk, that's all." He tried to lean around Xona to look at me, but she shoved him hard in the chest.

I could easily see this all getting out of hand quickly, so I touched Xona's shoulder lightly. "It's okay." I stepped around her and crossed my arms over my chest once I was face-to-face with Max. I surrounded him with my telek in case he tried anything. "What do you want?"

"Can we talk more privately?" He nodded toward Xona and Ginni.

I glared at him in response. "Anything you have to say to me you can say in front of them."

"Please, Zoe. Just a few minutes. That's all I'm asking for."

"Fine," I said, if only to hurry it up. I turned to Ginni and Xona. "I'll be fine. If he tries anything, I'll rip his arms off."

They backed away, but not before Xona gave Max a death glare and said, "We'll be close by if you need us."

"So," Max said after they backed away. "How are you feeling? I overheard at dinner everything you went through and—"

"Cut the small talk," I said impatiently. "What is it you want?"

He was quiet a second, then looked at me, his brown eyes earnest. "I want to say that I'm sorry. I'm so sorry for how I treated you when we were back in the Community and I'm sorry for all the lies." He looked down, his forehead scrunched up like what he was saying pained him. "I'm sorry for ever working with the Chancellor, and most of all," he looked back up at me, "I'm sorry for what I did to Adrien and then lying to you in the worst possible way by impersonating him."

"And," I said coldly. "Your point?"

He took a deep breath. "What I really want is to know if you can ever forgive me."

"No, I can't," I said curtly, then started to turn away. He put out a hand to stop me, but I froze it midreach with my telek.

"Can't I have a second chance?" he asked, his voice impassioned. "Doesn't everyone deserve that?"

I spun on him, my calm demeanor finally cracking. "You had a second chance. Ten times over! You could have come with us instead of staying with the Chancellor when we first escaped the Community. Then during the raid when the Chancellor told you to switch with Adrien, you could have chosen not to. She wasn't there to compel you. I would have welcomed you to the Foundation with open arms. You *chose* to do what you did that day. And then after you'd switched with him, you could have told us what you'd done so that we could have saved him before the Chancellor took a hacksaw to his brain!"

He winced and stepped backwards a couple steps. Only then did I realize that I was shouting. I didn't care. "But no, you never would have told me the truth if I hadn't *caught* you. So don't talk to me about second chances. At a certain point," I shook my head in disgust, "it's just too late. You deserve to pay for all that you did. And yet here you are, safe and sound, while people far better than you were captured or killed." I shook my head and grimaced. "Looking at you makes me sick."

"But I've changed!" he pleaded. "I'm trying to be a better man. I'm trying to make up for the things I've done. Doesn't that count for something?"

"Not enough." I overenunciated every syllable. "Never enough." The words echoed around the silent room. Looking around, I saw that everyone had stopped what they were doing to stare at us. Well, almost everyone. Adrien was walking in our direction.

Max didn't notice him. His face was red and his hands were balled into fists at his sides. "So you won't even give me a chance?"

"No."

"I shouldn't have come here." His voice was low as he narrowed his eyes at me. "You'll never believe me, no matter how hard I try to prove it to you. I don't know why I even bothered."

Before I could respond, Adrien reached us and slugged Max hard in the face. Even though Max probably had fifty pounds on Adrien, he was knocked off his feet and landed hard on the concrete floor. When Max looked back up at us, blood ran from his nose. Adrien shook out his hand. "I've wanted to do that for a long time."

Before I could do anything other than stare in shock at him, Adrien yelped suddenly, as if in pain. He clutched his head and dropped to the floor. His body quaked with an uncontrollable shaking. All the conflict with Max was forgotten as I dropped down and tried to brace Adrien's head as best I could so he didn't slam it into the concrete.

"What's happening?" Ginni asked, her voice high-pitched with worry. The others crowded nearer.

"It's a vision," I said. "Everyone stay back and give him some room. He'll be fine in a couple minutes."

His body finally stilled and I helped him sit up. He ran a

quivering hand through his hair as he blinked and tried to right himself.

"Can someone get him some water?" I asked. Ginni hurried to the sink and back. She handed him the cup and he drank shakily.

"What did you see?" City asked him.

"It was a split vision, like before," he said quietly. Everyone leaned in to hear him. "Two possible futures. It was even less clear than my last vision. I was present, but I'm not sure I was in my own body. It felt like," he paused, frowning, "like I was seeing through someone else's eyes, but I don't know who."

"Well, what happened?" City asked impatiently.

He swallowed hard. "In one future, the Chancellor is lying dead at Zoe's feet. In the other," his eyes darted up to meet mine, "you're dead at hers."

Chapter 21

I SWALLOWED HARD AND BLINKED rapidly. There it was, stated so blatantly. I'd known it would come down to this, if I was honest with myself.

"When?" I asked.

He shook his head, his eyebrows furrowed. "I couldn't tell."

I took a deep breath to steady myself. "How do I kill her?"

"She had a hole from what looked like a laser round burned through her chest."

I frowned. "A laser round? Why wouldn't I just use my telek?"

He shrugged, still trembling slightly as he recovered from the vision.

"So what makes the difference between the two visions?" Xona asked.

"Maybe like last time, the split hinges on some variable we don't know about," Adrien said. "Maybe even how we respond to the vision. Like whether or not you take a laser weapon with you because of how I saw her killed." Then he shook his head, brow furrowing. "Although it's probably more complex than that."

"Maybe that girl will be there," Ginni said. "The one who made all our powers not work."

I nodded slowly. That did make sense. I'd assumed the girl's power was like the techer's, unconsciously affecting everyone; in which case, the Chancellor would never keep her around. But what if the girl could direct her power only at certain glitchers? Though, if that was the case, how would I ever get close enough to the Chancellor for either of the visions to come true? Without my powers, Regs could easily take me out the second I got there.

I hated the thought that some decision I, or someone else, made in the future could be the difference between the Chancellor's death, or my own. When the time came, how would I know if I was making the right choice? Or what if it was something that was out of my hands altogether?

"Where is she right now?" I asked. "Ginni, you mentioned last night that she was in some compound where everyone else was imprisoned."

Ginni closed her eyes briefly. "She hasn't moved. And Zoe." She opened her eyes to look at me. "Your brother's there too."

I nodded, swallowing hard. I'd expected as much.

"All right," Henk interrupted, "now that all the fun's died down, I'm gonna make a supply run. We're running short on food, and we'll need full bellies before we figure out what's comin' next. I know a market supply center that's just beggin' to be ganked. Who's with me?"

"I'll go," Rand said.

Xona and Cole volunteered too, along with a couple Rez fighters. Max slunk off to the corner. I knew I needed more rest before I'd be of much help to anyone, so after a long blistering shower I climbed back in the med container and told Ginni not to wake me this time.

When I finally woke, it was midmorning the next day. Cole dropped a huge pallet full of rice and beans in the center of the room, and the others began unloading it. I went to help.

My legs felt strong for the first time in days and the overall achiness was almost gone. It was amazing what a solid night of sleep could do.

I was finally well rested and now our pantry was well stocked. We could stop worrying about simple survival and start planning out what our next move was going to be. I hefted a bag of flour over to the cabinet and set it alongside the others.

"How'd it go?" Ginni asked Rand.

"No problems. Henk's the king of thieves," Rand said, then tilted his head sideways with a grin. "'Course I helped too. Couldn't have made it through that thick guard fence without my skills."

City rolled her eyes. "Yes we could have, Rand. They're called wire cutters."

"Fine, but don't even say I wasn't helpful, melting a hole through those metal loading doors."

"And let's not forget," City said with a falsely sweet smile, "how you burned through half the merchandise when you accidently lit the stacks of wood pallets on fire in the back of the warehouse."

Rand shrugged. "It made for a nice distraction while we got away, didn't it?"

"Enough, children." Henk stretched and then clapped two hands to his stomach dramatically. "Where's lunch? I'm starved."

"I made some stew." Ginni pointed at a pot that was still bubbling on the stovetop.

Rand grabbed a spoon and dipped it in the pot. He blew on it a moment before sipping it. He made a face and pulled back from the pot. "Well," he grimaced, "it'll fill an empty belly, at least."

"And don't forget what we also picked up." Henk smiled

and held up a large cylindrical container. "Salt! Put enough on, and it'll make even the rankest food passable."

"Hey!" Ginni objected. Henk sent her a sideways grin, then grabbed a bowl and ladled in a large serving of stew. Those of us who had stayed behind let the people who'd gone on the supply raid go first. I looked around for Adrien. He stood at the end of the line, absorbed in a tablet he was reading from. I sighed and looked away. But then I frowned.

"Wait, where's Max?" I asked.

Several people's heads swiveled around, looking for him. Xona frowned. "I don't see him."

"Maybe he's in the shower?" Ginni said.

I stood still one more moment, checking every face both with my eyes and my telek until I was sure he wasn't in the room with us. When I hurried over to the bathroom to check there, no one was inside.

"Shunting bastard," I whispered under my breath as I walked back out to the group. "He must have snuck on the jet with you guys and then gotten off once you got to the supply site."

Henk let out a long string of curses, half of which I'd never heard before. "He knows about this hideout here. If he goes back to the Chancellor—"

I shook my head. "He won't. He wouldn't want to get anywhere near her and risk falling under her compulsion again. Especially after failing her on the last mission she sent him on. No, he'll probably go lose himself in one of the bigger cities where he can pose as a wealthy Upper and live in pampered luxury." I curled my lip in disgust. It was a fitting end to his story.

"You all have to see this!" called out a voice from the corner.

"What is it, Simin?" Ginni asked.

I turned to look as a dark-haired boy hurried to the middle

of the room. His face was pinched with concern as he set a small portable projection console on one of the tables.

The slight chatter that had filled the room quieted almost instantly. We all gathered around the table.

"What happened?" Henk asked.

"This just broadcast over the Link," the boy Ginni had called Simin said. He clicked the console on. A few people moved back so the 3-D projection cube would have a clear space to play over the table.

The calm face of Chancellor Bright showed on the vid feed. I winced and averted my gaze before forcing myself to look up and watch as she strode down the aisle of a large auditorium in Central City. A banner ran across the bottom of the screen: NEW CHANCELLOR SUPREME APPOINTED.

There was no mention of what had happened to the previous Chancellor, if he had died or been deposed or who knows what else Bright might have done to him in order to usurp his top position. This had always been her ultimate goal, even back when she was just the Chancellor of a single Academy in a midsized city. Hard to believe that was only a year ago. She'd compelled her way up to Underchancellor of Defense, and now was the supreme leader of the second largest of the eight worldwide Sectors.

The camera switched to an auditorium shot where Chancellor Bright was being sworn in, then did a quick pan of the other Officials who sat in the long panel at the back of the stage. Their faces didn't show any reaction. But then, Uppers were always careful not to display emotion when they knew the vid feeds for the Link were on. Couldn't let the drones see that the ideals about a passionless Community were actually just a load of propaganda, meant to keep them under control. Either that, or they were under the Chancellor's compulsion.

I looked at their empty faces and wondered what they

would look like if they knew she was a glitcher who'd just fi-
nagled herself into the top Upper position in the country by
using mind-control. Of course if they ever realized anything
was suspicious, the Chancellor could compel the thought away.

Bright walked up to a podium in the center of the stage.
Her dark brown hair was oiled and slicked back in a bun and
she wore the black tunic denoting those of highest rank. Her
face was blank, but unlike the Officials behind her, it wasn't
because she was under any compulsion. Cold and calculating
was her natural state.

"Subjects of the Community, I greet you as your new Chancellor Supreme. I stand here today to assure you of the continued prosperity of our great Community in spite of the menace
that has grown up among us like thorns. We have long reported the increasing number of anomalous-behaving Community members. When we asked for your help in reporting
any anomalous activity, you all responded admirably.

"We will not abide subjects exhibiting the destructive pas-
sions," she went on, "the very same violent outbursts that led to
the destruction of the Old World. They lie and cheat and com-
mit atrocities against their fellow subjects. If they had their way,
the perfect and orderly world we have created would be blasted
backwards into chaos and ruin." She tilted her head. "But I am
here to tell you today that during my tenure as Underchancellor of Defense and now as Chancellor Supreme, the virus is
being stamped out once and for all.

"For months we rounded up and disabled infected subjects.
Our techers were hard at work discovering the malfunction
in the hardware and how to repair it. And we finally discovered the answer."

She leaned slightly over the podium. "It was simple, really.
The problem lay in the adolescent V-chip itself. Our best
techers worked around the clock for months to develop a way

to implant the *adult* V-chip in infants instead, but without impairing natural neural growth as the subjects age. They have finally succeeded. This technological advance will herald a new age for humanity, one without fear of glitching hardware or anomalous behavior. Finally, we can all live in peace. Order first, order always."

The vid screen went dark. My mouth was open in horror at what she'd said. Adult V-chips, in children? It meant we wouldn't be able to ever recover anyone from the Community. We'd long ago accepted adults were lost to us. But there'd always been hope for children and teenagers under eighteen before that final invasive chip went in. Hope that we could free them one day.

If the Chancellor had her way, there'd be no one left to free and humanity's enslavement would be complete. I'd known the Chancellor lusted for power, but naively, I hadn't ever believed she was absolutely *evil* until now.

"Well, that answers that question." City broke the silence, taking a step back from the table. "No way we're gonna try and infiltrate to get the others if she's the Chancellor Supreme."

I looked at her in disbelief. Really? *That* was what she'd taken away from seeing the video? "What about the drones? What are we going to do about them? We can't let the Chancellor get away with this!"

City stared at me as if I was the one who was making no sense. "And what exactly do you think we can do about it? Nothing. It's time we accepted the fact that we're defeated and hide out somewhere we can be safe."

Henk stiffened. "The vid doesn't change anything. We're going back for the others."

"It changes everything!" City said. "Ginni said they're all in the same building as the Chancellor most of the time. We can't even imagine the kind of security detail she has surrounding her now that she's Chancellor Supreme. There's no way we'd be able to sneak in unnoticed."

"But we have to try," Juan said, putting down his bowl on the ground with a loud clank.

"I agree," Henk said. "It's Jilia." He looked around at the others. "You know she wouldn't hesitate to sacrifice herself if it meant a chance to get one of you lot back."

"Exactly," City said. "She wouldn't hesitate to sacrifice herself. You think she'd want you, us, anyone, going in after her and risking their life?"

"It's not just Jilia," Juan said. "It's Molla and the baby—"

"Would you stop mooning over her already? It's not even your baby. And she's in love with the traitor."

"City!" Ginni said, looking at the other girl sharply. "Don't say that. Juan was there for Molla. He was her friend."

"She was my friend too," City cut in. "But you have to leave people behind. It's what happens. Tell her, Xona."

I expected Xona to object and throw it back in City's face. But to my surprise, Xona just looked at the ground. "City's right," she said quietly. "I had to leave plenty of friends behind over the years. That's the life of living on the run. And the only way the Rez survived this long is because people have known when to duck and hide."

Ginni's mouth dropped open. "You can't believe that! Tyryn was captured too. Don't you love your brother at all?"

A vein pulsed in Xona's forehead. "Don't you say a shunting thing about my brother."

I was shocked at how all the camaraderie I'd just been watching had suddenly turned in on itself. I'd assumed it was a given that we'd go back and try to rescue the others.

And how was no one else even mentioning what the Chancellor had announced about the V-chip? I opened my mouth to bring it up again but then closed it. I supposed City was right in a way, we did have more immediate problems than worrying about the drones, but still. The Chancellor had to be stopped.

My mind flipped to the vision Adrien had yesterday. Was this the catalyst for what he'd seen? Because there was no way I could ignore what the Chancellor was doing and go live my life in peace somewhere. There would be no peace for me until she was dead and I'd rescued my brother. My chest cinched up even thinking about Markan. Had she done the procedure on him already, implanted the last deadening V-chip? I thought I'd have a few more years to get him back before the final chip was installed. Or would she keep him un-chipped if he was a glitcher with a useful enough Gift?

Meanwhile, the discussion raged on around me.

"The Rez has survived because we didn't leave our own behind," Henk glared at City.

"That's not true," City scoffed. "Look at what happened to Taylor when they went for Adrien. You try to rescue even just one person and the rescuers get killed instead. Whole Rez teams have been killed that way. And then what's the point of it all? Who's going to fight the next battle if we're all dead? You've said yourself that we're the only ones left, Henk. That means they win."

"So, what?" I interjected. "We just sit here and do nothing?"

"It's called living." Xona crossed her arms. "It's what the Rez has done for hundreds of years. Hiding out and staying alive." I thought about the promise she'd made to her brother as she went on. "We steal the supplies we need and stay on the move. There's gotta be some cells that haven't been cracked yet."

"None that I could find," Simin said.

"Yet," City corrected. "None that you could find *yet*. And it makes sense. Any operatives who've managed to escape the

Chancellor aren't going to be broadcasting it. It's protocol to go communications-dark when the situation gets hot."

"Yes, but there are other protocols to set beacons to let others know you're still alive," Simin said. "I pinged the beacon for the Rez in Sector Six, and none have been activated."

"Then we go to other countries," City said. "If everyone in the Rez in this Sector has been cracked because of the Chancellor, then we get as far as we can away from her. The other side of the globe if we have to. There are other groups we can find." She looked at Simin. "Have you tried contacting the Rez in other Sectors?"

He shook his head. "Not yet."

"There," City said, nodding her head. "Then that's what we'll do."

"That's *not* what we'll do," Henk said, slamming his hand hard on the table. "You're all just kids. You don't know—"

"Don't you dare patronize us." City's voice rose an octave. "We all heard Jilia talk about you. How you're irresponsible and don't think before you do things. You'd get us all killed if you were in charge."

"Did you forget whose bunker we're all sittin' in?" He gestured around him. "And whose jet is sitting outside?"

"Zoe was a Colonel," Ginni said. "She's the highest-ranking person we have left. She should be in charge."

"Because that turned out *so* well back at the Foundation," City said sarcastically. "Did you forget about the earthquake she caused that led them straight to us?"

My face burned both in anger at what she'd said and shame because I knew she was right.

"I say we vote about going back for the others or not," Rand finally spoke up. "It's the only way that's fair."

"Fine." Henk let out a frustrated blast of air. "Raise your hand if you want to set up a mission to rescue the others."

About half the group raised their hands, myself included. Cole frowned deeply, looking back and forth between Henk and Xona, but kept his hand down.

"And those who want to stay safe and not do anything foolish?" City asked. She raised her hand. Adrien, Xona, Rand, Simin, and Cole joined her, along with four of the Rez fighters. They outnumbered us by a single vote.

City let out a small whoop. "There you go. Nine to eight. No mission."

Henk shot to his feet. "This is ridiculous. It's not a democracy. I've got the jet and I'll go by myself if I have to."

"You can't take the jet and strand us here like that," Xona said, her voice hard. "You'd be sentencing us to death without a way to travel for more supplies."

"I've had enough of all of you." Henk's face was red. "These are the people we *love*. You do anything to save the ones you love. End of story. Instead, you're all letting fear turn you back into machines who can't feel a shuntin' thing!"

Cole winced at his words.

"That's enough, Henk," Xona said.

Henk stared at her hard, then threw his hands up in frustration and strode out of the room, banging his fist angrily against the doorjamb as he left.

It was deadly quiet in the room. Some stared angrily at one another. Others kept their eyes trained on the ground. People slowly shuffled to their feet. Those who'd eaten already put their dishes in the sink. Cole silently moved to start washing them. Others climbed back up into their bunks.

I was left alone staring in numb shock at everything that had just happened. I went back to the line for stew even though I wasn't particularly hungry. My mind kept whirring to the image of the Chancellor's smug face as she accepted the role as Chancellor Supreme. Replacing one corrupt, tyrannical system with another. One that was worse. I imagined the infants and children she'd probably already ordered to the upgrade centers. Children who'd never laugh or play or have the opportunity to feel any of the wondrous emotions I'd discovered over the past two years.

The Chancellor had always wanted power and so she'd taken it. More and more until she was the single most powerful person in the entire country. But that hadn't been enough. She wanted absolute, unchecked power. Would glitchers even still develop if she put the adult V-chip in children? Or was that part of the point? She didn't want anyone more powerful than herself to ever be able to challenge her. She'd condemn them all to a life of unending slavery just to secure her own position.

And would that satisfy her, or was she already scheming about ways to take over the other global Sectors as well? Would the Rez in the other seven Sectors fall as quickly as we had here? If they did, she'd rule the whole world. I shuddered. The breadth and depth of her evil made a cold chill settle on my chest. Adrien used to help me stay determinately hopeful, but it seemed more and more that hope was nowhere to be found.

I finally reached the front of the line and ladled some stew into my bowl, but didn't bother adding any salt. Tasteless was just fine with me right now.

Where did this leave the few of us outcasts who were left? We had powers, but we were powerless. We had no armies to command and no government officials to wield as puppets. The more I thought about it, the more I wondered about what Xona had said—that we should just *live*.

It was what Adrien had said back when we were in the wilderness, and it struck me as just as wrong now. Or maybe the truth was, I simply had no idea how to do that. Just live. I didn't know how people, free people, were supposed to live. There had been some kind of normal for humankind back when it was free hundreds of years ago. Then there had been the normal of drone existence. Normal for me had been all about my life with Adrien and fighting so that we could have a real future together. I'd always wanted to free the drones too, but at my core, it had been a very personal mission. I was fighting so that I and the ones I loved could live free.

And now?

Ginni tried to wave me over to sit with her, but I shook my head and went over to the corner where my med container was. I sat down with my back against it. I ate several spoonfuls of stew, barely noticing that it burned my mouth it was so hot.

I finally put down the bowl and looked across the room at Adrien, who sat eating on his cot, still reading from his tablet. He hadn't spoken to me all day. I moved my hand from my bowl to massage my aching chest. It hurt so much it felt like my heart was literally breaking. Because I loved him, both who he had been and who he was now. I loved all of him, and always would. But my love for him was only an incomplete half of a whole. He didn't love me back, and that meant the jagged gash that had been punched through my heart would bleed forever.

It didn't matter, I tried to tell myself. After our time in the wilderness, I believed more than ever that Adrien was going to be okay. Maybe if there was any hope at all, it was in that. He could live a full life now. A life without me.

The vote had sounded like a firm answer. Like it was settled. But seeing Henk stomp out of the room like that, I knew it wasn't. And City had been right too. I wasn't fit to lead, not when I'd always been such a danger to everyone around me. If I accidently caused another earthquake once my telek energy replenished fully, I could lead the Chancellor right to them all over again. I wouldn't let that happen. It was the same realization I'd had after the first quake. I'd ignored it or been too tired to think about anything other than getting to safety the past couple weeks. But the danger of my presence still remained. There was only one thing to do.

It would be my last gift to the ones that I loved.

I would leave them.

Chapter 22

EARLY THE NEXT AFTERNOON, I sat down beside Henk on his bottom bunk as he sipped a large cup of coffee. "I need to talk to you."

He winced at my words and put a hand to his forehead. "A little softer, love. My head's pounding."

I leaned in, worried. He'd slept in till almost noon, then had barely spoken a word to anyone while he warmed up his coffee.

"What's wrong with you?" I asked. He looked more ragged than usual. The circles under his eyes were dark and the scruff on his cheeks heavier.

Henk ran a hand over his face. "It's nothin' that won't heal with a few cups of coffee."

He seemed to sense that I still wasn't catching his meaning. He sighed. "I got piss-faced drunk last night after the vote. I keep a stash of gin on the transport."

So that was where he'd disappeared to after he'd stalked out last night. A few people had whispered at breakfast about him stumbling in right before sunrise.

"Well, no more of that," I said, my voice severe. "I need you alert. I wanted to leave tonight, but not if you're in this condition."

"Leave where?" he asked. Several people around us looked our way and I shushed him.

"It's not safe for everyone if I stay here." I kept my voice low.

He looked like he was about to object, but I silenced him with a look. Slowly, he nodded. "Guess that might be true."

"So I need you to drop me somewhere. And Henk," I put a hand gently on his forearm, "I'll do what I can to free Jilia and the others."

His head shot up in surprise, his eyes wide. "You will?"

I nodded. "The Chancellor has my brother too." Then I looked around furtively. "But don't tell anyone. I don't want anyone to know until I'm gone."

He stared at me, frowning, but then finally nodded his head.

"Lunch is ready!" Rand's voice boomed throughout the room and Henk winced again.

I looked at Henk one last time. "We'll leave early tomorrow morning then. It will probably be good for me to get another day of nutrition and rest anyway."

I stood up and headed toward the kitchen area. With nothing to do all day, mealtimes had turned into big events because they broke up the monotony. But unlike the past few days, no one was laughing or joking today. Several others had gathered around to get their sandwiches, but I noticed they weren't crowded haphazardly together like yesterday. Everyone bunched up according to how they'd voted last night. Half filled their plates and sat at one end of the room and the others arranged themselves at the opposite side.

I sighed, half tempted to go back into the container to see how many more hours I could manage to sleep before having to face real life again.

But I couldn't avoid being awake forever. Surely that was a lesson I'd learned by now. Life wasn't always pleasant, but you couldn't hide from it. Not in sleep, not in the Link. And this was my last day to be with my friends. I didn't want to sleep through it.

I made a quick sandwich by tossing a protein patty and some sliced tomatoes between two pieces of fresh-baked bread. I looked back and forth between the two groups. I guessed, according to my vote last night, I should go sit by Ginni and Juan.

But then I looked over at the other group. Xona was watching me. Adrien sat on the other side of Cole.

Ginni came running up from behind me. "Come sit with us," she said, her voice falsely bright. I let her drag me over to the group sitting nearest the kitchen.

"They're a bunch of cowards," Juan said to the others sitting with him. "Too afraid to risk their own precious necks."

I sat down cross-legged and put my plate in my lap. I thought about what Xona had said to me in the plane. I wondered if she'd explained her reasoning to everyone, or if it wasn't common knowledge. I glanced over my shoulder at the other group. If that was the case, it wasn't my place to share what her brother had made her promise.

"And now Molla's out there all alone, probably terrified." Juan put down his half-eaten sandwich as if he wasn't hungry anymore.

"Molla won't be scared if she's under the Chancellor's compulsion," I said, hoping that offered a bizarre sort of comfort. "And maybe the Chancellor has kept them all together. Ginni said they're all in the same compound. Jilia would take care of Molla."

"I just can't believe the others voted not to go back for them," Juan said.

"I know!" Ginni piped in. "Especially Xona. It's her brother—"

"Don't judge her so harshly, Ginns," I said. "She's your friend."

Ginni didn't look mollified. "A friend who apparently would leave me behind to save herself without a second thought."

"You haven't spent your life on the run like she has," I said. "And as much as I don't like it, maybe she's right. What would an all-out assault on the Chancellor's personal compound accomplish except getting you killed or captured under her compulsion, and lost yourselves?"

"I could make sure the Chancellor was away when we attacked," Ginni said, speaking so quickly in her eagerness that her words tripped over one another. "With all our Gifts, Henk's stockade of weapons, and with *you*, we'd have a fighting chance at freeing them."

"But there's still so much that could go wrong—"

"Are you suddenly switching sides or something?" Ginni's eyes narrowed.

I munched on a bite of my sandwich before responding. "No, I'm on your side. But I'm also on Xona's. The three of us have become best friends, just like you hoped when we first became roommates." I put the bowl down. "I hate to see this come between you."

Ginni hesitated a moment, then spoke firmly. "As soon as she sees reason, I'd be happy to be her friend again."

My shoulders slumped. I guessed I couldn't fix everything before I left. But I still could have a moment of good-bye, even if I didn't tell Ginni that's what it was. I moved closer and hugged her hard. She hugged me back, always so quick to give affection, always so hungry to receive it.

"Love you, Ginns," I whispered into her frizzy hair.

She giggled. "Love you too, Zoe." She pulled back, then popped to her feet. "Now come on. Let's see if there's any sandwich makings left. I'm still *starved!*"

Throughout the next few hours, I tried to unobtrusively make the rounds to each of the people who'd become important to me over the past year and a half. I was careful not to spend too long with Xona, afraid she'd see right through me and know what I was planning.

And finally, there was only one person left to say good-bye to. Adrien.

I walked up to him as he washed dishes. All day he'd been volunteering for whatever tasks needed to be done. Folding laundry, even scrubbing the floors of the small square entryway room. I didn't know if he was avoiding me or just wanted to keep his hands busy. Either way, I was determined to talk to him before I left. It wouldn't mean anything to him, but it was a memory I wanted to take with me. Maybe it was selfish. I pursed my lips. Okay, it was definitely selfish. But that didn't stop me from joining him at the sink as he washed the last few dishes. I watched him in silence.

"If you need the sink," he said, not looking at me, "I'll be done in a few minutes."

"I don't need the sink." I took a step closer. "I want to talk to you."

He glanced up in surprise, then tensed his jaw and went back to scrubbing the last plate in the sink. "I'm busy. I told the others I'd gather up another round of laundry when I'm done here."

He dropped the dish in the drying rack and turned to go. I shot out a hand and grabbed his wrist. "I need to talk to you now." And then, even though I'd sworn to myself not to give away my plan, I couldn't help more words spilling out. "Look, after tomorrow you won't have to worry about seeing my face again." It wouldn't matter to him anyway. He wouldn't care enough to try to stop me.

His mouth dropped open in confusion, and he let me tug him toward the entryway room. It was as alone as we'd get in the packed bunker.

"What do you mean, I won't see your face after tomorrow?" he asked. Only a dim light-cell flickered overhead. Even though I could hear the hum of voices from the adjoining room, it felt quiet in the small entryway.

"I talked to Henk about dropping me somewhere away from you all. I don't want another earthquake leading the Chancellor here."

"Zoe, you can't!" His face took on a look of horror. "We didn't work so hard keeping you alive in the wilderness so you could go get yourself killed now—"

"I'll be fine," I interrupted him. *Stupid*, I chided myself. I shouldn't have said anything. "I'll have the portable med container, so I'll be able to sleep. I'll find somewhere safe to hole up." I hoped he couldn't read the lie in my face. I had far clearer plans about what I'd do once Henk dropped me off, but considering how upset Adrien was getting, I knew it was better he didn't know. "I just wanted to say good-bye." I looked down. "And that I love you. I'm so sorry everything turned out the way it did, but I couldn't leave without saying it this one last time. I love you."

I finally looked up, bracing myself for his mask of indifference. Instead what I saw shocked me. Anger. Fury even. "Stop saying that," he seethed through gritted teeth. He turned away from me suddenly, his chest heaving. "You don't love me. You loved *him*. How many times have I told you that he's gone!"

"Adrien." I reached out a hand to touch his shoulder, but he spun away as if my touch was charged with an electric shock.

I dropped my hands to my sides, balling them into fists to help myself keep it together. This was so much harder than I expected it to be. "I know that, Adrien. I know you're not the same as you used to be. I've gotten to know you as you are now. *You*, Adrien. And I love you."

He swung back around to me with tears that he kept violently trying to blink back. "It's not true. You look at me and see him."

I put a hand to his face with trembling fingers, knowing this might be the last time I touched him. "I see all of you," I whispered, meeting his eyes. "I know you don't feel it back, but it doesn't change how I feel. I love you."

His mouth opened and his eyebrows cinched together, as if he was somehow scared of me. "It can't be true." His voice was the barest of whispers. "Can it?"

Then, before I could respond, he'd pushed me back against the nearby wall and was kissing me. I was so stunned, I barely responded for a moment. But then I started kissing him just as fervently. My hands rose to his chest. I wasn't sure if I wanted to push him away or draw him closer. Questions tumbled over themselves in my mind. Was this really happening? Was it only hormones, his body reacting to mine somehow? Could I bear the pain of his indifference if it meant nothing to him?

But then he tangled his fingers in my hair, keeping my face close to his. He nestled his cheek against mine. "I don't know if I can believe it that you care for me, the real me I am now. But I love you, Zoe. I've loved you for so long."

I froze and he must have sensed me tense up from shock at his words.

He pulled back a few inches, his bright gray eyes searching mine. "Yours was the first face I saw when I began to come out of the fog. When I began to *feel* again. It was your hand clasped on mine. Your voice reverberating through my dreams, whispering soothing words."

My mouth dropped open. "But then why?" I finally whispered. "Why didn't you tell me? Why did you push me away? We could have had all these months together."

"Because you kept talking about *him*. Talking about your memories together. It hurt so much to have you look at me with love but know it wasn't for me. Emotions were new, and the hurt cut so deep." He shook his head, trapping my hand against his chest when I tried to pull it away.

"I couldn't bear it," he continued. "I tried to harden myself. Deny I felt anything for you at all. I tried to convince myself that love itself was illogical. That it made me weak." His voice was low and raw. "So I forced myself not to touch you when you came to visit every afternoon. I forced myself not to look in your eyes. I wanted so badly not to love you. I'd even half convinced myself I didn't.

"But then when we were out in the wilderness," his words were a rush now, "and the rendezvous site was burned and I knew you'd go into an allergy attack at any moment, all logic fled from my head. I had to save you. I didn't question the impulse, not till later. And then when I did, it was so clear to me what I'd been denying all along." His eyes met mine. "I love you, Zoe. Every incarnation of me will love you, even when this body is just bones and dust."

Each time he said the words *I love you*, a flutter went through my stomach like some long-dormant bird finally taking flight again. I could barely believe what he was saying.

His eyes glistened in the dim light. "That night in the cave, I let myself forget everything except the feel of you against me. But then morning came, and as much as it felt like ripping my heart out of my chest, I knew I still couldn't bear to live like that. With you looking at me with love in your eyes, but really seeing him. Even if it meant I could be with you, I couldn't do it." His face darkened and he looked down. "Because I didn't ever believe you could love me back. Not when I'm so much . . . *less*. Less than everything he was."

I freed my hand from his so that I could nudge his chin up and make him look at me. "Don't ever say that." My voice was thick with emotion. "You're different now, it's true. But not at all any less. When I visited you every afternoon, it didn't matter to me that you weren't exactly the same—how could you be after everything that happened to you? All I wanted was for you to look at me like you used to, like I meant something to you." My voice broke and I looked down. "Ever since I started glitching I've loved people who couldn't love me back—my brother, my parents. But it hurt worst of all when *you* didn't love me, because I knew how it felt to be loved by you." I looked back up at him.

He looked at me uncertainly. "I'm still not sure I believe you." But before he could second-guess it or start to pull away again, I went up on my tiptoes and pressed my lips to his. He kissed me back, hesitantly at first. But then his arms slowly wound around my waist, pulling me up and into him. Our heartbeats drummed madly against each others' chests. I closed my eyes and sank into him, not coming up for air until our heads bumped against the ceiling.

Adrien pulled back, laughing. My eyes popped open and I realized I'd lifted us right up off the ground. We bobbed by the ceiling but I didn't drop us down; I just threw my arms around his neck, hugging him so hard I was probably about to crack his ribs. He didn't complain, though, and held me to him with as much intensity.

"Say it again," I whispered in his ear.

He didn't ask what I meant. He pulled back and looked me straight in the eye. "I love you."

I couldn't think about the uncertain future or about all my reasons for leaving, which were still completely valid in spite of this revelation. All I could think about was the singing happiness of knowing that Adrien loved me.

I'd never felt more complete than in this moment, not in my entire life.

And then several loud *booms* shook the compound.

Chapter 23

I LOOKED AROUND IN CONFUSION and dropped Adrien and myself back to the ground. He seemed just as bewildered as he pulled me back into the main room. Everyone was on their feet, scrambling to figure out what was going on.

"She did it again!" City yelled, pointing at me. "We have to send her away! She's gonna get us all cracked."

I looked down at my hands, then at my body. It didn't feel like I'd released anything. "I don't think—" I started to say, right as the techer, who was scanning through console script faster than I could read it, shouted, "It wasn't Zoe doing it. Henk's jet just got fired on from overhead."

Henk pushed past several people to look at the console screen. The techer turned toward all of us.

"It's the external camera feed," the techer said.

A fire lit the screen, so bright I could only barely make out the smoldering remains of the jet. Two more transports were beside it, and we all watched in frozen attention as Regs poured out the sides.

"No," Henk whispered in disbelief.

"Everyone, get your emergency packs," Xona said. "We gotta run again."

"Run where?" City's voice was frantic. "There's only one way out—through the hatch, and that's right where the Regs are."

"Are there or are there not some badass glitchers here in this room?" Xona asked. "We make a path through."

"With the techer's help, I could probably fly one of the Reg transports if we could get to it," Cole said.

I nodded, running over to the hatch and projecting my telek up beyond it. Xona was right. If we couldn't take care of the Regs, no one would be safe.

Adrien and several others followed right behind me.

I closed my eyes. "There are twelve of them." The hulking Regs crept outwards from their transports in a search pattern, weapons at the ready. "I don't think they know where the entrance is."

"They must not know it's you either," Xona said, coming up behind us as she hefted a supply bag over her left shoulder. "Otherwise they'd have sent an armada. It's probably just the normal response team to anomalous activity caught on the Sat Cams."

"But what would they have even seen?" I hissed. "We've all been underground."

"Not all of us," City said. She glared at Henk. "He's been out there. Did you wear the coolant harness when you stumbled in last night?"

Henk opened his mouth to make a response, but then his face went ashen. "I can't remember."

"Why would they even be monitoring this area?" I asked.

"It's not a person. It's a humanoid-motion-recognition algorithm," the techer boy said. "The Sat Cam compiles an alert and sends the daily report to the nearest Guard stations, then they send out two transports to investigate."

City swore and spun away to get another supply pack.

"Can you drop them?" Xona whispered to me.

I nodded. Stretching up with my power like invisible fingers, I reached into the Regulators' bodies and counted down

the notched vertebrae in their spines. Snapping their necks at
the C2 vertebrae should keep them from dying, at least if someone did a spinal reattachment surgery in the next twenty-four
hours.

As they dropped to the ground, I felt sick to my stomach.
I'd accidentally killed Regs before by doing this. Underneath
the metal, they were men. Getting to know Cole had taught
me that clearly. But I couldn't risk the lives of my friends, and
at least these Regs had a chance now.

"It's done," I managed to say. City pushed past me and hurried up the ladder. Rand and Henk followed.

"Adrien, go next," I said.

He shook his head. "Not till you go."

"I'll be right behind you. And I'll be able to concentrate
better, knowing you're safe."

He reluctantly nodded and took off up the ladder.

I ran back into the main room.

"Come on!" Xona called out to us. "Ginni, let's go."

"We've gotta get Zoe's bed," Ginni said, trying to fold the
unwieldy plastic bed in half.

Cole and the Rez fighters grabbed two heavy packs each,
then lined up to climb up the ladder and out of the compound.

I turned to Ginni as she wrestled with the med container.
"It should self-collapse." I felt along the surface of the lid until
I found the right button. It began folding in on itself. Ginni
and I stepped back.

The bed finally finished and I picked up the heavy plastic
square, about as big as my chest. I gave it to Ginni. "Take it
and go."

I looked at Xona. "What else do we need?"

"My console station," the techer boy said. He pointed to the
big pile of console components, several heavy machines and a
mess of cables.

"What do you absolutely need?" I asked.

He stared at me as if it was obvious. "All of it."

I wasn't sure if that was true, but since he was the only chance to try contacting other Sectors, I said, "Fine." I lifted it all with my telek and tugged it along behind me as I ran back to the entryway.

"Careful!" the techer shouted. "There's some very sensitive equipment, you can't just—"

"Shut up and get up the ladder." Xona grabbed the boy and pushed him in front of her. He clutched two personal consoles to his chest and made his way awkwardly up the ladder. I sent the rest of his equipment up after him with my telek.

"Go, Ginni," I said. She, Xona, and I were the only ones left. "I'll push my bed up after you so you don't have to carry it."

"Hurry," Xona said. "We don't know if those Regs saw something before Zoe took them out. If they com'd in, more could be coming."

Ginni nodded and disappeared up the ladder. I sent the bed up after her. The wide rectangle barely fit through the circular hatch opening. Right as I edged it past the metal lip, a red burst above blinded me.

The roof suddenly began caving in. Big chunks of concrete and red dirt rained down on our heads as the tunnel collapsed on top of us. I threw my telek upward to catch the rubble before it crushed us.

Another transport must have arrived. I'd been so busy using my telek for other things, I hadn't thought to check if any more were coming. *Stupid.*

"Take my hand," I yelled to Xona. She took it, and I gritted my teeth as I lifted us up off the ground with my telek. I pushed the rubble up what was left of the chute and we followed it out.

Red dust swirled all around as I set us on the ground. Xona

coughed and covered her face. Even though it was late after-noon, I could only barely see a spiral of electricity shooting out of the end of City's fingertips through the thick cloud of dust. Rand stood beside her, his arms raised. I couldn't see exactly what they were doing, but no more laser rounds fired down at us.

Others crouched among the rocks. Someone was lying flat out on the ground, but I couldn't make out who it was.

I put my hand over my eyes and tried to look up. The trans-port was almost right on top of us now, a sleek round-edged triangle with three blazing propulsion modules on the bottom. It wasn't quiet like the antigravity models Henk designed. It roared like an ancient monster over our heads.

City's electricity wove around the entire thing in an inter-locking web. As the cloud of red dust billowed away, I could see part of the bottom was melting off. A huge hissing glob of metal dripped off and plunked to the ground right in front of us. I jumped backward.

City yelled something at Rand, but I couldn't hear it over the sound of the transport. I started reaching out with my telek to help them, but just as I did, the shadow around us became bigger. I looked up and saw the transport was dropping out of the sky. It looked graceful as it fell. Until it slammed into the earth with the rippling force of an earthquake.

Everyone still standing was knocked off their feet by it.

"Zoe!" Xona's voice called out. We'd gotten separated when I dropped her hand and ran toward Rand and City.

"I'm here, Xona!"

"There'll be Regs inside," she called.

Right. Of course there would be. Everything was happen-ing so quickly, there was barely time to avert one crisis before another one rose up in its place.

I cast my telek outwards. There were six Regs in this larger transport, half of them ripped out of their harnesses and collapsed on the floor from the crash. I hurriedly counted down their spines and snapped their necks at the C2 vertebrae right as a couple of them started to stir.

"It's clear," I called. "Cole and the techer, get in one of the Reg transports and see if you can get us flying."

"Rand," I turned to him, "start melting all these transports down, including what's left of Henk's jet. If we're lucky, any more that come to investigate will think the two molten piles are their own transports and assume we got away in the jet. Hopefully it can buy us some time."

Rand rubbed his hands together, smiling. "My pleasure."

"Everybody else!" I shouted. "Gather up. We're gonna take one of the Reg transports, and I'm not sure how much of the supplies will fit with us. Grab what you can carry." There were only six Regs in each transport, and we needed to fit in seventeen people. Granted, one Reg was as big as two normal people, but still it would be a tight fit. "Xona, can you start arranging people inside the transport with only the necessary rations?"

"Wait," the techer asked. "Where's Ginni?"

The question seemed to knock the breath out of me. I'd been barking orders only because I saw clearly what needed to be done, but he was right, where was she? Ginni had barely made it out of the hatch before the blast that caved in the bunker, and she must have been standing close by when it struck.

Oh on no. I ran over to the person I'd seen lying on the ground.

It was Ginni.

Midway down the shin of her left leg . . . was gone. Blood gushed from the wound, but not so much that I couldn't see the splintered bone where her leg had been severed, just inches below her knee. The techer haphazardly put his hands on the wound, trying to stop the blood.

"What do we do?" I yelled frantically, afraid he was only making it worse.

Henk pushed us both back. "We gotta stabilize her leg and get a tourniquet on it to stop the bleeding."

"Oh, Ginni!" I dropped down beside her and held her hand. All the composure I'd felt a moment ago evaporated. Henk ripped off his belt and wound it tight around her leg.

"Simin?" she called, her voice high-pitched and hysterical. "What happened?"

"I'm here," the techer said. "You're okay. You're gonna be all right."

"It hurts," she said in a shocked whimper. Her eyes were wide, shifting all over the place like she couldn't seem to figure out what was going on. "It hurts so much."

"We're gonna take care of you, don't you even worry a bit," I said. Though, looking around, I had no idea what on earth to do. Every minute we stayed here was another minute we made ourselves vulnerable. I tried to keep my face turned down, because I knew Sat Cams would be recording this whole exchange now. I couldn't let Bright see that it was me when they reviewed the vid feed.

I cast my telek up and outward, to make sure I sensed any more transports before they arrived. The sky was empty for as far as I could reach. Still, that didn't mean they weren't on their way. I looked back down at Ginni.

"I'll load her in the transport." I tried to harden my emotions. My voice trembled anyway. "Simin," I said, using the name Ginni had just whispered, "the best thing you can do for Ginni right now is figure out how to get us the hell out of here."

He nodded, his face pale.

"Go!" I shouted.

He finally turned and hurried into the transport.

I lifted Ginni as gently as I could with my telek, but she screamed out in pain as soon as I pulled her off the ground anyway. I moved her through the air as quickly as I could, then set her down on the cold metallic floor of the transport. The inside was even smaller than I'd feared. There were no seats in the back, just harnesses along the wall where the Regs strapped themselves in during transport. The techer and Cole were already at work on the console in the cockpit. I cleared out all of the fallen Regs, and the rest of the group piled in around Ginni.

"Where's the med kit?" I frantically pushed through the packs we'd brought. "We need the healing acceleration gel and some pain meds. She doesn't need to be awake for any of this."

"Here." Xona pulled a square med kit out of one of the bags. She popped it open.

"Wait," Adrien said, putting a hand on her arm to stop her as she lifted the pain relief infuser. "Ginni, is the Chancellor at the same location she was yesterday?"

"Stop it, Adrien," I said. "She's in pain. We'll figure it all out later—"

"No," he all but shouted. "We need to know now."

"Yes," Ginni wheezed out, her teeth gritted against the pain. "She's in the same place."

"We'll take care of her," Xona said to me. "Go find out why we aren't off the ground yet."

I nodded once and spun in the direction of the cockpit where Cole and the techer were arguing.

"I'm telling you, we've gotta disable the tracker first," Cole said. "Otherwise it doesn't matter how far away we go, they'll be able to follow us."

"And you aren't hearing me!" Simin yelled, his voice half hysterical. "We can't. It's attached to the transport's central processor. If we fry the tracker, we fry the transport. As in, no more flying, got it? We'll just be sitting here like a stone, and we have to get Ginni out of here—"

"Disable the tracker," I said. "There's no more time."

Simin let out a furious noise. "Did you not just hear what I said—"

"Do it!" I ordered. "I know a way to get us off the ground."

Simin huffed again, but he typed frantically on his console screen. "I can't break through the firewall to insert a virus. We need an overload of energy, but I don't have that kind of equipment here!"

I knew where we could get some. "City," I called. "We need you."

She came up to the cockpit. "Why aren't we off the ground yet? They'll be here any second."

"I need you to fry the engine, blow all the circuits. Can you do that?"

She smiled and placed her hand against the console. The space underneath her hand glowed slightly blue and within a few seconds I heard elements snapping and crackling. The smell of smoke filled the cabin. "It's done," she said.

"Great. Brilliant." The techer threw his hands up in the air. "We're now officially dead in the water. Now what's going to happen to Ginni?"

"Got all the transports and the jet melted down," Rand shouted from behind us. "I sure can't tell which ones were theirs and which was ours."

"Good job," I called over my shoulder. "Help everyone get strapped in as best as you can."

Simin got up to go check on Ginni and I sat down in his seat. I gripped the armrests, letting my mind expand. I'd never tried moving something this, well, *big*. In theory, it shouldn't be a problem . . . But in reality?

I let my telek push through my fingertips and imagined the

way I'd seen City's electricity web weave around the other transport. I did the same, but instead of electricity, I laid a web of energy. The projection cube burst to life in my mind and I could sense the entire transport and all seventeen bodies crammed inside. I memorized the feel of it, the slightly acrid smell of smoke in the air and the smooth texture of the steel armrest underneath my fingers. The back door clanged shut. Everyone was inside now.

And then I whispered, "*Up.*"

The people behind me let out surprised yelps and gasps, but I ignored them. I was entirely in my mind now, lifting the triangular object off the ground and up into the sky. Like I'd done when it had just been Adrien and me, I kept my mind's eye focused on the ground.

But the physics of flying a transport compared to moving two bodies was a very different thing. For one, the wind resistance was different. It caught the wings in ways I didn't expect and sent us tipping left and right. People screamed and yelped behind me. I bit down on my lip and compensated.

I tried to get a feel of how the wind worked. Right when I thought I'd gotten a handle on it, it would gust at strange times with another updraft.

After another few minutes, I'd gotten the basics down, at least enough to keep us mostly steady. "Henk, tell me you've got another transport hidden somewhere close."

"'Course I do." He came up behind me and put a hand on the back of my chair, staring out through the window. "Can't believe it. You just made a dead bird up and fly."

"I need you to direct me to the other transport. It won't take them long to realize what happened. The melted transports might throw them off for a little bit, and maybe if we're lucky they'll think we took off on foot. But I'm sure soon enough they'll go back to the Sat Cam logs and watch this one take off. They might already be tracking us."

He nodded beside me. He looked at the projected map the techer had set up on his personal console, depicting our position and altitude. "'Kay, you need to turn left, and head straight that way about a hundred miles."

I turned the vehicle slightly and hit another updraft that made the whole transport wobble for several long moments before I compensated.

"Too far," Henk said. "You gotta adjust back to the right a smidge."

I did, more gracefully this time, and then threw all my concentration into gathering speed. Finally the comments and terrified gasps behind me quieted. I hoped I wasn't banging Ginni around too roughly. I didn't dare a glance backwards to check. Sweat beaded on my forehead already. I couldn't split my focus in any more directions.

Henk and I kept at it, him giving me directions to nudge me one way or another until finally, only ten minutes later, I felt the landscape that had formerly stretched out flat in all directions begin to jut upward. I opened my eyes to look, because I didn't understand the topography I felt with my telek.

"You're taking us into a city?"

"Look closer," Henk said. "No one's lived there for a couple hundred years." As the transport drew closer, I saw what he meant. What I'd thought at first were normal buildings stretching up into the sky, I could now see were ruins. The whole city looked like it had been burned out. Half the ground was covered in rubble, the other half was made of buildings on the verge of collapse.

"What is this place?"

"Used to be a tourist destination in the Old World. It was one of the few cities that actually got hit with a bomb on

D-Day. Since it's out in the middle of the desert, it never got rebuilt. It's just been fallin' to bits since. Makes for a good hiding place though. Look," he said, and pointed to an area that was clear of debris. "Drop altitude and settle down in that flat bit o' ground down there. You see it?"

I nodded, then closed my eyes again. I needed to do more than see it.

"I feel it." I tried to decelerate the transport as gently as I could but still heard some *oof*s from behind me. I ignored them and set us down in the tall grasses that sprouted from the concrete.

"No time for restin'," Henk said. "We gotta get into the next transport fast or they'll be on us. It's not much roomier, but it's got cloaking. We'll be invisible as soon as we're off." He looked up into the sky as the others opened the back hatch. "Frankly I'm surprised we ain't seen no one yet."

Almost as soon as he'd said it, I felt them coming. "Two more transports are headed this way."

"If they get one good blast at us, we're all dead," Henk said.

That decided it then.

I cast my telek out, latching onto the transports as they blasted nearer. I thought about the beating hearts inside of the Regulators who had once been men. And then I pushed that thought away and, using their own momentum, yanked them off course. Their transports flew straight into the ground at full speed and exploded with an earth-shaking *boom*. I bit down hard on the inside of my check, trying to ignore the rush of emotions flooding me.

When Xona dropped the back hatch open, the air was warm and ashy from the exploded transports. Rand and Xona lifted Ginni down. Henk dropped after them, taking huge strides with his lanky legs and motioning us to follow. Simin hurried beside them, holding Ginni's hand while I searched the rest of the sky. It was clear. No one else was coming. Yet.

We ran down an alleyway between two teetering bombed-out buildings. The late-afternoon sun cast long shadows that covered the alley, and we had to be careful to avoid tripping over chunks of concrete and junk that had piled up on the ground.

"Is the new transport close?" Cole asked. "Next time they won't just send two investigative units. They'll send an armada."

"We'll be long gone by then," Henk said. He pushed ahead of us and then banged open a rusty door with his shoulder.

"Is this safe?" City asked.

Henk didn't respond, he just disappeared into the darkness beyond the door. I paused and let the others who were carrying Ginni pass.

We all hurried after Henk. The windows on the opposite side of the building had been blown out. Henk ran across the debris-strewn floor and led us to an old stairwell, blackened by fire and covered in dust.

"I've got Ginni," I said, grabbing her body and lifting her with my telek so we could all get up the stairs faster. We ran up the four flights and Cole helped Henk kick open another door.

And there it was. A pristine transport, perched on two slabs of concrete. The floor looked mostly solid, even though everything else in the room was demolished down to the steel girders. The walls were completely gone, open to the sky.

As we all hurried out onto the floor, the whole building above us creaked loudly.

"Shunting hell, Henk," City said. "Is this building even stable for us to be in?"

"'Course not," he said with a grin. "That's why it made

such a good hiding place for my flier. So walk lightly. Whole bloomin' thing's like to fall on top of your heads."

"Ignore him," I hissed. "Focus on the task at hand. Henk, get the rear door open."

The building overhead gave a long *creeeeeeeak*. Rand let out a high-pitched yelp of fear. If we weren't in such a life or death situation, I was sure City would have teased him about it mercilessly. But then the structure around us shuddered. The girders began to visibly vibrate.

"Everyone *in*," I yelled. I didn't know how Henk had managed to get a flier in through the narrow struts of the open wall, or if the floor was as steady as I'd first thought. Maybe when I'd crashed the incoming fliers, the vibrations had weakened the building more than it had been when Henk had first hidden the transport here.

Now if we could just get out again before the building collapsed on top of us.

Henk jumped to the front console. Adrien joined him since they both had the most experience flying. I helped everyone else in behind us, glad to relax into a hard metal seat for a moment. But I kept my telek split three ways between my mast cells, the building on top of us, and out into the air searching for more approaching fliers. I closed my eyes hard against the strain of trying to keep it all together in my head.

Xona strapped herself in beside me, and I looked at Ginni, lying on the floor. For a second, I let my eyes travel down to her stump leg.

"Is she gonna be okay?" I asked.

Xona pursed her lips and looked at the ceiling. "The bleeding in her leg stopped, so that's a good sign. And she's been out ever since we gave her the meds."

"Good." I leaned my head back against the hard wall of the transport. No lush comfort chairs here; this transport was all hard metal lines and chairs meant to efficiently pack in the greatest number of people.

I spared a glance toward the front. Henk was hunched over the console intently. He pushed a button and it roared to life beneath us. "All right," he said, raising the vehicle up off the ground.

But the transport bumped into the ceiling overhead accidently, and the building that had been only previously creaking in disagreement suddenly began to crack. The girders in front of us buckled, and loud popping noises sounded on all sides.

I tried to cast my telek out to hold it up, but the building was so *huge*.

"It's coming down on top of us!" City yelled, but Henk didn't flinch. He leaned hard on the maneuvering stick. The next second we were in motion, shooting out the side of the building right as we heard the huge roar of steel beams breaking. As we zoomed out into the night sky, I glanced back and saw the building crumbling in on itself, throwing off huge pluming clouds of dust and debris as it sank.

"Wow, Henk, you might as well have handed them a map and a written invitation," City said tightly.

"Won't matter," Henk said as the transport cut expertly through the sky. "Got the cloaking on, there'll be no trail to track."

I breathed out and relaxed my body into the hard seat. A few moments of reprieve. I'd been barking off orders like I knew what I was doing, and maybe at the time, I had. I shook my head and blinked hard. Had it finally happened then? I'd finally turned into a leader? Everyone had listened to me, even City. It felt unreal. I pinched my hands around the bottom of the chair until the sharp edge cut into my skin.

We were nowhere near safe. Would everyone keep looking

to me now? Could I do it? Maybe after a good night's rest, I'd feel more up to it—

My eyes flew open. I hadn't thought about it until now, but when that blast had hit the entrance to the compound, my med container had been destroyed too.

There would be no night's rest for me.

"Adrien," I called out. His head swiveled back from the front seat to look at me. I waved him over. "Come here, I need to ask you something."

He frowned and chewed on his lip a moment before unbuckling and making his way back to where I sat, stepping carefully over Ginni. He crouched in front of me since there were no open chairs nearby.

"You asked Ginni if the Chancellor was still at the same location. You think it's supposed to happen soon, don't you?"

He looked up at me, a tortured expression on his face. "Yes," he finally whispered. "But the Chancellor's always on the move. She could be gone by now."

I looked down at him sharply. "You don't really think so. You know my sleep container was destroyed. You know what that means." I saw in his eyes he knew exactly what it meant: I had to try now, before I was weakened again by several days of sleep deprivation.

"No." He put a hand on my leg. "There's every chance you'll not die. I just found you again. I lost my mom, I can't lose you too." He leaned forward and pulled me into a hug. He spoke into my ear. "We'll find another place to hide, find another oxy-safe med container. We'll hide out and be together." His voice was low and rough. "I don't care if the whole world crumbles so long as I have you."

It was what I wanted too. All that I wanted. But then I remembered another boy who'd asked that of me. It was what Max had always said, that the problems in the world were too big for us, small as we were, to make any difference against.

At the time, I'd been so sure that we still had to try and change it anyway, no matter what. The Chancellor had offered me something similar too—a place at her table with other glitchers in her employ, living safe with the people I loved while she ruled over all the drones.

And I'd asked myself the same question I did now: How could we, when so many others were suffering? How could we live happy and free when the rest of the world was enslaved?

But I'd been so young and naïve back in the beginning. I hadn't seen the world, hadn't yet experienced how crushingly difficult life could be. I hadn't known what a lucky and precious thing it was to have someone who loved you by your side, or how quickly you could lose them.

And now? The idea of going somewhere quiet, hiding out, having Adrien hold me every night . . .

I was so, so tempted.

But there was a chance I could make his first vision come true. I could kill the Chancellor and save my brother. It might not free everyone like I'd always hoped, but without her, the Rez could have a chance to rebuild. We could start rescuing glitchers again and try to come up with another plan to subvert the Link system that enslaved so many. If I survived.

"Right, then," I said. My throat felt suddenly dry. I looked around at all the faces of the people gathered around us. I knew what I had to do.

"No, Zoe," Adrien pleaded. "Don't."

"What?" Xona asked, looking back and forth between us. "I don't get it."

I clenched my jaw. "I'm going to go kill the Chancellor."

Chapter 24

"JUST DROP DOWN ANYWHERE, HENK. I can fly myself there."

Adrien turned away, as if he couldn't look at me. I steeled myself against all my riotous emotions. Surely he knew I wasn't rejecting *him*. This was something I had to do. Something I was maybe even destined to do.

"Zoe, we're on the other side of the Sector right now," Henk said. "At least let us fly you within a hundred miles so you can save your energy. We'll drop you then."

"And we'll stay nearby and wait for your signal," Cole said. "If you take out the Chancellor and there's no risk of us falling under her compulsion, the rest of us can move in. Ginni said the other glitchers are still there too, in the same compound."

I looked down at the unconscious girl. Ginni's chest moved up and down steadily. The laser had partially cauterized as it cut. As we all spoke, Xona worked with Simin to apply the gel that would disinfect and stimulate skin regrowth. A necessary part of every med kit when you lived in the Rez.

Cole continued. "If you're successful, then we can join you and—"

"But we voted," City objected. "We all agreed we wouldn't risk trying to rescue them."

"Well, I change my vote," Cole said.

Xona's head snapped to look at him. He put a hand on her shoulder. "You feel bound by your promise, but I know it's what you've wanted all along."

Xona stared at him a long moment. "That's that then," she said, taking his large hand in hers. "Now the vote is nine to eight in favor of rescuing the others."

"What?" City said, straightening in her seat. "There's still a bunch of us who don't want to. Rand." City spun to where he sat, nearest the back door. "Tell them. They can't do this."

Rand's forehead was scrunched up in thought. "We've got a chance now, Citz. If the other vision comes true . . . you know, the one where Zoe doesn't make it," he avoided my gaze, "then we won't move in. But if she does, then everything will be chaotic. And you and me can take on whatever security they got."

City's jaw tensed as she looked back and forth at all of us watching her. "Fine!" She sat back and crossed her arms. After a few more seconds, she said, "Well, I guess I haven't gotten to fry anyone in a while."

Simin finished wrapping up Ginni's leg with soft bandage, then wound adhesive tape gently around the bandage to keep it in place. His eyebrows knit together in concern as he looked down at her.

"Can someone give me the coordinates for where we're heading?" Henk called back over his shoulder from the cockpit.

Simin put a hand gently to Ginni's face, then stood and headed down the aisle to the front of the transport. I followed him to the cockpit. He pulled out a tiny box from his console bag, slid out a chip, and plugged it into the dash console. A projection cube immediately popped out. He flipped through several screens and a map rose with a pulsing red dot indicating the Chancellor's location. He zoomed in closer so I could see a Sat Image of the building.

Adrien's voice came from behind us, startling me. "That's the building I saw in my vision." I turned to look at him. His face was pale.

"All right." Henk swung the tip of the transport around and headed in the opposite direction. "The Chancellor's all the way in the east-most part of the Sector, along the seaboard. Should take a couple hours to get there, so rest up."

I went back and sat down. Everyone around me fidgeted in their seats. I could tell they were scared, but there was also a palpable adrenaline rush at the thought of heading into battle. Adrien looked at me from several seats down across the aisle, his face drawn in worry.

I forced myself to close my eyes so I couldn't see him. It was the only way I'd be able to mentally prepare myself for what I was about to do.

"Does anyone have a laser weapon?" I asked, opening my eyes ten minutes later. If the Chancellor was supposed to die by a laser weapon, I needed to have one.

Adrien stayed silent but reached into the pack at his feet and pulled a small weapon out. He handed it Amara, gesturing for her to hand it to me.

"Here," Xona said, leaning over and unclipping the holster at her ankle. "Take this so you can conceal it."

I nodded and took the holster, wrapping it around my own ankle. I'd seen Xona do it enough times, but my fingers still stumbled as I tried to click the small clasps along the side closed. I finally got it and slipped the weapon into it.

I sat back up, balling my hands anxiously into fists. There was nothing else to do but wait.

Last time I'd seen the Chancellor six months ago, she'd

crippled me with an allergy attack I'd barely survived and then she'd flown away in her transport before I could finish the job. Not this time. This time there would be no hesitation. She would die, and I would stand over her fallen body.

I'd have thought such an image would make me feel powerful . . . but all it felt like was relief. If I could kill her, finally I could live again without fear for myself and for my loved ones. I'd get my brother back and the Rez could re-build. We might have a real chance at trying to come up with an idea of how to free the drones without worrying about the Chancellor compelling Rez agents to tell her what we intended before we ever got a plan off the ground.

After another half hour, I noticed Adrien riffling through the bag at his feet again. His back seemed oddly stiff as he bent over to look through it. I wondered if he was angry at me. He'd said he loved me and asked me to go away with him. I'd said no. I hadn't meant it as a rebuff, but maybe that was how he'd taken it.

I unbuckled myself and walked down the small aisle to where he sat at the back. The small twin telepath boy, Jare, watched me as I went. He must be wondering if I'd be able to do what I'd said. If I could kill the Chancellor and free his brother.

"What're you looking for?" I asked Adrien when I got to him. There was an empty seat beside him, so I sat.

"Nothing," he said, still not looking at me.

"Oh." I didn't know what to say now that I was here. I took a deep breath. If I didn't . . . survive, I couldn't have our last words in this world be angry ones.

"Adrien—"

He surprised me by turning toward me and taking my hand. "I love you, Zoe," he said. "All I want is for you to be safe. You know that, don't you?"

I nodded. "I know. And I know you might not believe it right now, Adrien, but I love you too. This is just something I have to do."

He smiled and lifted a hand to my face, caressing my cheek. Then, to my surprise, he dropped his lips to mine. I knew everyone was watching, but I didn't care. I wrapped my arms up around his neck and his slipped around my waist, pulling me in tight. I wanted this one last moment with him.

For those few seconds, I let every other care and worry fall away. The touch of his lips lit me up like a spark of electricity tracing up and down my body. It was enough to consume all other thought.

But then I felt a sharp pain in my back. I gasped and pulled away from Adrien.

His face wasn't warm and loving anymore. It was completely blank. I twisted to look at what was wrong with my back, then screamed in pain. But not before I saw that there was a kitchen knife lodged hilt-deep below my kidney.

I pulled it out, blinking and looking at the small bloody knife in shock.

What—?

I turned back around just in time to see City raising her hands toward me. I felt the buildup of her electricity crackle in the air the instant before she released it.

Nothing made any sense, but I threw my telek outwards against her. If she let out that stream of electricity in the tiny metal-encased space of the transport, we'd all be dead. I tossed her backwards hard. Her head hit the wall with a sickening *thwack*.

I didn't have time to check if I'd overdone it, if I'd hurt her badly or even *killed* her on accident, because Rand and Cole had both launched themselves at me. Rand held his hand out toward me. I could already feel the heat pouring off him, and

I knew he was only just warming up. If he actually touched me, the burn would almost surely kill me.

I stopped them both midair and wrenched Rand's arm upwards instead of at me. The metal over our heads quickly turned red hot.

Everyone attacking me all at the same time could only mean one thing. The Chancellor. But she was still hundreds of miles away, how was she compelling them—

Suddenly we were all knocked off our feet as the transport dipped down, aiming straight at the ground. I fell hard into Cole, Juan, and Xona. My head banged into the metal of Cole's chest, but he'd been slammed into the back of the cockpit seat and for a moment was just as disoriented as I was, so he didn't renew his attack. Then again, he didn't really need to. In a few more seconds, we'd all be a pile of fiery wreckage, our bodies indistinguishable from the twisted remains of the transport.

I pushed myself off of Cole.

My mind spun as I tried to figure out what was going on. The Chancellor's power didn't extend more than a few city blocks, maybe a mile at most. How was this happening? How did she even know where we were?

I tried to grasp the transport with my telek, but we were dropping so fast, I couldn't seem to get a clear hold before it all spun out of my mind's grasp again. It didn't matter how it was happening. All that mattered was that I stopped us in time. But when I tried to move so I could grab the controls, I tumbled past Henk in the driver's chair and my backside smashed into the glass windshield at the front of the transport.

The reinforced windshield didn't crack, but I was woozy from the pain of hitting right where the knife had gone in.

The transport was spinning now as it fell, throwing me from one side of the dashboard to the other. I kicked Henk in the face accidently, and he let go of the transport controls all together. At the same time, Cole had reached up and ripped off the guide stick at its base. He lunged for me next, but I pushed him back with my telek.

I could see the ground now, closer every second. I closed my eyes, trying to ignore the screaming pain in my back, the nauseous sensation of spinning out of control, and the thought that this was my worst nightmare coming true—tumbling through the horrible open sky, empty space on all sides except for the unforgiving ground that was rushing up all too quickly to meet us.

I ground my teeth together. The projection cube blinked to life in my mind, and I hurled my telek outward until I was not only out of the chaotic cockpit, but was outside the transport too. The cube enlarged and I reached blindly for another surface to hold on to so I could orient myself. And there it spread out beneath us—the ground.

I braced myself against the earth with my telek and then felt out the spinning contours of the tiny transport falling through the huge unending sky. It was like a child's toy tossed through the air. I caught it and steadied it out until we stopped spinning.

It was the strangest sensation, because I could feel the momentum slowing in my outer body while simultaneously slowing the plane's fall in my mind. I couldn't think about the mind-twist of it though. I poured more energy into curbing our speed, slower and slower, until when we finally got to the ground, we landed gently on a grassy field.

Cole's metal-encrusted hand immediately reached toward me, but several of the others were clogging the entrance to the cockpit between us. He tossed them aside like they were no more than paper dolls.

I'd been chased by Regulators before. I knew they never stopped. I pressed my telek against the windshield and blew it outward. I tumbled through the hole I'd opened up and landed painfully on my side. I looked down. My tunic was covered in blood from the knife wound. I tried to get to my feet, but stumbled and fell back down again. I may have cast my mind out beyond the spinning plane while it was falling, but my body had felt every turbulent moment. I was so disoriented I could barely tell which way was up and which way was down. I tried to get to my feet and again crashed into the ground.

I let out a pitiful gasp as I looked at the downed transport. Cole was crawling through the hole I'd made in the window. He'd be on me in seconds.

No.

It couldn't end like this. Adrien's vision. I was supposed to at least have a chance to kill the Chancellor.

I abandoned trying to stand on my own and closed my eyes, pouring my energy into the only one of my senses that seemed to be working at the moment—my telek. I lifted my body up off the ground and into the air right as Cole got to the spot where I'd just been. He reached his arms up after me, almost catching the edge of my tunic. I flew higher right in time.

The others had opened the door of the transport and spilled out. City was one of them, grabbing her head and walking a few clumsy steps before collapsing to the ground again. A sweep of relief rushed through me. She looked like she'd be okay.

"Zoe, wait," Adrien called. "Stop! I'm sorry, I must have been under her control, but it's gone now. Come back, Zoe!"

I wanted to believe he was telling the truth. But I knew it was much more likely that these were just the Chancellor's words coming out his mouth. Trying to lure me back so they could attack me again. I pushed myself farther into the sky before City figured out how to use her electricity again.

My mind felt thick with cotton. I'd flown away from the

wreck as fast as I could, but now I wondered which direction I was heading. I thought about dropping back to the ground, but instead I pushed on. I lifted my left arm in front of my face and clicked through to the compass function on my arm panel, like I'd watched Adrien do so many times when we'd escaped the Foundation.

Okay, I was headed north. I tried to remember exactly where the Chancellor's facility had been located. It had been to the east, I knew that much. But I'd never be able to find it without the map. I slowed my momentum and finally stopped, not sure what to do.

I was weak and hurt, and if I tried to go kill the Chancellor now, there was a high chance I'd fail to even locate her. But if I didn't, there was no way I'd be able to find a safe place to sleep, and that was only if I didn't pass out from blood loss.

I had to try. The others were lost to her compulsion. I couldn't let it all be for nothing.

I wasn't sure if it was an actual decision so much as grim determination. I turned around and went back the way I'd come.

I didn't go close enough for anyone from the downed transport to see me. Just close enough so that I could feel the outline of the plane. I could sense the shapes of my friends, walking aimlessly in the field, looking upwards in the direction I'd flown away. The techer had pulled Ginni out of the transport and was checking her vitals. I prayed she was okay. She must have gotten tossed around like crazy during the tailspin.

I stayed behind the trees where they couldn't see me and cast my telek outward. I was able to focus enough to push through the broken window and down to the small drive plugged into the dash console. I was surprised it hadn't been knocked off in the fall. I tugged it out, then paused for a moment and reached through all the tossed contents in the back of the transport. I grabbed the healing gel and a roll of bandage wrap, then pulled all three items out through the window. I kept the objects hovering close to the ground before launching them up into the sky when they reached the tree line. No one even noticed the small bundle flying through the air. It sailed and landed in my hand.

I flew farther away again, wincing in pain as I lifted off the ground and set myself back down several miles away. I peeled up my bloody tunic and opened the tube of healing gel. I barely kept myself from crying out as I twisted around to apply the gel to the wound on my back. It wouldn't be able to heal the internal bleeding the knife had caused, but at least it would help the outer cut seal closed and scab up.

Then I opened the spool of bandage and wrapped it as tight as I could bear in several loops around my torso. When I'd bound the wound as well as I could, I dropped the roll to the ground and took several deep breaths. I felt a little lightheaded from blood loss, but there was no time to waste. The Chancellor had somehow compelled my team from far away, even though I still didn't know how she'd found us. She'd be sending a transport to pick them all up soon.

But Adrien had said the building where Ginni'd located the Chancellor was the same one he saw in his vision. She must still be there, or she'd be returning soon.

I steadied myself, then plugged the tiny drive into my arm port and watched the map appear in the glowing display. Now I knew where to go.

I took one moment to look over toward the trees that separated me from the jet. I was so close to Adrien. I couldn't leave him here, knowing he was under the Chancellor's control. Who knew what she might do to him? The last time she'd had him, she'd cut out part of his brain. But there was nowhere I could take him to be safe from her, I saw that now.

The only way to truly ensure his safety was to kill the Chancellor. I swallowed hard and lingered one moment longer. I imagined Adrien's comforting hand in mine and then launched myself up into the sky.

Chapter 25

I RACED TOWARD BATTLE WITH no army and already wounded. The odds were not on my side.

But there was my anger. That I still had, that I could cling to. Rage, fury, the hottest and brightest-burning of emotions. I fed them until wrath pulsed through my veins. It was different than the last few months when I'd been trying to swallow all my emotions down and make myself steel. I embraced the anger now and pulled it over myself like a mantle. It made me stronger.

My speed increased as I ticked off each wrong the Chancellor had done to me and to the ones I loved. She'd lobotomized Adrien, imprisoned Markan, killed who knew how many Rez fighters, and now was planning to implant adult V-chips in children. When I couldn't feed the anger anymore myself, I imagined the rage of centuries of people whose lives had been stolen from them by people just like the Chancellor. I carried millions of ghosts in my wake like a cape billowing out behind me.

The wind ripped at my hair, pulling it out of its braid and whipping it back in a mad rush of black curls. I pressed on, letting no more thoughts enter my head. I emptied myself out. I had never been so single-minded in my entire life.

And then I saw the ocean. It stretched out even vaster than the sky. I couldn't fathom all the crashing water that battered the coastline. I turned my thoughts from it and focused only on the building perched on a high hill that matched the blinking dot lighting up on my arm panel map.

The Chancellor's compound stood out like an ugly metallic sore against the beauty of the horizon. It was a long burnished steel rectangle, only two stories high but covering at least a quarter mile. I must not have been paying attention to the scale of the schematics the techer had shown us, because the building in front of me was far bigger than I'd expected. I flew toward it and let my rage expand even further.

As I neared, I sensed gun barrels click to life on the top ledges of the building. Both laser fire and projectile missiles streaked toward me. I banked and launched myself straight up into the sky, dodging the lasers and catching the other missiles midair with my telek. I forced them out to the sea and then rammed them into each other. The explosion created a huge fireball over the water. Next I ripped all the guns I could see off the building.

People began pouring out of the front doors. They were too small to be Regulators, which meant they had to be glitchers. I needed to disable them before they attacked me, but at the same time, any one of them could be my brother, Markan.

I remembered training with Tyryn. He'd always said the key to knocking someone out with one punch was the speed of the blow. I'd practiced tossing dummies against a pressure panel and had been confident at the time that it was a skill I could use whenever I needed it. But now, with adrenaline pumping through my veins and knowing that any one of the figures rushing out the door could be Markan, I was less sure.

I reached forward with my telek. As soon as I could feel the shape of their bodies, I threw them all headfirst into the metallic slabs that made up the outside of the building. Some stayed on the ground, out cold, but others got to their feet again.

More poured out the door. Even as ten bodies slumped to the ground, ten others replaced them. I felt the tingling that signaled an assault on my mind and threw the new wave of glitchers against the walls.

Still more came.

The next moment, laser fire blasted toward me from a second round of guns that had previously been hidden. I barely dodged the disorienting flashes of red, dropping low to the ground to escape the blasts.

I ripped the guns from the wall before they could get off another shot. I landed on my feet and ran a few steps so I could direct all my telek toward the building.

But before I could do a sweep to check for more weapons, a familiar figure held her arm out toward me, a blue orb in her hand.

It was Saminsa. She released the orb and I tried to jump up to fly out of the way. But the orb expanded as it went and I was blasted straight in the chest by the wave of blue energy. It knocked me sharply backward, disorienting my telek. I put out an arm to brace my fall but hit the ground so hard that I heard the crack of bones in my right forearm even before I felt the searing pain. I let out a deep howl of rage and looked back up.

Just in time to see a stream of fire burning toward me.

I tried to jump out of the way, but I wasn't fast enough. The fire caught the outer side of my left thigh. My pants and part of my tunic went up in flames.

I dropped to the ground and rolled several times to put the fire out. But not before it burned through my tunic and pants down to my skin. I screamed in pain, both from rolling over my broken arm and from the burns. I didn't look down to see how bad it was but the smell of charred skin filled my nose.

Somehow I had to ignore the excruciating wounds because I could see Saminsa gathering another orb. I lifted myself up into the air again to avoid another wave of fire while I focused in on her. Saminsa was a friend so I tried to be delicate; I reached into her body to look for the blood vessel to close off so she'd pass out easily. But she released the second orb before I could. It sent me spinning through the air end over end.

As soon as I'd righted myself, I saw the fire boy gearing up to send yet another stream at me. I was already half-delirious from pain. I couldn't handle getting burned again, so I did the first thing I could think of; I grabbed hold of his body and Saminsa's and slammed their heads together. They crumpled to the ground and I could only pray I hadn't hit them too hard.

A loud jarring noise exploded in my ears, disorienting me so that when I tried to stand, I only stumbled a few steps before falling to my knees again. I tried to look around for the explosion, but there was none, and I realized a second before another screeching sound hit that I felt the telltale tugging at my brain. Mind-workers.

I looked back up. I'd taken out everyone I could see, and no more were rushing out. But their power wouldn't be halted by walls any more than mine was. I reached forward with my telek, pushing past the flimsy barrier of the outer wall.

Just as I sensed a group of bodies huddled in a main corridor, I froze and toppled forward into the packed dirt. I hit the ground face-first. Blood gushed out of my nose and the burned side of my body was ground into the rocky dirt. My vision blurred from the pain. I tried to jump to my feet, but I couldn't get up, couldn't move at all. I was completely vulnerable, lying paralyzed in the middle of the open field in front of the building.

And then I started drowning. I gasped in panic but only swallowed more water. I coughed it out, only to have my throat fill back up again.

I tried to stay calm. This was part of their strategy. Assault me from enough angles and I'd be so distracted, I wouldn't catch the one attack that killed me. But every rational thought I managed was punctuated by another flicker of terror. I was drowning, I couldn't breathe! I squeezed my eyes shut and forced myself to ignore my panic.

I held my breath and searched the wall with my telek. My instincts had been right. More guns dropped from where they'd been hidden encased in the wall, taking aim at me. I ripped them off only seconds before they could fire at my prone body.

Still, when I tried to move again, I was as immobile as if I'd been wrapped head to toe in steel bands. I choked out the water in my mouth and managed another quick breath before my throat filled back up again. I didn't know if the water was real or just a hallucination, but if I didn't get more than half a breath soon, I'd pass out.

Worse, in addition to the jarring noises still blasting in my ears, I suddenly felt the prickle of a thousand crawling insects all over my body. I shuddered internally and counted to ten to calm down, in spite of my desperate need for air. I could hold my breath for a minute more, and my mind at least was still unbound.

I reached back into the building with teeth-grinding determination. I was done letting the Chancellor use these innocent people as weapons against me. Not to mention I was so battered, I didn't know how much longer I could keep this up. I let out a growl of anger as I sent the energy outward from my body. It passed easily through the wall and then into the thirty waiting bodies, knocking them backward.

It must have been enough to startle the mind-workers from their focus, because suddenly I could both move and breathe again. I took in a gulp of air and then jumped back off the ground, biting back a scream from the pain that lit up my body. I flew as fast as I could toward the main entrance. I could sense some of the bodies starting to move, so I reached in again, more surgically this time, pinching the blood vessels leading to their brains until they all passed out.

Then I moved on to the Regs lined up behind them, poised to attack in case the glitchers failed. Their standing in such orderly ranks was actually a help to me as I reached through each body, counted down their vertebrae, and all at once, snapped their spines where I knew they could survive until spinal reattachment surgery was done. They immediately toppled to the ground in a single wave. I flew through the doorway and over all the slumped bodies.

I wanted to stop so badly to see if Markan was among them. But I was exhausted and battered. Blood from my broken nose dripped into my mouth, the wound in my back had bled through the bandages, my right arm was broken, and the burns on my leg and torso screamed in pain with every move I made. Still, I had to keep going and find the Chancellor. I'd come this far and there was no going back. I cast my telek outward, hoping I could sense the shape of her body. Maybe now that I'd taken out most of the glitchers and Regs, she'd be easy to find. I dropped down to my feet and searched both the floors above and below with my telek.

And then my heart lurched in my chest.

There were hundreds upon hundreds of Regulators all around me. They filled the two elevators and all four stairwells, all heading to the ground floor with their heavy hydraulic-reinforced legs pounding out a terrifying rhythm.

In the seconds before they burst out the doors at the end of the long wide hallway, I felt the shape of the building in my mind. It went down six floors, so deep that my telek became too fuzzy along the edges to tell if the Chancellor was down there. Even if I sensed the shape of a body, what if she'd already escaped and simply left a body double behind?

I hadn't seen or heard any transports taking off, though, and she had to know she'd be a vulnerable target if she tried to escape like that. I could easily bring a transport crashing to the ground before she ever made it out of my telek range. No, she would have stayed here and burrowed deep into the ground like the snake that she was. She'd trust in her army to protect her. It was how she operated—compelling others to do the dangerous work in her stead so she never had to get her hands dirty.

Either way, there was no way I'd know for sure until I stood over her dead body, just as Adrien's vision foretold. I tried not to think about the other fork he'd seen, the one where she stood over me.

I snapped the cables on the elevators right before the doors opened and sent them tumbling down six stories. A loud crash echoed up the elevator tunnel right as the doors at the end of the corridor flew open. I could sense Regulators charging down the side hallways toward me from all sides of the maze-like central level. They'd make it to the main corridor where I stood in less than a minute. No more time for thinking.

I closed my eyes and reached out with my good arm as if to guide my mental aim at the Regs pouring from the stairwell in front of me. At first I tried counting down their spines like I had with the others. I took down ten that way, then twenty, then forty. The downed Regs clogged the doorway from the stairwell, but I could feel more and more in the other hallways coming for me. As soon as they rounded the corner, they'd have a clear shot.

There were too many. My breath came in and out in panicked gasps. I looked left and saw Regs make it around the corner and raise their laser-leaden arms. I only managed to avoid being hit straight in the chest by flinging a couple of downed Regs into the path of the oncoming fire.

There was no time to be delicate with the lives of the Regs attacking me anymore. So much was happening, I couldn't even spare the emotion to feel bad about it. I just started twisting their necks so hard a couple of heads came completely off. They thunked to the floor until they were kicked by the Regs charging by, like some macabre version of a children's ball game.

I swallowed down my horror at the gruesome sight and focused instead on disabling the attackers right as they turned the hallway corners and could get off a straight shot at me.

But while I was staving them off and piling up a mountain of bodies, I wasn't getting any closer to my goal. Splitting my focus in so many directions and using so much of my power at once was exhausting me quickly. A few moments here and there I even started to feel lightheaded from the pain and exertion. I couldn't keep this up forever. The stairwells were choked with Regs, there was no way I'd be able to get down that way.

Then I looked at the elevator doors right beside the stairwell. Of course. I could easily drop down the six-story opening and get to the Chancellor with only minimal obstruction.

If I could get to the elevators.

I simply didn't have enough left in me to keep taking out Regs from every direction simultaneously. I had to switch tactics if I was going to survive this.

I yanked ten of the fallen Regs closer and then held them shoulder to shoulder around me, creating a monstrous shield out of their dead bodies. I stacked up another layer of ten outside those, then let go of my focus on all the Regs coming at me from behind.

I heard laser fire start to rip into the bodies at my back. The armor coating the Regs had could withstand laser blasts only up to a certain point. But with enough concentrated fire, they'd start to disintegrate. I had to work quickly. I flew forward, making sure to keep my shield intact around me. With fewer targets to focus on, I was able to move faster down the long corridor. I reached the elevator doors and wrenched them open with my telek.

I leapt down the opening, letting my shield of dead Regs fall behind me. I dropped quickly and then slowed my speed. Shunt, I'd forgotten the elevator was still lodged in the bottom of the shaft from where I'd crashed it earlier. I was going to have to waste more energy getting through.

I could feel the Regs above me pushing through the open elevator doors. I took them out as quickly as I could, hoping I'd clog up the opening so no more could get through. But all I managed to do was send several Regs tumbling through the opening. I caught them right before they fell on top of me. The elevator doors from other levels were opening too, with more Regs leaning down to fire at me. I yanked them through as well, snapping their necks as they fell. I kept them suspended overhead, building another shield.

I tried to split my focus again to rip off the ceiling of the elevator below me. But I was already so depleted, the exertion sent a searing pain through my head. I roared in anger and pain and managed to tear away a small portion of the elevator's top. I quickly disabled the Regs who'd survived the fall, then dropped through the opening. The elevator was little more than a steel cage. The huge bodies of the fallen Regs covered every inch of ground. I was forced to step on top of them while I pushed the elevator door open.

As much as my body begged me to stop and rest, I forced myself to keep moving. My eyes stung and when I wiped at them, my hand came away covered in blood from a head wound I hadn't even realized I had. I blinked several times as black spots darted across my vision. I grabbed the doorway of the elevator to steady myself. The anger had drained out of ine. Grim determination was all I had left. I winced in pain as I dragged myself out of the elevator and into the small six-by-six-foot concrete entryway that led to a door of triple-layered reinforced steel. I could feel more Regs on the other side of the thick door, but thankfully, it didn't feel like many, only about forty.

Still, at this point, forty seemed like two hundred. I sagged against the concrete wall while I crushed, twisted, and snapped all of their necks until I finally felt no more movement. There were only two figures left standing, huddling at the end of the corridor beyond the door. I could tell by the shape of them that neither was a Reg. The Chancellor must be keeping a glitcher with her. I shuddered, knowing that if she kept a glitcher as a personal bodyguard, it wasn't anyone I wanted to face.

I tossed the smaller body against the wall and yanked the weapons out of the Chancellor's hands before I started working on the door. If I'd been at full strength, I could have ripped it off without a thought. As it was, I had to take almost half a minute pouring my telek outward and then yanking several times before it burst free.

I stepped through, careful to keep most of my weight on my unburned leg. The Chancellor cowered at the end of the small hallway, her eyes wide as she watched me approach. I froze her hand as she reached to push a button on the wall console behind her. She was probably trying to open the reinforced doors from the other stairwells so the Regs could come and save her. I kept her completely immobile. Being so close to my goal sent a surge of adrenaline through me.

I pulled the huge metal door behind me shut with my telek, lodging it slightly off kilter so any Regs who managed to make their way down here would have more difficulty getting it open again. It wouldn't stop them, of course. Nothing would stop a Reg on a mission. Even with the rush of adrenaline, my power was almost depleted; I wouldn't be able to hold them off.

But I'd have enough time to kill the Chancellor before they got through. After that, nothing mattered. I would die, but that had always been an inevitability, even if I'd never wanted to face it. After all, Adrien's vision hadn't extended beyond the moment he saw me standing over her. My mind was strangely calm now that I was here at the end of things. Without the Chancellor and her compulsion power to turn Rez operatives against their own comrades, the Rez could rebuild again in secret. Adrien would be safe. He'd find a way to survive.

Cole was always talking about redemption. Maybe this could be mine. Even if it didn't atone for all the people who'd been hurt or killed because of me—I thought of all the dead bodies piled up in the building above me—I could still hope that this sacrifice was one that mattered.

I turned to finally face the Chancellor. She stood against the far wall, her body still paralyzed by my control. I locked eyes with her as I limped forward, stepping around all the fallen Regs between us. Neither of us said a word. I stopped a few feet away from her. Without anyone to control with her power, she looked so small, so ridiculously impotent. Her cheeks were pale. Her hair that was normally slicked back so perfectly in a tight bun had come loose and hung across her face in stringy chunks.

I reached my telek fingers through her chest and lifted her up by her spine. The boy on the ground beside her was faced away from me, but he twitched as if in pain.

I looked back at the Chancellor, suspended in the air. I thought I'd feel some great rush during this moment—finally having her under *my* control. But all I felt was a weary determination to finish it. Just as I was about to snap her spine and be done with her forever, she screamed, "Stop! You cannot kill me without killing your brother!"

Her words brought me up short.

No.

The boy on the ground twisted again, and I could see his face as he blinked and slowly sat up, clutching his head.

Markan.

Chapter 26

"MARKAN?"

Could it really be him? I blinked hard, not trusting my eyes. This might be a hallucination. The person beside the Chancellor could just as well be a mind-worker as it could be my brother. She'd used one on me before, and I knew just how lifelike the hallucinations could feel.

I closed my eyes and felt out the contours of the boy in front of me. The details of the face matched exactly what I saw, the rounded nose and sharp cheekbones. He'd grown. I hadn't seen him in over a year. He'd been still so much a boy when I'd last seen him but now he was clearly edging toward manhood.

"We have to get you away from here!" I reached for him.

"Stay close to me," the Chancellor ordered and he remained unmoving on the ground. She laughed. I glared at her with hatred. She would not laugh for long.

I slammed her hard against the wall. Markan's body contorted and he screamed in pain, just like the Chancellor did.

"What I said was true," she said, looking at me through her stringy hair as she gasped for breath. "Another glitcher has an ability that has linked your brother's life thread with mine. If you kill me, you kill him. Will you have another brother's death on your conscience?"

It was a lie. I couldn't trust a thing she said. I tightened my hold on her and squeezed her throat shut so she couldn't spout more poison. She was so fragile. It would be nothing to snap her neck and watch the life drain out of her eyes. I cinched my grip tighter still. Her hands went to her throat and Markan's did the same. His eyes bulged wildly, and it made my heart stutter. The Chancellor could just be compelling him to act that way, I tried to reassure myself. Still I lessened my grip so she could breathe, and Markan's breathing seemed to ease as well.

"You're only saying that to save yourself!" I yelled at her. "You will die today for your crimes."

"Then you'll kill your brother as well," she wheezed out, her voice raspy from my earlier crushing grip. "And I will have a sweet death, knowing this will haunt you forever. You'll never know peace. The murder of both of your brothers will be on your head."

"Stop talking!" Doubt began to creep in. Because what if it wasn't a lie? Glitcher Gifts were all so varied, what if one of them *did* have the power she spoke of? I loosened my grip on her and lowered her to the ground.

The Chancellor, always so attuned to watching her manipulation at work, took advantage of it. "Markan, attack your sister. Kill her."

Markan pulled a laser weapon out of his boot and got to his feet.

"No!" I put up my hand, freezing them both where they stood. I ripped the gun out of his hand and flung it behind me. Now that Markan was standing, I could tell he'd gotten so much taller in the past year and a half since I'd last seen him. He was fourteen now, almost fifteen.

What was I going to do if what the Chancellor said was true? Adrenaline had carried me through the last few minutes, but it began to fade. I sagged against the wall as the pain throbbing in the background now came sharply to the forefront again.

The Chancellor eyed me critically. "You don't look so good, Zoe. I must admit, I am surprised you made it this far. I used the telepathic twin's connection with his brother to locate you on the transport. I was sure I'd be able to kill you then and there. But you've always had an uncanny ability to survive."

So that was how she'd found us. It was an oversight on our part. Thinking back, it was clear that we should have kept Jare sedated or at least blindfolded. But there was nothing we could do about it now. So many mistakes. Especially the most glaring mistake of all: not going back for my brother before it had all come to this.

"But it looks like it's all taken its toll," the Chancellor went on. She pointed at my blood-soaked tunic where Adrien had stabbed me and the blood still seeping from my head wound. "Just how much blood have you lost? Look at you. You're so exhausted you can barely stand on your own feet."

The pounding of the Regs battering against the wall behind us got louder.

"And listen to that." A cold grin etched itself on her face. "Seems like the Regulators are breaking through your paltry barriers. You won't be able to hold them off for much longer. In fact, I imagine you're going to pass out very soon." She leaned in and I immobilized her again with my telek. "Stop fighting it. If you give in now, I'll have Markan grant you a quick death. I promise that I'll spare the ones you love. I've already sent a transport to pick up your friends. They're on their way back here as we speak.

"What I told you all those months ago is still true," she went on. "All I want is a world in which glitchers rule according to their superior Gifts. There will be no more war. Let that thought bring you peace."

The screech of twisting metal made me snap my head around to look behind me, just in time to see Regs breaking through the door from the stairwell. My face scrunched up in pain as I held them back, snapping necks and crumpling their arm weapons before they could fire. Between keeping my brother and the Chancellor still, forcing my mast cells in check, and holding the wave of Regulators at bay, the last ounces of energy I had were fading quickly.

I looked back at the Chancellor, then over to my brother's face. I had to kill her. My brother was mindless under her control. Wasn't that in itself something like death? And even if it wasn't, surely the sacrifice of one boy's life was worth it to rid the world of the Chancellor forever. I had to harden myself against thinking of him as my brother. He was collateral damage, just like all the Regs I'd already killed today.

There was no other choice.

Tears poured out of my eyes as I again reached for the Chancellor's neck in a stranglehold. Her eyes widened in shock. She'd been so sure I wouldn't do anything to harm my own brother.

I wanted to close my eyes as Markan began to gasp like the Chancellor. But I couldn't. I watched my brother. His face, even changed as it was, was still so familiar to me. Memories rose up until I was tumbling through them: every morning sitting at the table with Markan, and how, after I'd started to glitch, I would sometimes sneak into his room to watch him sleeping. I'd always had an overwhelming urge to protect him.

And then there were the memories of my other brother. The one I'd betrayed as a child. He'd haunted my nightmares ever since. I'd called out his name to the Regulators and he'd gotten killed even though all he was trying to do was save me from the Community. Because he loved me. Yet here I was now, about to let another brother die.

Only this time I'd be actively murdering him.

Cole's words suddenly rang in my ears about hearts of stone

being turned into hearts of flesh. Could I really allow my last act on this earth, before my strength failed and the Regs stomped toward me, be the murder of my own brother? Would I let the Chancellor take this last bit of humanity away from me right at the end?

And I knew I couldn't do it.

I couldn't let Markan die even if I knew it meant damning the rest of the world to slavery. It was simply a thing I could not do. I thought of Xona's and Tyryn's promises to each other. Well, this was the thing that I had sworn. I'd sworn to protect Markan. It was my deepest promise to myself, the absolute truth that I'd built the rest of my life around after I'd started glitching: I would do everything in my power to save the lives of the people I loved.

The last of my rage seeped away and I was left broken. I released the Chancellor from my hold and she stumbled forward several steps. The cold smile grew on her face as she realized my decision.

I drank in each of Markan's features as he walked toward the laser weapon I'd pulled out of his hands earlier. His jaw had become more pronounced, his shoulders broader. He was becoming a man. I should have tried harder to get him out of the Community, should have done so many things differently. I felt the exhaustion of the past two days and every inch of pain from all my wounds. I was dizzy and lightheaded. This was it then. This was how it ended.

The Chancellor grinned wickedly. She'd won, and she knew it.

Markan was only a few steps away from the gun now. I didn't stop him. I inhaled several quick breaths as I fought to hold on to consciousness. Death had always seemed far away even though I'd come close so many times. But it had never been so certain before. One moment alive and thinking and breathing, and the next, a cold slump of a body on the ground.

But no, I couldn't think about that. It was life that I should be celebrating. Markan would live, and I believed the Chancellor would keep her promise to keep the others in my group alive. They had such valuable Gifts after all. It would be in her best interest to keep them safe.

Markan's fingers closed around the gun.

But then suddenly a burning red light erupted from the center of the Chancellor's chest. Laser fire. The Chancellor fell to her knees and looked down in disbelief as the red stream cut off. It had blasted a fist-sized hole through her chest.

"No!" I shouted, not understanding what was happening. I looked back at my brother, terrified I'd find a similar hole through his chest, but he was unharmed. He did not crumple to the ground. He didn't even look like he was in pain.

The Chancellor *had* been lying after all. Their lives had never been linked.

My eyes flew back to her. She blinked and her body twitched a couple times. Blood gurgled up out of her mouth.

Then another burst of light came from beside me. Markan had fired his weapon, but not at me. At first I thought it had been him who'd killed the Chancellor somehow and now he was firing at her again, though I could have sworn he hadn't even had his arm raised at the time.

But when I looked back at the Chancellor, suddenly it all became clear.

A body materialized behind her, covered in blood.

"Max!" I screamed.

My brother's weapon had sliced Max across the lower part of his abdomen, completely severing the top half of his body from the bottom. It must have been the Chancellor's last command to Markan before she died—to kill the person who had killed her.

I ran over and dropped down beside Max. He'd been invisible, but she must have still figured out that her attacker was right behind her. Markan dropped the laser weapon the next second, stepping back in confusion. "Zoe?" he asked in a small voice from behind me.

I ignored him and tried to use my telek to keep Max's blood from pumping out of his body all over the floor. The laser had cauterized as it cut, which helped, but not enough to stop some of the largest blood vessels. Max gasped in shock, his eyes open wide.

"Max, hold on," I said desperately. "Just hold on, we'll get you fixed up." But even as I said it, I wasn't sure it was true. Blood spread in a pool where his body was sliced in half. I clamped as many arteries shut as I could, but he'd already lost so much blood in the few moments it had taken me to realize what was happening.

I just had to get him back together again. I tugged the bottom half of his body over with my telek and tried to line it up with the top half like a gruesome puzzle. Then I threw my mind forward until I was lost in the mass of tissue and vessels, trying to knit them back together with my power.

But I didn't know how, and there was just so *much*. I was already pulling on vapors at the end of my power reserve to keep the Regs back. Maybe if I got the important vessels—

"Zoe," Max rasped out.

I kept working, trying desperately to fix him. I bent over him as if proximity alone would help. My brother and I were alive, and Max was alive, and if I just fought a little harder . . . One of my tears splattered on his cheek. "Max, you stay with me—"

"Zoe . . ." He coughed and blood spurted from his mouth.

"Shh, Max, don't try to talk!" I whispered. I lined up his spine and matched several large blood vessels, holding them flush together and trying to force blood through them.

Max looked up at me, his face pale and his eyes glassy. I'd barely studied human anatomy, I didn't know what I was doing, but I kept trying to work my way through the material of his body.

"I told you . . . I could be . . ." he rasped out, pausing with another choking fit and then continuing, ". . . a better man. I came to kill her. Keep you safe. But couldn't get inside till you came. Followed, but so many Regs . . ." He expelled a long breath. Talking was taking every last ounce of strength, I could see it.

"Stop talking. You can tell me all about it later. You're going to be fine, Max," I said, still working as fast as I could. But my control was slipping. Several arteries I'd clamped off had pulled back open again. There was so much blood on the ground already. Too much.

"I'm not," he said, his eyelids fluttering weakly.

He was right, of course. I finally stopped trying to piece him back together and just held everything in place for as long as I could. Even with all my power, there was no way. The pool of blood I sat in grew larger every second. Sobs wracked my chest as I took his face in my hands.

"You are a good man," I said. "I always knew you could be."

His eyelids fluttered again, and I could tell he was fighting to hold on a few more moments.

"So you . . . forgive . . . me?" he gasped out, only a whisper.

"Yes." I nodded my head furiously. "I forgive you."

"I love you," he said with his last breath, and then he stilled. The eyes that had been so full of life and always chasing after more were now horribly vacant.

I crumpled, sobbing into his unmoving chest. I'd been so

angry with him for so long. I'd hated him for the things he'd done. But he'd been telling the truth the last few months. He, like me, had been searching for redemption.

And he'd come here. He hadn't run away to save himself like we'd all assumed. He'd been practicing expanding his power so that he was totally and completely invisible to people with powers like mine . . . and the Chancellor's. Her compulsion hinged on her ability to sense the minds of those near her. Max must have become so proficient that he could make himself invisible not only from sight, but also from mind.

But even he couldn't sneak through locked doors. He must have followed me in, but had to hang back. It was *his* decision to come here that had been the hinge of Adrien's vision.

I wiped my eyes, smearing Max's blood on my cheek. He was my first friend, and I'd always felt he was part of my true family. That had never meant much to him; he'd always wanted more. But there were times when it had been everything to me.

I sat back against the wall, exhausted and dizzy. For a second my telek blinked out and I could feel my throat start to swell shut. My eyes shot open again. It took me a few gasping moments before I managed to eke out a little more power to keep my mast cells intact. But my hold was wavering. I'd taken out enough of the Regs that they piled up in the doorway and for about ten more feet beyond. I couldn't even imagine how Max had managed to sneak his way through them.

I could feel other Regs pulling away the crumpled bodies, cutting their way through. I wouldn't last much longer. I turned my eyes back toward my brother.

"Markan," I said. He still stood frozen where he'd fired the weapon. He hadn't moved the entire time, he'd just watched everything with his face contorted in confusion. I waved him over. Halting, almost hesitating, he made his way toward me.

"You don't know how good it is to see that you're safe." More tears ran down my cheeks. I wasn't sure I'd be able to stand up, so I dragged myself across the ground away from Max's body toward Markan. "I've thought about you so much all year, wondering if you were okay. I'm sorry I didn't come back for you. I should have, no matter what."

He stepped back and watched me like I was an animal about to bite him.

"I won't hurt you," I said. I stopped crawling and rested my back against the wall. I probably looked terrifying crawling across the floor, covered in Max's blood. And who knew what lies the Chancellor had filled his head with? Or maybe she hadn't even bothered. Maybe she'd compelled him constantly, giving him no room to think for himself at all. It was more her style.

After a few more seconds, he nodded and sat down beside me. I reached forward and hugged him hard with my good arm.

The second I touched his skin, though, I yelped in surprise. The dim buzzing of my telek became instantly as loud as a howling screech. I expanded beyond the room, beyond the compound, and then for miles and miles around until I was reeling from the flood of information. I could feel the long coast stretching on in both directions, and the miles of trees and hills behind me that eventually became mountains. Then there were the cities full of people. So many souls squirming in bodies like ants in an ant pile.

Markan pulled away abruptly and stood up. "You just want to use me like she did."

My heart beat rapidly at the shock of being encapsulated back in my body again. He backed away from me.

"What *was* that?" I asked, astonished.

"You don't know?" He sounded cautious.

I shook my head.

"It's my power." He nodded toward the Chancellor with an infuriated look. "She called me an Amplifier. She kept me with her all the time. Always with her cold hand locked around my wrist." He shuddered.

I stared at him in astounded shock. So that was how she'd been able to compel my team from hundreds of miles away. And how she'd cracked so many Rez cells so quickly over the past few months.

"It's okay," I said. "She can't use you anymore. I just wanted to hug you. It's what I've wanted for so long."

"Everything feels . . ." He looked around at the blood and the bodies on the floor before looking back at me with a face as bewildered as a child's. "So *much*."

My heart broke as I watched him. He hadn't had time to sort through all the emotions that came with glitching, that was clear. He'd never had the chance. The Chancellor must have pounced on him almost as soon as he started showing anomalies.

The noises beyond the clogged-up door were louder now. The rest of the Regs would be here any moment. I was barely keeping my mast cells in check. I wouldn't be able to stop them. My head drooped against my chest. Markan stood a few feet away from me, still looking disoriented.

"Move to the other side of the room," I said, gesturing with my good arm. "Stand straight against the wall. Don't panic when they come in. They won't have kill orders for you. You're gonna be just fine."

"But—" he started. There was no chance for him to finish. Several Regs had pushed through the blockade. I tried to send my telek toward them, but I absolutely had nothing left now. I was only managing to pull on the tiniest thread to ward off an allergy attack, and that was all I could do.

They raised their forearms, weapons gleaming in the stark overhead lights.

"Shut your eyes!" I shouted to Markan. "Don't watch!" I didn't want him to have memories that turned to nightmares like I'd had of watching our older brother die in front of me.

Then I shut my own eyes and waited for the blasts to slice through me. If they aimed for my head, it would be a quick enough death.

One second passed. Then another.

Was I dead? Had it happened so quickly that I hadn't even realized I'd shed my mortal body and now my soul was going wherever it was that souls went? But no, I still felt the pain in my back and thigh. I peeked one eye open.

The Regulators had stopped their assault. They stood halfway in the room, their eyes full of wonder, with strange awed smiles on their faces.

It was such an incongruous expression paired with their weapon-encrusted arms, for a second I could only stare.

Then I heard a voice. "Zoe! Are you down there?"

Adrien. It was Adrien's voice.

"We're here!" I shouted back, still staring at the Regs in confusion. Then it hit me. The team was here. And Amara was with them. She must have cast her web of bliss over the Regulators. I almost laughed at the absurdity of it. She'd overcome these programmed killing machines by giving them an overwhelming taste of joy.

"Zoe! Where are you?"

"Bottom floor," I shouted back. I hauled my exhausted body off the ground and went over to my brother. My legs were weak, but knowing Adrien was close gave me one last burst of strength. Markan looked more confused than ever. I reached toward him and took his covered elbow so he would know I wasn't trying to touch him for his power.

"Come on," I said, laughing with relief and a sudden giddiness. The Chancellor was dead. Help was here. We'd won. I led Markan forward and together we moved through the smiling Regs, closer and closer to the stairwell door.

"Zoe?" Adrien called again, his voice closer now.

"Here!" I shouted back.

We finally got to the threshold of the door. Adrien hurried down the steps, elbowing his way past Regulators. I did the same and we met at the bottom of the stairs. He threw his arms around me and lifted me up off the ground in a giant hug.

"Ow," I said, laughing even though it hurt. I couldn't believe he was here. That I was here. That I'd *survived*.

He immediately put me back on the ground. "I'm so sorry I stabbed you. She took over and I couldn't stop it." He pulled back and finally got a good look at me. His eyes widened in fear as he took in my blood-soaked clothes. "Oh my god, Zoe, what happened?"

"It's okay," I said, lifting my hands to his face for a brief moment as if to make sure he was real. "It's okay, I'm safe now. Most of it is Max's blood. He didn't make it." A wave of grief swept over me again, but I tried to swallow it back. There would be time for grieving later. "And there's someone I'd like you to meet." I gestured behind me for Markan to come forward. "This is my brother."

Adrien nodded a greeting to Markan. "And the Chancellor?"

"Dead." Now that it was all over, the exhaustion was getting the better of me. My legs gave out, and Adrien only barely caught me before I hit the ground.

He spoke into his arm com. "Ginni, have you found Jilia yet?"

Ginni's voice responded. "Yes, in one of the cells on sublevel four. Rand is melting the door open as we speak."

"Get her to the top of the stairs. Zoe's in bad shape. Xona,

Juan, see if you can find an infirmary or anything that might have some epi so she can sleep safely."

Adrien swept me up in his arms and started to head back up the stairs. I looked over his shoulder and waved at Markan to follow us. We threaded our way slowly through all the still blissed-out Regulators and continued up the stairs.

Pain radiated through my body with each jarring step. I could feel myself on the edge of consciousness.

"Adrien." My voice must have radiated my fear, because he started going faster. And then, right when I was sure I couldn't handle another step, sure I was going to pass out from exhaustion and pain, we stopped and came into the larger open space of the ground floor.

When we got there, Jilia was waiting. She immediately rushed forward. Adrien laid me on the ground, gently maneuvering me to my side and pulling away the bandage so Jilia could see my back wound. Then her calm, cool hands were on me.

I winced and let out a small yelp. Her touch stung at first, but then the pain lessened and lessened, until I could barely feel it at all. Adrien eased me onto my now-healed back and rested my head in his lap. Jilia moved on to my burned thigh, then to my broken arm, knitting the bone back together, and finally to the wound on my forehead. I sagged back against Adrien once she was finished, the pain only a dull soreness.

He and Jilia stripped off my dirty, bloody clothes, and helped me into a clean tunic Jilia had brought from the prisoner's quarters. I was too exhausted to be embarrassed. Once I was changed, Adrien cradled me against him.

I heard other footsteps come into the room, but couldn't stop staring up at Adrien's face. It all still felt surreal, like a dream. He looked at the others who'd come in. "Did you find any epi?"

I finally dragged my gaze over where he was looking.

"No," Xona said, "but we found something better." Rand, standing beside her, held up a silver box. "Tyryn was in the cell beside Jilia, and he said he thought the Regs had brought all the gear from their crashed pod back when they took them prisoner. We broke into storage and found it all. Including one med container in perfect condition."

Adrien leapt up and within moments they'd set it up. Xona helped me stand up and get me situated in the box.

"There's so much to tell you all," I mumbled tiredly.

"It can wait," Adrien said firmly.

"But—"

He took my face in both his hands and leaned down to plant the gentlest kiss on my lips. "You are worn-out and broken and battered, and I can see you're about to pass out any second now. So do it someplace safe, here in the med container." He planted another whisper-soft kiss before pulling back. "I love you, Zoe. Now go to sleep."

He clicked the lid closed and, in spite of myself, I settled back onto the inflated pillow. I made sure to stay awake long enough for the vacuum process to finish clearing all the allergens out of the space and start pumping in fresh oxygen, but within a few breaths after the beep signaled the air was clear, I was fast asleep.

Chapter 27

I SHIFTED, SLOWLY WAKING UP and blinking my eyes blearily at the insistent knocking on the top of my sleep pod. Then I remembered where I was and all that had happened. My eyes snapped open. I poured my telek inward to control my mast cells, then popped open the top lid of the container. Adrien was there, reaching out a hand to help me stand. I was sore and stiff, but overall felt remarkably better.

"What is it?" I asked. "What's going on?"

"Everything's fine," Adrien reassured me as I stepped out of the container. "But we need to decide what to do next."

I looked around. When I'd gone to sleep, the central room had been littered with Reg bodies. Now it was clear.

"How long was I asleep?" I turned to Adrien with a frown.

"Twenty-four hours. Come on, everyone's in the dining area." I followed him as he led me across the sleek black floor and down one of the hallways.

"What did you do with all the Regs?" I asked, my voice subdued. I didn't know how I was going to look Cole in the face after what I'd done.

"Cole and Xona have been clearing the dead out all day. Simin was able to hack into the Chancellor's control console, so he's been feeding new instructions to the rest of the Regs so they didn't start attacking us once Amara got tired. But it only works for the Regs who were here under the Chancellor's personal guard."

"And Markan?"

"He's fine." Adrien squeezed my hand. "He told us what happened with the Chancellor . . . and with Max."

I took a deep breath in and out. I had to keep it together. As much as I might want to go curl up in my sleeping container and forget the world, people would be looking to me for leadership. And I could tell there was more Adrien wasn't saying yet. He was tense.

"Adrien, what's really going on?"

He nodded toward the doorway ahead. "Everyone will want to talk about it at the same time."

Now he really had me worried. I went into the room and saw a crowd gathered inside, locked in a tense discussion.

I straightened my back and tried to exude a strength I didn't feel as I strode to the center table. "Okay," I said, working to make my voice sound confident. "What's the situation?"

Juan moved out of his chair and offered it to me. I sat down, and looked around the table at Tyryn, Jilia, Xona, Henk, and some of the other glitchers on my team. I was relieved to see that those who had been captured by the Chancellor didn't look any worse for wear. Markan sat at a nearby table, his expression less fearful and suspicious than it had been yesterday. I barely managed to stop myself from going over and hugging him.

Xona spoke up first. "We're under attack. The Chancellor sent an alarm signal when you breached the walls. Saminsa's keeping the armada back with a huge protective sphere surrounding the whole building. But City was just out there with her." She turned to City. "What's the latest report?"

"We've rallied the other glitchers who are willing to work with us voluntarily," City said. "They've been working with Rand and me to take out attack transports all night. But

Saminsa's getting tired. She won't be able to hold the shield for much longer. Especially now that they've moved into high-payload missiles."

I jumped to my feet. "I need to go out there. I can take down transports with my telek—"

Adrien put a hand on my arm. "We agree, but first we wanted to have a meeting to figure out what our next step is. We can't just stay here under siege forever. Saminsa will be fine for a while longer until we get a game plan together."

I sat down. He was right. "So what's our next move?"

"That's what we've been talking about—" Adrien started.

Xona snorted. "You mean arguing about."

"What are the options you've come up with?" I asked.

Henk spoke up first. "I say we oughta bug out of here. We can keep the transports busy long enough to escape. The Chancellor has three attack transports of her own in the back bay. We can escape with those. We'll split everyone up and all head in different directions. Without the Chancellor around, we'll finally be able to go to ground and start rebuilding the Rez from scratch."

"And I say we need to stand and fight," Xona said. "Guerilla warfare has gotten us nowhere in the past two centuries. The Rez is all but wiped off the map at this point. We've got an army of glitchers at our command. We ought to take those transports and attack Central City. If we take out the heart of the government, we have a chance to finally start the revolution we've always dreamed about. We can hit a few key focalized areas where Zoe can crush drone V-chips so they can fight with us. Starting with the academies right outside Central City."

"All that's accomplished in the past is to get the people she freed killed within a day," Henk said.

Xona was undeterred. "But that was before. Now we'll be there to back them up militarily. What's your range up to, Zoe? How many chips do you think you can take out at once?"

My mouth popped open as everyone's gaze swung to look at me. For once I didn't feel out of my depth. I knew exactly what we needed to do.

I glanced over at Markan. He was looking on with interest. He must have been watching everyone for the past twenty-four hours. He'd gotten a glimpse of the Rez at work. Hopefully it was enough to convince him to help us.

"I have a plan," I said, "but first I need to talk to my brother."

An hour later, I sat in the attack transport behind Henk with my brother and Lundris, a boy Adrien had found among the glitchers as he was taking his meticulous survey of their powers. Lundris was short and blond, and couldn't be more than fifteen. He sat quietly in the seat by the window, awaiting instructions. Adrien said he'd had a vision of our mission and that it was imperative that Lundris came with us.

I looked over at Markan. "Are you sure you're ready for this?"

His eyes were wide, but he nodded anyway.

"And you?" I asked Lundris.

Lundris sat straight in his chair, still used to the posture required in the Community. He met my eyes. "You freed me from the woman who took my mind away from me. I will follow you."

"Ready to lift off," Henk said. He looked back at us, a grin on his face. "Alrighty. Let me know when you've cleared a path, Zoe."

I nodded, feeling nerves twist up in my stomach. I reached out a hand to my brother. He swallowed hard, but then took it.

Immediately I was bowled over by all the information and data assaulting my mind. What had begun as a small projection cube in my head suddenly exploded outward, flooding to encompass the entire building, then the fields full of attack transports surrounding us, then out to the shore and ocean beyond. To the west, my reach extended hundreds of miles inland.

Panic bubbled up. It was so much information. I grabbed my head with the hand that wasn't clutching Markan's. But after a few calming breaths, I was able to let all the data saturate my mind. In a way, it was exhilarating. I was spread out so far. I could sense so many things. Humans, machinery, trees, the ocean, tiny animals scampering across the ground. Hundreds of thousands of heartbeats all thrumming out a strange syncopated rhythm. For several moments I just lost myself in it.

Then I tried to ground myself again. It was easier when I focused in on concrete objects. I plucked all the transports surrounding the Chancellor's compound right out of the air as if they were no more than gnats. There were about fifty of them. I swung them through the air, crumpling the large propulsion modules along the bottom in on themselves. Then I flung them through the sky several miles into the ocean.

Next, I tried to filter through all the information and focus only on the humans. I used their heartbeats to help me key in on them. In a way, it wasn't that different from what I did with my mast cells every day. I'd learned to differentiate mast cells from amongst all the other billions of cells. I could do the same to identify people. Once I'd grabbed hold of all the human shapes in range, I let myself drift up from their pumping hearts to their brains. I grimaced, biting hard on the inside of my cheek. I could not let all the sensory data overwhelm me. I *had* to make this work.

There. I zoomed in through the soft putty of brain matter and finally could feel the contours of the hardware inside the hundreds of thousands of heads. I'd long ago studied and gotten familiar with the differences between the bigger adult

V-chip with its snaking metal filaments connecting to places all over the brain, and the pre-eighteen chips, which were much smaller and had less invasive wirework to allow for normal brain development. Most of those with the smaller V-chips were all clustered together. It made sense. They'd be together in their various Academies at this hour in the day. That was good. They'd have strength in numbers once I freed them.

I sifted through those in my search radius and let go of everyone with the larger V-chip. Then, anchoring myself in all the smaller V-chips left, I squeezed Markan's hand tighter and pushed the radius out even farther. There were millions now. Millions of thumping hearts and millions of V-chips. I sorted through and again latched on to those with the smaller hardware.

Finally, when I felt like my head was going to split wide open from being pulled in so many directions, I took one last deep, calming breath, then crushed the smaller V-chips all at once. Almost immediately, chaos erupted as the previously staid groups of people began to respond to their crushed hardware. They were all seeing color for the first time, all beginning to feel emotions at once. I couldn't let myself imagine what they would be going through over the next few days.

These people were only the beginning. I slowly pulled my energy back into myself and then let go of Markan's hand. I thought I'd feel an extreme exhaustion as soon as I lost connection with him, but to my surprise, I felt fine. It was as if the power I used while connected to him sapped only as much strength as it did when I was on my own in my normal smaller sphere of control.

I blinked my eyes open. Henk and Markan were both watching me.

"It's begun," I said. I grabbed Markan's hand again. Henk

turned back to his controls and we lifted off the ground and flew out of the wide bay. Saminsa's bright blue shield vibrated in front of us as we approached the perimeter.

Henk spoke into his arm com. "Release it, Saminsa."

The blue orb suddenly exploded outward, dissipating as it went. There were no more transports in range, so everyone still in the building would be safe for the several moments it took us to fly up and out of the compound.

For the next three hours we covered the entire country, all of Sector Six. By the end, I'd crushed at least a hundred million pre-adult V-chips, maybe more.

"More incoming," Henk shouted from the driver's seat. A loud beeping filled the transport as another missile that had been fired at us came into our air space. We'd been fielding them almost incessantly since we took off.

Henk swore loudly. "This one's a nuke. Mother of god."

In spite of the fact that I'd been fielding missiles for the last few hours, my heart still jumped into my throat. With the previous missiles, I'd just detonated them by ramming them against each other, into the ocean, or into the ground in secluded areas. When Adrien had told me his vision, I'd balked, saying surely no one would be foolish enough to release a nuke, no matter what. But here we were, flying over a huge metropolis no less, with nukes headed toward us. I was infinitely glad Adrien had made us bring Lundris along.

"It's coming on fast, Zoe," Henk shouted. "Tell me you've got it."

I abandoned my control over the subjects in the city below and gripped Markan's hand tight as I surrounded the nuke instead and gently slowed its momentum, bringing it to a stop right outside the back hull.

"Two more are in range now," Henk said.

I reached and plucked them out of the air as well. "Got them." I held them completely still in the air, feeling along the contours of their long, cold shells with repulsion. "Open the back hatch," I called to Henk, then stood, dragging Markan along behind me and signaling to Lundris.

"You know what you have to do?" I asked the towheaded boy. He nodded. Henk had brought the transport to a hovering standstill as the back hatch opened. It was surreal to see the deadly warheads bobbing mere feet away from us.

I took Lundris's hand as well, and lifted all three of us up off the floor of the plane, flying through the air so we could get close enough to the nuke to touch it. The wind was calm today, and since we were hovering still, there was only a cold breeze tugging at our tunics. Markan's eyes went wide as he took a quick look down at the empty air below us. Then he squeezed his eyes shut hard.

Lundris was calmer. His gaze was focused only on the nuke in front of us. I held my breath as he reached out his thin fingers toward the metal casing. I winced when he made contact, but nothing happened. I'd known in my head a simple touch wouldn't be enough to detonate them, but still . . .

Then, before my eyes, the gleaming metal turned to solid gray stone. Lundris could manipulate the molecular structure of any object he touched. And he'd just turned a deadly warhead into a warhead-shaped lump of rock. He repeated the procedure with the other two, then I sent them to rest gently on the ground a thousand feet below.

When we got back in the transport, I marched up to the front where Henk was sitting. "Who launched the nuke?" I asked, my voice cold. An icy fury swept through me that anyone would risk the kind of destruction a nuclear weapon promised.

"Sector Five, looks like."

I sat back down. "Then we'll be heading to Sector Five next. We'll shut down the V-chips in every country that has nuclear capability first."

Henk looked back at me, a frown on his face. "That's six out of the eight worldwide Sectors."

I met his eyes with a steely gaze. "We end this today. For everyone."

Epilogue

Three months later

A knock on the top of my sleep pod woke me. I took one last deep breath of safe air, then surrounded my mast cells with my telek and pushed the release button. Jilia said we'd try immunotherapy again to help my allergies once everything settled down, though she didn't know if it would work or not. Like so many things these days, it was an unknown. In the meantime, I slept in the med container. The top pulled up and slowly retracted. I smiled when I saw it was Adrien, and then smiled even wider when I saw the tray full of food behind him.

"You got in late last night. Are you sure you don't want to sleep a little longer?"

I stepped out over the side of the med container. "Too much to do today."

He laughed. "Every day, you mean. But still, you need to eat." He held out a chair for me. We'd stayed at the Chancellor's compound. It made for a good base of operations and had lush personal quarters on the top floor. One wall of the room was made entirely of windows that overlooked the ocean, but I couldn't see anything much since it was still dark out.

"Have you gotten the daily reports yet?" I asked.

"Not yet." He smiled. "Most people don't get up as early as you."

"You do."

He reached, almost shyly, and took my hand. "I like your face to be one of the first things I see every day."

I blushed and looked down. It had been three months since I'd freed all the drones young enough to handle their V-chips being destroyed. It had been chaos at first. The freed people didn't know what to do without the V-chip directing their actions and emotions. The intensity of suddenly being able to feel had resulted in a lot of violence initially. We'd quickly released all the imprisoned Rez cell leaders and positioned them around the Sector to gather as many recruits as they could from among the newly released subjects. In large part, they'd been able to gather the former drones and pretty easily convinced them to direct their anger at the Uppers instead of uselessly against each other.

I ran my finger around the tip of my coffee cup and looked out at the slowly lightening earth. It had been far from a bloodless revolution. There was still heavy fighting going on in some of the other Sectors around the world. After I'd freed all of the drones with the pre-18 V-chip, Resistance factions in each global Sector had led revolutions with varying success. The Community Corporation that had ruled the world for two hundred and fifty years was decimated and each of the eight Chancellor Supremes had been deposed. But in some poorer countries like Sector Four, there was still heavy fighting going on among the survivors about who would rule next.

Here in Sector Six we'd had a wide, unified Rez presence after we emptied the Community prisons, so the fighting had mostly died down. Xona and Cole led the army that took control of the Southern front a few weeks ago, where the Uppers had made their last stand. While pockets of violence still occasionally erupted, we'd subdued and imprisoned most Uppers and taken charge of the government. Many of the Uppers had surrendered in the end, especially after Simin finally accessed the Regulators' separate Link programming channel and ordered them to stop fighting.

The challenge now was to rebuild.

"I didn't get to talk to Jilia yesterday. Any developments in her research with the adult V-chips?"

Adrien took a bite of his omelet. "Not yet. But she has better research facilities than ever before, not to mention the best minds in the country are on her team working on it."

I nodded. I knew it might take a long time before we could figure out a solution to free the adults from the V-chip as well. Maybe someday even my own parents. At least the next generation would grow up free, and the generation after that would be born and never have any hardware put in their heads at all. Adrien often reminded me of that. That even if we never found a way to free the adults, we'd given their children a future, and their children's children.

In the meantime, as much as I hated to think it, it was helpful to have all the adults continue working so the infrastructure of the country didn't collapse. We lessened their work hours and the techer boy had taken over the Link programming.

I'd hoped that introducing vids over the Link of what was really happening instead of the lies the drones had been fed all their lives might help, but they still mindlessly performed their tasks. There was no way we could explain how to *feel* while the V-chip still controlled their limbic systems.

On the upside, it also meant that small children who'd been freed were still being cared for by their parents, food was still being produced, and necessary products were still shipped around the Sector. I was working with other Rez leaders to begin introducing a system of commerce so we could pay them for their work.

Ginni was recovering well with her new bionic leg and had

started a daily news hour that was broadcast both over the Link and the external networks. It finally put her gossip impulse to good use as she tracked down stories and tried to cover the revolution both here and across the globe. She was also investigating what was happening to glitchers worldwide. In some Sectors, it had been protocol to immediately deactivate any subjects who started showing anomalies. Sectors One and Two were the only others that had a significant glitcher population. After the fighting died down, they'd begun setting up schools similar to the Foundation.

Everything moved slower than I wanted. I wished I could just wake up one morning to the new world already fashioned and working. Disputes about the divvying up of land and resources were already cropping up. And everyone looked to me for answers. It was my face being plastered on the vid screens as savior and leader. Ginni said people needed a figurehead and that seeing the face of their leader helped them feel safe, so I went along with it.

"How did the negotiations go yesterday?"

"Diederich was less than willing to agree to our entrance into his weapons facility." Diederich was the leader of Sector One now, the largest Sector in the world. He was the highest-ranking officer in their Resistance movement, but he'd been hardened by his losses over the years. "He outright refused when I said I was coming to take away his nukes."

Adrien lifted an eyebrow. "And yet you managed to persuade him?"

"Markan went with me." I skewered a dripping peach on the end of my fork. It wasn't the reunion I'd imagined with my brother. We spent almost every day together lately, fighting in our Sector and traveling all over the world to help out when other Sectors needed it. Facing hordes of Regs together did create its own kind of intimacy, and we'd had a couple good conversations while we hunkered down on some battle-field or other. But still, I hoped someday soon we could get to know each other without the threat of danger around every corner.

"So I froze all three hundred people in the facility where they stood while Lundris did his thing," I continued.

Adrien choked on the orange juice he'd been drinking. "I thought we agreed we needed them as allies."

"Not at the cost of letting them keep nuclear weapons," I said, my voice hard. "They can rule themselves, that's fine, I won't interfere. But I refuse to let another D-Day happen. There's already been so much blood." I put my fork down, my appetite suddenly gone. In the spirit of free press, there'd been plenty of vid footage of the rebellion. And I'd witnessed far too much firsthand as well.

So much violence. All started because of me. I'd been naïve not to realize at the beginning what it would take. During the heaviest periods of fighting, like back when we were trying to take Central City, I was on call constantly to push back arma-das of Regs. Cole was busy rehabilitating the younger Regs-in-training who hadn't gotten the final V-chip installation yet. He hated sending them back out into the fighting, especially when they'd have to face off against their own, but in the end, he agreed it was the best way to achieve peace long-term.

Even with Markan at my side, I couldn't be everywhere at once. Inevitably, whenever I arrived on a scene, dead bodies already littered the ground. It kept me up at night, until I'd asked Jilia for the strongest sleeping meds she could give me. We couldn't afford for me to have a nightmare that accidently unleashed my power and ripped our compound apart. Because I was using so much of my telek reserve every day, I didn't think I'd have enough leftover to erupt at night. And it seemed like my power was finally leveling off, like the eruptions had just been part of my growing pains. But I didn't want to take any chances.

I couldn't take back the blood, and I couldn't give life back to the dead, but I *could* do everything possible to make sure another D-Day never happened. As much blood as had been spilled, no nuclear weapons had been fired in the worldwide revolution. I intended it to stay that way.

"Hey," Adrien said gently, reaching over and taking my hand. He had an uncanny ability to know what I was thinking about, especially when dark moods struck. "It's okay. Let's just think about all the good we'll do today. Only today matters, not yesterday, not tomorrow."

I looked over at Adrien. We were taking things slowly as well, but I didn't mind. As long as he was by my side. His logical mind had become invaluable as I tried to solve problems and mediate disputes.

He was different from the boy I'd first known. But every day I got to know the new him more and more. And I thought maybe, just maybe, he was starting to completely believe me when I told him I loved him. His hand lazily held mine, rubbing gentle circles with his thumb. The touch sent a warm tingling sensation all the way down to my toes. I closed my eyes for a moment and focused only on it. No yesterday. No tomorrow. Just now, this moment.

"Oh, look—it's time," Adrien said, his chair squeaking as he pushed it back and stood up. I opened my eyes and couldn't help but smile. The sun broke over the horizon, splaying warm pinks and oranges across the ocean.

I stood at Adrien's side. It was our ritual, whenever we could manage it, to watch the sunrise together. I reached for his hand and interwove my fingers with his.

There was so much left to do, and the future was still uncertain. Not even Adrien could see how this would all work out.

He told me that he didn't want to know. He avoided touching Markan at all costs.

I glanced up at Adrien. He had changed, it was true. But his gentleness had never left. He'd been strong enough to re-discover his humanity and hold on to it in spite of everything. It was his idea to watch the sunrise together each morning.

"I love you." I turned to look at him. "Do you believe me yet?"

His eyes were lit brilliantly by the light. He didn't waver from my gaze.

"I do." He dropped his lips to mine.

As we kissed, the sun rose and bathed the earth in light.